CAN'T TEXT THIS

TEAGAN HUNTER

Cover Design by Emily Wittig Designs

Editing by Editing by C. Marie

To Teagan's Tidbits.
Thanks for always being there to brighten my day.

 # CHAPTER 1

MONTY

"OW!"

"Shit. You okay?"

"I'm good, just hit my head on the soap dispenser. Don't stop."

The stranger chuckles. "Didn't plan on it, Monty."

I giggle when he says my name, partially because I'm a little tipsy, and partially because it reminds me of when he first said it.

"Hey, I'm Monty."

"Hi Monty. Wanna see my python?"

He uttered the words with a cocky grin, and I was a goner.

In my defense, that was the best pickup line out of all the guys tonight, and since I'm determined to enjoy myself since starting fresh in a new town, here I am: perched on the bathroom counter at a dive bar named Lola's with a guy I only just met.

He's a new adventure, and I'm enjoying the exploration.

His touch is gentle, yet firm in the best of ways. Large hands grasp my waist, holding tight enough for him to leave red marks but not bruise. It's sexy, makes me feel safe, warm, *alive*.

Or that could be his lips roaming over my jaw. His stubble rakes over my skin, and I live for this moment.

I'll be the first to admit this isn't *me*. I'm not this girl. I don't make out with strangers. Heck, I don't even pick up guys in bars. I'm your average Mary Jane, the girl next door.

I know it and I own it.

I don't have a single *come hither* bone in my body, but there was something about the way this man's eyes slid over me that made me feel worthy of his kisses.

Or it's the booze talking.

Yeah, it could be the booze.

His lips travel down the side of my neck and I lean into him, enjoying the contact more than I probably should. The kisses are slow and wet and perfect. He runs a hand up my back and into my hair, wrapping it around his fingers and pulling lightly until my head is tilted just where he wants it.

He runs his nose along the column of my neck, and I'm so stupid over this, thinking it's the hottest thing ever.

"You smell like beer and sweat and flowers." A soft kiss. "Why flowers?" he mutters.

I don't answer him.

I can't.

He's captured my mouth with his again.

He moves his lips slowly against mine, learning and teasing, seeing what he can get away with, seeing how we fit together.

The hand that was entwined in my hair is now cupping my face, and the pressure he's putting on my jaw is...*hot*. It's not too much, but it's not enough either.

His tongue finds its way inside my mouth and I nearly come apart. Such finesse. Certainty.

This guy *knows* how to kiss.

I mean, I've only kissed three guys in my lifetime, but I'm certain he's the best kisser on earth. With the way he's setting my skin ablaze, there's no way there's anyone better.

He pulls his mouth from mine and his lips find my jaw again, this time traveling up to that spot just behind my ear.

I giggle at the contact and he laughs, the vibration against my neck making me squirm.

"Shut up. It's been a while."

"Uh huh. That's not the reason you're reacting the way you are, though," he argues.

"You're right. It's because I'm super into you because I know you so well."

He tsks. "Was that sarcasm I detected? Someone's got

a mouth on her." His lips meet the shell of my ear. "I like that."

I want to push him away and pull him closer all at once.

Push because this isn't me. This isn't who I am. I don't lash out with sharp words, and I sure as hell don't make out with strangers in bathrooms.

Pull because I don't think kissing could ever get better than this.

There's also a little dose of shame.

"I'm not usually this...forward with guys."

He runs a hand over my sweater, pulling at the collar of the crisp white shirt underneath it. "I couldn't tell."

"Are you making fun of me? I'm sitting in the shame corner over here and you're making fun of me?"

He withdraws a bit, and I miss the feel of him against me. I curl into myself, trying to regain some semblance of warmth.

"Shame?"

His dark brows are slashed together. He stands there, hands settled on either side of me, waiting for me to answer.

Under the yellow glow of the light overhead, I take a good look at the man who was just firmly planted between my spread legs.

His olive skin is covered—and I mean, every single inch, right up to his thick neck—in tattoos, ones I can't quite discern in the shadows but look beautiful none-theless.

There's delicious stubble lining his strong, angled jaw and plump, rose-colored lips. I can't make out his eye color clearly, but right now he has that glassy look about him. He's had a few too many drinks too.

"There's nothing to be *ashamed* of. We're adults, and we're enjoying each other's company—no shame in that."

I squirm beneath his scrutiny.

"Unless you're not into it..."

"I am," I say too quickly.

Another grin. "Yeah? Then what's the big deal?"

I shake my head. "There isn't one. I'm being dumb."

He pushes himself off the counter and it creaks under the shifting weight.

That's another thing: he's huge—like, muscles on muscles kind of huge, the kind that tells me he's probably hiding a six pack under that tight gray shirt of his.

The thought overwhelms me because I've never seen abs in real life. My fingers itch to touch him, and before I know it, I'm pulling him back between my legs. My hands fan out on his stomach and he shakes his head.

"What are you doing, Monty?" he whispers, his breath brushing over my lips.

"Abs."

"Huh?"

"You have abs—I'd guess eight."

He hisses when my hands collide with his bare skin,

and I love the way it sounds. It's like he can't get enough of our contact either.

I run my fingers over his middle.

"One...two..."

His chest begins to move rapidly.

"Three...four..."

He reaches out and stills my movements, locking eyes with me. There are so many shadows between us I almost can't see him.

And it's making this encounter all the more enticing.

"Six. It's six, Monty."

I frown. "You ruined the surprise."

He crushes his lips to mine and I gasp at the contact. The movement is so rushed that I slide forward on the counter, my butt now barely hanging on to the edge. I wrap my legs around his waist for more support, and right behind me, following him into the bathroom earlier, it's the smartest move I've made all night.

His erection brushes against *all* the right spots, and it feels just like the python he called it.

"*Fuuuuuck.*"

I've heard many curse words in my life. I'm not against cursing it's just never sounded right coming out of my mouth, so it's not something I do.

But that word leaving his lips? That didn't sound like any curse I've ever heard. It sounded like a prayer.

And I'm praying right along with him.

His hands slide up my bare legs and under the knee-length skirt I'm wearing. I don't stop him when he reaches my thighs, or when he reaches the edge of my panties.

I'm too lost to acknowledge that I shouldn't be doing this with a stranger, too lost to care when he runs a finger along the band lining my thigh, too gone when his knuckles graze my swollen lips.

He buries his face in my neck as he fingers the hem over and over again. I want to combust every time he brushes against me. He's unsure if he should press forward or not.

I'm not.

"You can touch me, Robbie."

Another prayer and one of his fingers dives into my underwear, seeking out my center.

"You're so wet," he whispers before taking my mouth with his again.

My body heats at his words—or at his kiss. I can't tell which, but I know I'm not used to hearing words like that.

He adds another finger and I lose all ability to move. He glides his fingers in and out of me, and I gasp in shock when his thumb presses against my clit.

What the...

"Do that again."

He lets out another throaty laugh at my instruction and obeys, circling his thumb and teasing the bundle of nerves with just the right amount of pressure.

"Again."

He obliges.

"Don't stop."

He doesn't, and I ignite.

There's no other way to describe it. I unravel beneath him, legs quaking, breath stuttered, eyes rolling into the back of my head.

I've read about this in those magazines my sister reads, heard it's the most euphoric feeling in the world...and they weren't wrong.

I cling to Robbie as I come down from the high, my breathing returning to normal, his fingers still languidly stroking my clit.

"Are you okay?" he asks quietly.

"I'm..."

A pounding against the door yanks me out of the haze and clears my foggy brain in an instant.

Oh god.

What have I done? I'm in a *public* restroom with a *stranger*! I just let him...let him...do dirty things to me!

My heart's racing, this time for all the wrong reasons, and I can't seem to catch my breath.

I push at the big wall of muscle blocking me in, and he moves out of my way as I hop off the counter, frowning at me.

"Monty?"

"I... This... We..." I huff, annoyed with myself for not being able to get the words out. "I cannot believe I just let you do...*that!*"

He smirks, and I hate how sexy it looks on him. He

takes two steps closer, his hand coming up to cup my face. I gasp at the touch, and it makes me so mad that I react at all.

His lips brush against my ear. "Touch you, Monty. I touched you. I put my fingers inside you and rubbed your sweet little clit until you came undone beneath me. That's what I did." He trails his lips along my face until they're resting against my mouth and he's kissing me all over again.

And I let him. I let him consume me, take control, and move his lips over mine in whatever way he pleases. I don't know what's come over me, and in this very moment I don't care.

Until another loud knock sounds on the door.

"No. This isn't me. You...you don't understand." I laugh humorlessly. "How could you? You're a stranger."

He lets out an irritated sigh, and I can't blame the guy. I got my rocks off but he's still standing there with a boner. "I thought we discussed this already."

"We did...but I just...I can't. This isn't me."

"You keep saying that. What does it mean?"

I wave a hand down my body. "See this? See my outfit? Does this scream *bathroom sex* to you?"

His hard eyes rake over me and I can feel the heat licking my skin.

It's a slow perusal from head to toe. He scans over my freckled face that perfectly complements my long red hair, my black cashmere sweater with the white shirt underneath, the knee-length floral skirt I'm wearing, right down to my perfect white Keds.

I don't look like I belong in this bathroom, let alone this bar, not with someone like him, and we both know it.

He doesn't say anything, and I take that as my cue to leave.

I hastily straighten my clothes and spin toward the counter, looking for the cross-body purse I was wearing when we rushed in here. I glance in the mirror and regret it.

My lips are swollen, cheeks flushed, eyes hazy, and my red hair is a complete mess.

I look like I've been up to something naughty—which, of course, I have.

When I spot my purse, I drag it closer, unzipping it to make sure I'm not missing anything. My eyes land on a pen.

Part of me wants to run from this bathroom and never, ever see Robbie again. I'm embarrassed by how easily I gave in to him, mortified by how vulnerable he made me in such a short amount of time.

The other part of me wants to give him my number and let him kiss me whenever he pleases.

Which is *so* unlike me.

What has gotten into me? *Liquor.*

That's it—it *has to* be the booze. I'm not a big drinker, and tonight I had already slung back three shots before Robbie even stepped foot in the bar. It's the reason I danced, the reason I talked to so many guys, the only thing that could make me lose my inhibitions the way I have.

Alcohol makes me brave.

And stupid.

Before I can let anything else enter my mind, I do something I'd never do in a million years.

I write my number on a paper towel, thrust it into his hand, and run.

# CHAPTER 2

ROBBIE

THIS IS the fourth morning in a row I've woken up with my balls aching, and I'm getting damn sick of it.

It's all because of her.

Monty.

I spotted her from across the room, an easy feat with her bright red hair, and I had to draw closer. Now, gingers have never been my thing. I've always gone for girls with dark hair and big tits and even bigger asses. I have a type, and Monty is not it.

Yet I couldn't stop my feet from dragging me closer.

From a distance, she was cute. Up close? *Beautiful.*

Her porcelain skin was dotted with freckles. Eyes were wide with wonder, bright with intoxication, and green as the sea.

Then my gaze traveled south, and I wanted to laugh. She didn't belong in Lola's. Her place was somewhere comfortable, like the library or some shit, not a dive bar.

She was too...*untouched* for that.

I knew I wasn't any good for her, but that didn't stop me from hitting on her. We clicked at once, keeping the conversation light and fun. Only names were shared, nothing else.

"I'm going to say something very forward, and you'll have to excuse me for this—it's the alcohol talking."

She sipped from the straw sticking out of the bright blue concoction she was drinking and didn't wait for me to respond.

"You have the most kissable lips I've ever seen in my entire life, and I want to kiss them."

I grabbed her hand and led her back to the women's bathroom, knowing the men's was a disaster, and lifted her onto the countertop.

"You wanna kiss me?" She nodded. "Then kiss me, Monty."

Holy *fuck* did she kiss me.

I was surprised when she let me touch her, and even more shocked when she ran out of the bathroom, leaving me standing there with a raging hard-on.

I glance to the paper towel sitting on my bedside table.

It's the same one she shoved into my hand, the one that has her number hurriedly scrawled across it.

I haven't done anything with it. Based on her quick departure, I'm not sure I should, though this multiple-day bout of blue balls is telling me something different.

I can't stop thinking about her, can't get the image of

her—head thrown back, long hair a crumpled mess, coming apart on my fingers—out of my head.

My dick twitches at the thought, and I reach under my sheet to adjust myself.

Think about something else, Robbie. Anything else.

The last thing I need is—

"*Daaaaaaaad!*"

That.

That's the last thing I need right now.

My seven-year-old son bursts through my door and I quickly throw a pillow over my junk.

"Dude, what'd I tell you about knocking?"

His shoulders slump. "Oh crudders. I forgot."

He backs out of the room and shuts the door. It's not even three seconds later when I hear his knuckles rapping against the door.

"Who is it?" I say, playing his smartass game right back.

"Xavie. Your son. I'm hungry."

"Come in."

He throws the door open once again and beelines for my bed, crawling up into the heap of blankets I threw off in the middle of the night and making himself comfortable.

"I want food."

I roll to my side and stare at my mini-me. Some days it still amazes me that I'm a father. *Me.*

I didn't plan on that happening until a lot later in life,

a good ten to twelve years from now when I was ready to settle down—not at nineteen before I was even legally able to drink, before I'd hit that decade of my life that was supposed to be reserved for partying and fun, not changing diapers and three AM wake-ups.

I guess that's what happens when you decide to throw caution to the wind and not wrap your dick up. You get girls pregnant and then your entire life changes in a flash.

I'm not going to pretend I wouldn't go back in time and change things, do them differently, be smart, because I would. I know many others who've found themselves in my same situation would too, but that doesn't mean I don't love Xavier—or Xavie, as I like to call him—with my whole heart. He's my everything and I'm thankful he came into my life, no matter how unplanned he was.

"Oh, you want to eat?" He nods. "No one ever said I had to feed you."

He furrows his brows. "Toys, love, *and* food—those are things dads give their kids."

I chuckle. "Is that so?"

"Yep. Momma said so."

"Did she throw the toys in there or did you?"

He grins and shrugs before scurrying off my bed. "She did. Now come on—I'm not getting any younger."

Xavie runs out of the room, his curly hair bouncing the entire way.

I pull myself up and hit the bathroom. I kick away the

toys lining the tile, reminding myself to have Xavie clean his mess before he has to go to his mom's later tonight.

"Are you coming?"

I give my dick a good shake and wash my hands while trying not to let out a weary sigh.

If anyone in the history of ever said kids aren't exhausting, they're a damn liar.

Xavie is the most exhausting thing to ever happen to me. He's needy, he's pushy, and he can be *so* annoying.

But he's mine, and I'd die for the kid.

"Hold your horses," I tell him as I dry my hands.

"I can't. They're out of control!"

I amble through our small apartment and head into the kitchen, where I find him already sitting at the counter, ready to eat.

"Whatcha want, Xavie?"

"Waffles...bacon...sausage...biscuits   and   gravy. Pancakes too!"

I lift a brow, and he giggles.

"Okay, okay. Just waffles."

"With peanut butter and strawberries on top?"

He nods enthusiastically. "Please."

"Coming right up."

I pull open the freezer door, grab the bag of pre-made waffles, and begin preparing them. I used to spend my Sunday nights in front of the latest gaming console with a burrito in one hand and a joint in the other. Now I use them for meal-prepping and making lunches.

Parenthood does weird things to a person.

The doorbell chimes and Xavie hops off his stool, running to the front door as fast as his little legs can carry him. "I'll get it!"

"Make sure you look out the peephole so you know it's not a creeper."

One of the biggest selling points for this apartment was how kid-friendly it is. They have an adult-level peephole and one for kiddos—that shit is brilliant.

"Is Uncle Zach a creeper?" The kid's voice is full of excitement because he is in love with my best friend.

In a weird turn of events, I met Zach the same night I got my ex-girlfriend pregnant.

I ran into the back of his way-too-expensive car at the stoplight outside a strip club. Instead of being mad, Zach took me inside and bought me a lap dance because he'd had a good damn day at work.

Sure, it was only one of those eighteen-plus clubs, and it was only four in the afternoon on a random Thursday so the best of the best wasn't in the lineup, but we bonded over titties like you wouldn't believe.

Haven't looked back since.

Xavie wouldn't be here without him either, not only because Zach is the best support system in the entire fucking world, but because that lap dance he bought me led to some crazy sex with Xavie's mom.

Life is strange.

"The biggest one I know. Don't let him in."

"I'm not a creep. I'm awesome," Zach says once Xavie opens the door. "What's up, buddy?"

I chuckle every time he says this because he sounds exactly like Pauly Shore. One day when he's older, I'll have to introduce my son to the actor that ruled my childhood so he can finally understand why his Uncle Zach is both the coolest and lamest guy ever.

"It's weird not having to pick up your dirty socks. You should come hang with me and Delia sometime soon, maybe give your dad a break from your special brand of crazy."

He's not wrong. It's been a few months now, but I'm still getting used to living on my own. We were roommates up until recently when Zach met "the one" and kicked his first love—me—to the curb.

Kidding...mostly.

In all fairness, when I noticed Zach was ready to take the next step, I opted to move out. Besides, it was time. I'd spent too many years living with him, and if I was ever going to start taking my adulthood seriously, I needed to fucking scoot.

So, here I am: twenty-six and in my very first two-bedroom apartment with my seven-year-old son. We're making it work, and I'm doing a damn good job...most days.

I mean, I *did* just almost have sex with a stranger in a bathroom four days ago.

It's called balance.

"I'm not *that* crazy," my son argues back.

"I beg to differ," I say.

"Keep it up and I'm gonna move in with Uncle Zach."

As they stroll into the kitchen, I pull the waffles from the microwave and plate them, then grab the peanut butter and strawberries from the fridge. I place them out on the counter with a butter knife and point a finger his way. "Don't make promises you can't keep."

"Worst. Dad. Ever," Zach says, taking a seat at the bar. "I'll take two, please."

"You'll make your own."

"Come on, be a good sport."

"Yeah, Dad. Uncle Zach drove *all* the way over here to have breakfast with us and you won't even feed him? I thought that's what dads are supposed to do—give toys, food, and love."

"To *kids*."

"Uncle Zach is the biggest kid I know."

Zach fist-bumps him. "Right on, little man. Right on."

I stare at my best friend, mouth hanging open in shock. "You've turned my own spawn against me? That's messed up, man."

He shrugs and reaches across the counter to grab two waffles. "Can you pass the peanut butter?"

"I hate you," I mutter as I slide it his way.

He opens the jar and begins slathering the creamy substance on his waffles, grinning. "I love you too."

"Aww," Xavie teases, and I throw a hand towel at him.

He giggles and dives into his own breakfast.

"So, how are things? I haven't talked to you in days, man."

"Things are..." I start, memories of Monty flashing before my eyes.

I should talk to him about her. Zach's a female whisperer or some shit like that. For being such a huge nerd, the dude has game that makes even *me* swoon.

"Xavie, how about you take your waffles into the living room."

His little eyes widen to twice their normal size. "The living room? With food? And TV?" His voice is about two pitches higher than usual because I *never* let him watch TV while he eats his breakfast.

Today I'm making an exception. I need help getting a certain ginger out of my head, and I need my best friend to help me. The last thing my son needs to hear is details of the weekend I had while he was at his mom's.

"Yep. TV too. Just this once though."

"Can I have some juice?"

That's where I draw the line. "Out there? No way. Juice stays in the kitchen."

I grab a cup from the cabinet and the orange juice from the fridge, pouring him half a glass. He chugs it down quick.

"Thanks. I'll come back when I want more."

Then he grabs his plate and takes off for the living

room. I've never seen a kid walk so cautiously before. He knows he better not drop a single crumb on the floor.

Zach chuckles. "You've got that turd trained."

"Someone needed to."

"What's up? Why'd you kick him out?"

"Well..." I rub the back of my neck, trying to figure out how I want to phrase this.

"You got someone else pregnant."

I cross my arms over my chest and glare at him. "No. Stop it, you ass."

He presses his lips together, trying to hold in his laughter. "Right. Sorry. What then?"

"I met someone."

"What about Holly?"

Up until two months ago, I thought Xavie's mom would be my endgame. I thought me finally getting my shit together and getting a place of my own was the icing on the cake. We'd stop our back-and-forth, on-and-off bull and take a real stab at being a united front for our son, maybe even fall in love and get married.

But that's not how it happened, and I'm done trying.

Holly and I aren't destined to be together, and I've finally accepted that. As much as I don't want my son to grow up with a broken family, I can't force things with his mother. That'll be worse for him than if we just call it what it is and do our own thing.

We promised we'd stand united, even went back to court and reworked the custody agreement so our time with our son was split right down the middle. So far, it's worked out great.

"We're done for good."

Zach's lips tilt up in the corners, and then a full smile spreads across his face. "I'm happy to hear that."

He was never a fan of Holly. Shit was bad when Xavie was first born, and we were both so young that we didn't deal with anything in a healthy manner. Zach's never forgiven her for it, which is crazy because he isn't really one to hold grudges.

It's his love for my son, who truly is practically his nephew, and for me that keeps him angry at her.

I kind of love the moron for it, but I also wish he'd just get over it and be friendly with her since she's still such a big part of our lives.

He takes a bite of his waffles and chews before saying, "This girl then—what about her?"

"We sort of...hooked up."

He mumbles something, but I can't make it out through the food jammed in his mouth.

"In the bathroom at Lola's."

He sputters, choking on his breakfast. Loud coughs fill the room and I grab a bottle of water from the fridge, sliding it his way.

He nods and cracks it open, taking a drink.

"Is Uncle Zach dying?" Xavie calls out from the living room.

"We hope so! I think I'm in his will."

"Yay, money!"

Laughter bursts out of Zach and water covers the counter.

"What in the hell are you teaching your child?"

I shrug, grabbing a new towel and cleaning up the mess. "I don't know where he gets that shit."

"Uh huh." He takes another drink. "Okay, now details. I need details."

I rest against the counter and lean his way so we can talk quietly without little ears hearing all this.

"I got her with a one-liner, man. We clicked, she said she wanted to kiss me, I took her into the bathroom, and... yeah. Shit happened."

Zach squints. "What does 'shit happened' mean exactly?"

"It means..." I can still remember the way her legs quivered around my waist as she came, the way she squeezed her eyes shut—all of it. Can't get it out of my head. "It means we, you know, fooled around."

He peers over his shoulder, eyes darting to the living room to make sure Xavie isn't within earshot. When he turns back to me, he mimics a blow job.

I crack up laughing and shake my head no.

Then he sticks his tongue out, moving it around in a chaotic fashion. It's disgusting and hilarious all at once.

"If that's *your* version of what I think it is, I feel bad for Delia."

He grins. "Nah, she loves it—but is that the 'shit' that happened?"

"No." I lift my hand and wiggle my fingers his way.

"You fisted her?" His ass comes off the seat as he whisper-yells the question, now leaning over the counter just inches from my face, mouth slackened and eyes wide.

I shake my head in disbelief, laughing as I smash my hand to his face and push him away.

"I cannot believe I'm friends with you. No, you moron."

"Oh." He sits back down, brows squished together in concentration. Then it clicks. "*Oh!* Finger-banging, huh? That makes more sense than fisting on the first date."

"Or fisting ever."

He gets this wistful look about him. "I remember one time with Delia—"

"Nope. No. Not hearing about you two fisting."

"No, not fisting. Fing—"

"Still not hearing it."

He rolls his eyes. "Whatever. What's going on then? Why are you bringing this up now? We've been at work together all week and you're only just now talking about it. What gives?"

"Because I've woken up with a hard cock every fucking day since it happened. After she came all over me, she bailed."

"And you're all hung up because you didn't get your rocks off?"

"I...well, shit." I scratch at my week-old beard, knowing I should probably shave today. "That could be it, could be why I can't get her out of my head."

"She's the one that got away."

"In a sense."

He narrows his eyes. "What's that supposed to mean?"

"She left her number."

"And you haven't called her because..."

"Because...she's different."

"She doesn't look like the girls you're always after—so what? Big deal. Call her anyway."

"Zach, dude, I'm telling you—"

"She's different—yeah, I got that. How?"

"Monty is...innocent. She just has that look about her that says girl next door. She's all buttoned up and... reserved." I hold my tattooed arms out. "I'm clearly not."

Zach stares hard at me, and I wonder what's going through his head.

We both know I'm not one to go for the girls who have clearly spent more time hidden inside their safe little bedrooms than in bars.

He might be onto something here. Maybe the reason I can't get Monty out of my head is because we didn't finish what we started. Maybe it's because I don't know what she'd feel like beneath me and I *need* to know...for research purposes. Science and all that shit.

Yeah. That's totally the reason.

"Get your phone out."

My attention snaps to Zach and his hardened expression. "Huh?"

"Get your phone out. You're texting her."

"I am not."

"You're taking this Monty broad to Funkytown whether you like it or not. Phone—now."

I shake my head. "No. She ran for a reason, dude."

He gives me one of his famous all-knowing grins, and I want to slap the glasses off his nerdy, handsome face. "She gave you her number for a reason too."

He's not wrong.

I pull my phone from my pocket.

> **Me: Hey. This is Robbie. From Lola's.**

"Smooth," Zach murmurs.

"Shut the fuck up."

I carefully fold the paper towel I got her number off of and slide it back into my sleep pants. I don't know why I want to keep it even though it's now saved to my contacts, but I do. There's something about it that feels so...old school. No one writes their number down anymore. It makes me a little sentimental.

We watch my phone like two insane people, agonizing every time the three familiar dots appear and disappear.

"Maybe if you had opened with something better, she'd have a responded already."

"I already used my best one-liner on her when I met her."

"What was that?" He gasps. "You didn't use the angel one, did you? Because that one is *horrible*."

"No. I asked her if she wanted to see my python."

He nearly falls off the stool from laughing so hard, and I love that I didn't have to explain it to him at all.

"Fucking genius," he says, pulling his black frames off his face and wiping away the tears that have formed in his eyes. "Even I would have followed you into the bathroom after that one."

I smirk. "I wouldn't have to use any lines on you."

"Only because I'm easy."

"I'm sure Delia loves that."

He snorts and stands, grabbing his plate and walking it over to the sink. He also rinses it and puts it in the dishwasher like the good little houseguest he is.

He tugs the fridge open and pulls out the leftover pizza from last night, flips open the lid, and shoves a slice in his piehole.

"Sure, help yourself, man."

"Thanks." Or at least that's what I think he says through the mouthful of food.

My phone vibrates against the countertop and I freeze.

Then I spring into action. I snap it up and dance my fingers over the screen to enter my passcode, eager to see what she's responded with.

> Monty: Oh.

"What the..."

I show Zach my phone and he shrugs.

"Beats the shit outta me, man."

I quickly respond.

> Me: I can't tell if that's a bad "oh" or a good "OH".

> Monty: It's a surprised oh.

> Me: A good surprise?

> Monty: Good.

> Monty: I think.

> Me: I was going to call...

> Monty: I would not have answered.

> Me: Um...okay.

> Monty: That sounded so rude. I'm sorry. I just meant I wouldn't have answered because talking on the phone makes me want to vomit. I can't handle it.

> Me: I like that answer much more.

> Monty: Me too.

"See, you just needed to break the ice. Now you two are chatting and you can throw in there how you wanna bang her and all that. It'll be great."

I stare blankly at him. "How in the hell did you ever get a girlfriend?"

"Ah, ah, ah—a *live-in* girlfriend."

I briefly squeeze my eyes shut and try not to laugh at his enthusiasm. "Right. My bad."

"It's because of my ass. That's what sealed the deal, really."

"Dad, Uncle Zach said ass. You said I couldn't say ass. Why does he get to say it?" He walks back into the kitchen and sets his plate on the counter, then rolls his sleeves up before getting to work rinsing his plate and putting it in the dishwasher. He knows I'm here to take care of him, but he has to clean up after himself. It's teamwork.

Zach looks at me, eyes innocent and face red with held-in laughter.

"Get the hell outta here, man. Wait, why *are* you here anyway?"

He lifts a shoulder. "I was in the area. Met with that client at the ass—"

"Hey!" Xavie says, jumping off his stepstool and pretending to punch Zach's stomach.

Zach pretends to take the hit and makes all the proper noises. He's the best fake uncle ever.

"I meant *butt*, you little turd. Calm down." The kid backs away but is ready to strike again if necessary. "Anyway, I met with him at the *butt* crack of dawn and knew you'd be up getting this rascal ready for day camp, so I thought I'd stop in and see him since it's been a while." He nods toward my phone. "Apparently that was a good idea. It's like I had bestie intuition or some sh—stuff. Why, did you think I was here to see your ugly mug?" He scoffs. "Like I need more of you in my life."

"Shut up," I retort, then turn my attention back to my buzzing phone.

> Monty: So, Robbie from Lola's, why'd you text?

> Me: I can't stop thinking about you.

> Monty: Wow. Straight to the point then.

> Me: I'm not one to beat around the bush. Not my style.

> Monty: Good to know.

> Monty: If I'm being very honest, and even though I can feel my cheeks heating just thinking of admitting this to you, I've thought about you as well.

"Who you texting, Dad?"

"Business."

"Business?"

"Yeah, none of yours."

He props his hands on his hips and scrunches his face up. "That's not nice."

"Fine. It's Santa Claus. Homeboy just told me if you don't go brush your teeth and get dressed, you'll be missing a present under the Christmas tree."

He lifts a brow. "Santa's old. He'll forget by Christmas time. It's *July*, Dad."

"He might forget, but I won't. Scoot!"

The little smartass lets out a sigh but obeys, trudging off down the hallway to get ready for the day.

When he's out of the room, Zach sidles up next to me. "That her?"

"Yeah. I don't know what else to say."

"I told ya, tell her about the banging thing."

"Please leave."

He laughs and claps me on the shoulder, giving me a good shake. "You'll figure it out. Let me know if you need any more pointers. I'm gonna say goodbye to the rugrat. I'll see you at the office." I hear him shuffle down the hallway and into Xavie's room. "I'm out, kiddo. Here's five dollars for letting me in. Make your dad get you some ice cream or something."

"You're the best, Uncle Zach!"

"I know." I picture him dusting off the shoulder of his leather jacket as he says this, because that's *so* something Zach would do.

He gives me a wave when he walks back through the apartment.

"Don't be late! Your boss hates that shit!" he hollers over his shoulder before the door clicks shut.

"Uncle Zach said shit! You said shit was a bad word!" Xavie yells.

I groan and remind myself to kick Zach's ass when I get to work. "I know. Just get dressed. We'll talk about it on the way to school."

I begin cleaning up the small mess left over from breakfast and grab Xavie's backpack. I'm in dad mode now, putting in the final additions to his lunch—writing out the joke I always slip inside the box—and grabbing the miscellaneous school supplies scattered throughout the apartment. *Kid is a mess.*

I head back to my own bedroom and make quick work of shucking my sleep clothes and exchanging them for my work ones. Thank god Zach is chill and doesn't make us dress up. I love being able to work in jeans and a polo.

Right on time, I meet Xavie in the hall. I grab his backpack and he grabs his lunch, then we slip our shoes on and off we go.

We have our routine down to a science by now. When Holly and I agreed to an every-other-week custody agreement, I was a bit nervous. As bad as it sounds, I was only used to having Xavie around every other weekend and each Thursday, not for an entire week at a time.

But, we got the hang of things fast, and now I wish I had him every day of the year, not just when the court allows.

We buckle into my car and head about eight miles down the road to his school for the day camp he's taking part in this year. I both love and hate it.

I hate it because it takes time away from *us* and love it because it allows me to spend time with him and still pay the bills.

Luckily, he's forgotten all about the *shit* incident with Zach, and we just jam out to some Parkway Drive.

What can I say? My kiddo loves some metal.

I park in front of the school and hop out of the car, pulling Xavie's door open.

"Be good. Be smart. Be kind."

"Be good. Be smart. Be kind," he repeats.

We bump fists twice. "Love you. See you at three."

"Love you too!"

He runs off to his friends and I head to work.

It still feels weird not driving to Zach's, where our headquarters used to be, but I couldn't be prouder to pull up into my very own parking space at Embody Positivity.

Delia's climbing out of her car as I park, lifting two boxes of donuts and two trays of coffee from inside.

"Hey!" she calls when I step out. "I heard you finger-banged some girl in the bathroom of a bar."

"I fucking hate your boyfriend."

She gives me a look telling me she doesn't believe a word I say. "Are you two still texting? You know that's my and Zach's thing."

I realize then I never texted Monty back. I pull my

phone from my pocket and see I have four unread messages.

> Monty: OH GOSH. That was SO embarrassing. I'm sorry. I probably just made this so darn awkward for you. I'm sorry.

> Monty: I don't know why I apologized...TWICE.

> Monty: I'm so stupid.

> Monty: Just ignore me. Pretend I don't exist. We'll just forget the other night happened and go on our merry ways in three...two...one. GOODBYE FOREVER, ROBBIE!

CHAPTER 3

MONTY

I HAVEN'T BEEN able to stop thinking about Robbie since I ran out of that bathroom.

I ran right to Denny, my twin sister, and demanded we leave. She didn't argue, just grabbed her purse and got us a cab. I didn't mention Robbie once the entire ride home.

When we got back to the apartment we share, I showered and crawled into bed...only to awaken three hours later from one of the hottest dreams I've ever had and an ache between my legs.

The same dream has been on repeat for days.

I've been kicking myself for two reasons: not getting his number and not staying.

I finally told Denny about it yesterday, and that conversation went exactly as I had expected.

She didn't believe me.

On one hand, I can't blame her. It is *me*, after all. I'm

not known for making out with strangers in bars, let alone letting them...you know...*do* things to me.

It took about twenty minutes of convincing, and eventually I had to unbutton my pants and show her the fading bruises on my bum.

That set her off on a whole new tirade that took a good five minutes to talk her down from. The bruises came from the sink, not Robbie.

When he first approached me, I was ready to reject him based on his appearance alone. He stood so tall above me that it almost scared me, and his tattoos made him look...menacing.

Then he flashed a bright white smile and I melted.

Don't even get me started on his deep, rumbling voice. It's so...*sexy*. I don't think I've ever personally heard anyone with that heavy of a baritone. It's warm and inviting but a smidge authoritative, a whole different level of hot, especially with his massive, muscled arms wrapped around you.

There's a commotion outside my door and I peek out the window.

A classroom full of kids goes rushing by with Mr. Donahue—or Brandon, as us adults know him—following closely behind. They're on their way outside for whatever creative activity he's come up with this time.

"Oh, hey there, Miss Andrews. What are you doing here today? School doesn't start for another month."

He slides up next to me, and I can't help but compare him to the last man who stood this close to me—Robbie.

They're nothing alike, and not just when it comes to looks.

From what I've gathered about Brandon in the few short weeks I've been attending the weekly new teacher luncheons, he tries too hard to be liked, has no qualms about lack of personal space, and is crushing on me...hard.

Though he is the exact type of man I *should* be interested in—professionally dressed, manners out the wazoo, would never take a strange girl into the bathroom and touch her in her most private spots—I'm not.

The last guy that was "my type" turned out to be the worst thing to ever happen to me.

I take a step back, hoping he doesn't notice, and give him a polite smile. "Just taking a few pictures of the room so I can start buying some supplies and decorations."

"I bet your room is going to be beautiful because"—he waves a hand my way—"you know."

I don't, but I say nothing. I simply nod and point toward my room. "I'm going to get back to it. Just wanted to see what all the noise was out here. Better catch up with the kids."

"I-I...oh, yes, of course. I'll see you around, Monty."

I have no reaction to the way he says my name, not like I did with Robbie.

My phone buzzes in my hand as I walk back into my classroom, and I almost fall down in surprise.

Python: You're not stupid and that wasn't embarrassing. I said it first so if there's anyone who should be embarrassed (and there's not), it's me.

Python: I don't want to say goodbye just yet. I'd kind of like to talk to you some more, if you'll let me.

Me: You want to...talk to me? Seriously? After all that?

Python: If we're being perfectly honest here, I want to do much more than just talk to you, Monty.

Me: Oh.

Python: Yeah, OH. I want to taste those sweet lips of yours again, want to wrap my hands in your long, red hair, and I don't want to stop there.

Me: I don't think I'd want you to stop there either.

What? No, no, no, no. Stop it, Monty!

Me: But you should. I'm at work right now and I can't be doing...THIS while I'm at work.

Python: So? I'm at work too.

Me: Yes, but do you work with a bunch of children?

Python: Actually, yes, though they aren't here right now.

Python: I'll stop.

Python: But Monty? The moment the clock strikes 5, it's on.

Heat charges to the apex of my thighs and I squirm. *It's on.*

Who the hell says things like that to a stranger?

Well, I mean...I did let him do certain things to me, so I guess we're not complete strangers now.

But still.

Me: Change the subject, Robbie.

Python: Why'd you leave me your number if you thought I'd never use it?

Python: Or were you HOPING I'd never use it? Did you give me your number as a pity thing?

Python: Do you think I'm a bad kisser, Monty? Because I don't think that's the case, not with the way you... Oh, wait, I promised I'd stop.

Me: I am blushing so hard because now I can't stop thinking about you kissing me.

Me: No, I didn't give you my number as a pity thing. If that were the case, I would have given you a fake number.

Python: So why were you surprised I contacted you?

Me: Because I just left you there after...

Python: After what? And, please, be specific.

Me: I am not saying it!

Python: Chicken.

Me: The biggest chicken you'll ever meet.

Me: Can I be honest with you?

Python: Please do.

Me: You're not my type, not even close, and let's face it, I'm not yours either. We simply LOOK like we don't belong together. I gave you my number because I felt like I HAD to after I let you do what you did. Also, because I liked the way you kissed. A small part of me hoped you'd reach out, but I was mostly hoping we'd both move on and forget it ever happened.

Me: I'm sorry if you hoped for more, but I'm not a random hookup kind of gal.

Python: What makes you assume I'm a random hookup kind of guy? What makes you assume you're not my type? Because of the way I look? Tsk, tsk. So judgy, Monty.

Python: For the record, I've had random hookups in the past and they didn't work out in my favor (i.e., I got a girl pregnant).

Me: You're a father?

Python: I am.

Me: I...I did not see that coming.

Python: Is it a bad thing?

Me: No, not at all! I love kids.

Me: Not that I plan on meeting YOUR kid or anything like that. Just in general.

Me: I guess I just also didn't think dads did...well, THAT with strangers in public.

Python: Are you ever going to just say it?

Me: NO!

Me: I don't talk like that.

> Python: Fine, I'll say it: I touched your pussy, Monty. I led you into the bathroom, kissed you senseless, and rubbed your clit until you were panting in my ear, and you liked every damn second of it. You came undone from my touch alone. Your hair was wild and your eyes full of satisfaction. Your cheeks burned a scarlet red and I can't fucking stop thinking about it.

> Python: I want to see you come again. BAD.

> Python: I know I said I'd stop but I couldn't help it, not when you keep talking around it like you didn't enjoy it just as much as I did.

Holy crow.

My heart is hammering in my chest, sweat beading up on the back of my neck. I'm suddenly so glad I wore this skirt today because man, oh man, is it hot in here.

I gather my long hair and twist it into an artful bun then pinch at my boatneck shirt and fan it, trying to give myself some reprieve.

I want to send so many things back to him—like my address, for starters.

The need to see him again, to kiss him again, to let him *touch* me again...is strong. I don't get what's come over me.

Don't get me wrong, I've had plenty of sexual encounters before. I've just never "gone all the way".

I'm a twenty-three-year-old virgin who was saving herself for marriage while her fiancé was giving himself to anyone and everyone.

Even though I've fooled around before, I can safely say I have never been so turned on by someone. I believe if we hadn't been interrupted that night, I would have gone home with him in a heartbeat. Alcohol fueled a good part of it, and maybe the public setting too, but there was just something about Robbie that was different.

He felt...off limits.

Forbidden.

All kinds of wrong, and *so* right.

"Hey, a—"

"Ahhhh!"

My phone goes flying from my hands at the unexpected interruption. I bend down to quickly retrieve it and inspect the damage—a chip in the corner.

And of course, I just got it.

I let out a frustrated groan as Brandon crosses the room, taking four long strides to reach me.

"Oh, hell. I'm so sorry, Monty. I didn't mean to frighten you."

"It's fine." *It's not.* "No big deal." *It is.* "What'd you need?"

"I-I..." he sputters, nervous now. He clears his throat, stands straight, and tries again. "I wanted to invite you out to dinner tonight."

He must see the fear in my eyes because he's waving his hands and launching into a pitch within seconds.

"It's a group thing, you know, drinks downtown—nothing too crazy."

I tilt my head. "So our weekly luncheon, just for dinner instead?"

He looks nervous again. "Um, no. It'd be with my buddies and their, uh, girlfriends. I figured you might want to meet some new people, you know, not just the staff here at Wayward Elementary..."

Oh.

The polite girl my parents raised me to be knows I should say yes, should accept the invitation. I should be friendly, social, engaging.

But I don't want to.

The whole reason I moved out here to live with Denny was to leave my "yes" life behind, because that's all my life has ever been.

Yes, I'll take care of the baby at three AM.

Yes, I'll go to the college you pick.

Yes, I'll marry you even though you cheat on me.

I almost did too, was so close to it. Then one day I woke up and realized I wasn't living *my* life. I was living for everyone else and I couldn't keep doing it. It was wearing me ragged, something a twenty-three-year-old shouldn't be feeling.

Denny was the smart one out of the two of us. She left the moment we graduated and didn't return for her entire four years of college...or after. I wish I was brave enough to do that, but I couldn't leave Chuck, our younger brother, behind. I was too chicken.

After what happened with my ex and me almost walking into *that* kind of future, though, I knew I had to do something.

So, I called my twin, packed my bags, and was gone a week later.

My parents have called every day for the four months I've lived here, demanding I return home.

I refuse.

Just like I'm about to refuse this invitation to dinner.

"Thank you for thinking of me, Brandon, but I have plans this evening."

His shoulders slump. It's not the answer he was looking for.

"Perhaps another time?" The words leave my mouth before I can stop them, and I want to slap myself silly. All I'm doing is giving Brandon hope, and I shouldn't be doing that, not when there's no chance of anything between us.

"I'll hold you to it."

Oh crud.

I reach for my purse and slide it around my shoulder, trying to get out of here without making more promises I don't intend to keep.

"I'm heading out now. It was great seeing you." I move toward the door and he stumbles to race me there, holding it open just as I expected he would.

"You too, Miss Andrews. I'll see you next week at the luncheon?"

I nod and brush past him, exiting the classroom.

"Of course."

I don't look back as I power walk down the hall toward the exit, not giving him a chance to say anything else. I wave to the receptionist then push my way out of the building.

I toss my purse into the car, set my phone in the center console, and insert the key into the ignition.

A loud scream escapes me when my phone violently vibrates against the cup holder.

Python: Did I lose you?

Me: No.

Python: I was worried I scared you off.

Me: You didn't. I was trying to blow off a coworker.

Python: Um. Okay then...

Me: What?

Me: Oh! Oh goodness! No! Not THAT kind of blowing off. Holy cats & dogs!

Python: I'm laughing so fucking hard right now.

Python: Not just because of your blunder but because I don't think you ever cuss, do you?

Me: No. It doesn't suit me.

Python: Yeah. You didn't look like a cusser.

Python: I'm sorry if my potty mouth offends you.

Me: It doesn't. It's sort of...hot.

Python: Yeah? Good. Because I wasn't going to suddenly stop cussing. It suits me just fucking fine.

Me: Shouldn't you be working?

Python: Shouldn't YOU be working?

Me: I'm finished for the day.

Python: Already? How?

Python: Wait—does this mean I can talk dirty again?

Me: No!

Me: And I'm already done because I'm not technically working right now. I don't start for another month. I was taking pictures so I know how I need to decorate.

Python: Ah. That makes sense.

Me: Why aren't you working?

Python: Oh, I am. I'm just multitasking.

Python: Also because my best friend is my boss and I don't really HAVE to work.

Me: That doesn't sound right.

Python: It's not. It's just what I tell myself to make me feel better about slacking off and not doing my job.

Python: Actually, I should go. I've spent too much time not working already.

Python: But, Monty?

Me: Yes?

Python: Can I text you again?

I don't respond right away because I honestly don't know what to say.

I want to say no because, though I don't know him

well, I can tell he's all kinds of wrong for me. He's crass and direct and out of my league.

But I want to say yes for all the same reasons because it's the exact opposite of anything I've had before.

If I'm starting over fresh in a new state, might as well do it with a bang—maybe even a literal one.

Me: Yes.

CHAPTER 4

ROBBIE

> Me: Can we go back to Saturday? I cannot stop thinking about you up on top of that counter. It's a sickness at this point.

I AM A DISGUSTING, shameless man.

But a very prompt, disgusting shameless man.

I waited until 5:01 PM to text Monty again.

Sure, my opening line could use some work, but I'm not lying to her. I've been halfcocked and ready to go since Saturday night.

In fact, no amount of masturbation—and there has been plenty—has been able to touch this need inside me.

I reflect on what Zach said earlier, and perhaps he was right on the money: I didn't finish things with Monty, and if there's one thing I am in life, it's a finisher.

The fact that she walked away without letting things come to a natural, satisfying end with us is killing me. I can't handle it.

I want more. I need more.

Monty: 5:01, right on the dot.

Me: Did you expect anything else?

Monty: I don't even know you, but I can safely say no. It's exactly what I expected you to do.

Monty: Shouldn't you be driving home from work and not texting?

Me: I've been off work since three, thank you very much.

Monty: Shoot, maybe I should go work for MY best friend. Those are some nice perks you got there, Mr... Wow, I don't even know your last name.

Monty: That realization just made me feel so...dirty.

Me: Cross. My last name is Cross.

Monty: Hi Robert Cross. I'm Montana Andrews. Even though you've already had your tongue down my throat and your hand up my skirt, it's nice to officially meet you.

Me: Likewise, Montana.

Me: Okay, I'm just gonna say it: that's a weird name. What gives?

Monty: It's where I'm from.

Me: No, it's not.

Monty: Is too.

Me: You do not look like you're from Montana.

Monty: How exactly does one look like they're from Montana?

Me: You know, lots of jean jackets and cowboy hats and boots. Everyone rides horses and chases bulls there.

Monty: Is THAT what people think of us?

Me: The geographically challenged, only lived in one place his whole life people do.

Me: That's me, in case you didn't catch that.

Monty: Golly, I'm so glad you explained that one to me.

Me: Smartass.

Me: You're sexy, but you're a smartass.

Monty: You like it.

Monty: ^^I've never said anything like that before.

Monty: Moving on. So you've lived here your whole life?

Me: Yes, around these parts. We lived in a few different towns but finally settled here.

Me: How'd you end up on the east coast? Work?

Monty: Life. I had some…relationship troubles and decided to start over, so here I am.

Me: That's a big move. I hope the "relationship troubles" weren't anything too serious.

Me: And in case you wanted CliffsNotes for that text, I meant please fucking tell me your relationship troubles don't involve an abusive ex.

Monty: Oh, gosh. No, nothing like that. He just wasn't good at sleeping in one bed at night is all.

Me: Good. I'm glad to hear that.

Me: Annnnd that came out wrong.

Monty: LOL I knew what you meant.

Monty: It's fine though. I'm enjoying the eat couches now.

Monty: EAT COATS

Me: Please, tell me more about eating couches and coats. I'm intrigued.

Monty: EAST COAST

Monty: That was exhausting.

Me: It was very enjoyable on my end.

Monty: You're probably just laughing your bum off over there...

Me: Bum? You don't even cuss in text?

Monty: *blushes* Erm, no.

Me: Is it weird that I find that hot?

Monty: I find your cussing hot, so perhaps not.

Me: Perhaps.

Me: You sound so...buttoned-up.

Me: Which I also find hot, and that makes no sense to me.

Monty: Me either.

Monty: Out of curiosity, what type of girls are you normally attracted to?

Me: The exact opposite of you.

Me: I don't mean that to sound harsh, but it's true. I've only had two real relationships in my life and both were with women who were bold and didn't require an entire bottle of sunscreen to go outside.

Monty: That last part made me laugh because it's so true. Being a ginger is a real struggle.

Monty: The first part reaffirms my whole we're not each other's type thing. I don't know why we're bothering texting.

Me: Scroll back through and read my message from 5:01. Then you'll know why.

Monty: Oh.

Me: Yes, "oh".

Me: And because it intrigues me that I'm still thinking about you.

Me: My best friend Zach has a theory about this...

Monty: Your best friend that's your boss?

Me: Same one.

Monty: YOU TOLD HIM ABOUT WHAT WE DID?!

Me: Nooooooo, definitely not.

Monty: You're lying. I don't know how I know it via text, but you're lying.

Me: Fine. You caught me.

Me: But can you blame me? Our time spent in the bathroom was HOT!

Monty: I told my sister.

Me: See? Now we're even.

Monty: About this theory...

Me: Right. (You get me distracted so easily...) His theory is: we need to bang.

Monty: EXCUSE ME

Me: You read that correctly.

Monty: We need to "bang". That's his advice to you?

Me: Yes, and he's a certified woman whisperer, so I trust him.

Me: Fun fact: he and his—as he'd want me to phrase this—live-in girlfriend met via texting.

Me: Good things can come from random encounters.

Monty: You're advocating for us to bang?

Me: Yes.

Me: What do you say?

Monty: No.

Me: Hm. I didn't see that coming.

Monty: YOU DID TOO!

Me: Fine. I did. But what do you say we get to know each other a bit and then see about the banging?

"You still texting her, man?"

I grin at my best friend. "Yeah. I brought up your banging idea."

We're in Zach's basement, our old office, where a video game marathon is happening. Xavie liked the idea of spending time with Zach and Delia so much he demanded I drive him over here after camp was over for the day.

I gave in easily, only because I wanted Marshmallow snuggles.

The pygmy goat is the only one who likes me out of the three. Milk Chocolate and Graham Cracker snub me every time I try to get close, the little shits.

As if he knows I'm thinking about him being my favorite, Marshy snuggles into me closer, and I run my hand down his back. *At least someone loves me.*

"I wanna bang!"

Zach's eyes bulge from his head. "Uh..."

"My friend Marty from school bangs all the time. He and his dad love doing it."

"This is getting worse," Zach mutters from beside me.

"Sometimes they bang so loud it wakes the neighbors up."

"That, um, that sounds interesting, buddy."

"Can we get some drums so we can bang hard too?"

A relieved look crosses Zach's face and I clap him on the shoulder.

"Way to save face, dude. You did good."

"How did you keep a straight face during all that?"

I shrug. "Practice, and because I kind of figured he was going somewhere with it. 'Banging the drum' is what they call it at Marty's. His mom is kinda hippie-ish and they have bongos out in the garage the kids love to play with."

He glares at me. "Could have warned me, you douche."

"And miss the look on your face? Nah."

"Ass."

"Dad, Uncle Zach said—"

"Yeah, yeah. I heard him." I glare over at him. "But he won't say it again, right?"

Zach shrugs, a grin firmly in place.

Fucker.

He nods toward my phone. "What'd she say?"

"It's...uh... I don't think it's promising."

"You're you, Robbie—of course it's promising."

"I don't know. She's not falling for my usual charm."

"You have charm?"

"Shut up."

He laughs at his own joke. "You told her you wanted to bang her—that's not having charm."

"*You* told me to tell her that!"

"And you listened to me? I can't believe that."

"I hate you."

"Gromble, gromble, gromble," he teases.

"It's grum, moron."

"Same-same dif."

I groan and shake my head. "You make me want to take a nap, and I hate napping."

"Weird, Delia says the same thing."

He shrugs and continues kicking my kid's ass in the racing game. Zach's a big enough nerd not to grant the kid any mercy...even if he is only seven.

My phone buzzes on my knee and it spooks Marshy, sending the goat running.

"Ah, hell. Sorry, buddy!" I call out, and Xavie runs to grab him before he gets loose up the stairs.

"It's fine. Xavie, can you let him out? Just right there out the back door."

He coaxes the goat outside to be with his brothers,

much faster than I'd ever be able to, and returns to his video game like nothing happened.

"Hey, Dad," he says, controller in hand, eyes locked firmly on the screen.

"Eye contact, bud," I remind him.

He presses a button on the controller and sets it down, turning my way. "Sorry. I wanted to ask you a question. Can I?"

"May you, and although you technically just did, yes. What's up?"

"Can I stay the night here tonight?"

I clutch at my chest. "And leave your old dad to fend for himself? Absolutely not."

His lip juts out. "Aw, man, but I wanted to stay here with Uncle Zach again."

"You'd pick Uncle Zach over *me*? Where did I go wrong with you?"

Xavie exhales sharply. "I'd pick you first, but Uncle Zach second...or maybe Marshy."

"You'd put my own goat in front of me? That's messed up," Zach says.

"BURN!" I yell. "But, seriously, kiddo, you want to stay here?"

He bobs his head up and down. "Like old times."

Ah, that's it—he's missing being here with Zach.

I have to admit, I do too sometimes—but only for the super cheap room and board, not the actual living with Zach part, of course.

"Um, allow me to chime in here right quick." Zach points to Xavie. "You are not allowed to stay here...*ever*. Not again."

Xavie's bottom lip begins to tremble. "W-Why not?"

"Because you *shat* on my bed, that's why."

"I sharted!"

"I know!" Zach hollers back. "And it got all over my bed."

"I didn't do it on purpose!"

"No one sharts on purpose, Xavie. No one."

"What if I promise not to shart again?"

It takes everything Zach has not to laugh. I can tell by the way his lips are twitching and his eyes are beginning to crinkle around the edges.

"You promise? Like really, *super* promise?" Zach pushes.

Xavie nods enthusiastically. "Really, super promise."

"Pinky swear? You have to say it. Say, 'Uncle Zach, I promise to never shart in your bed again.'"

They hook pinkies and my son stares him right in the eyes as he solemnly says, "Uncle Zach, I promise to never shart in your bed again. I didn't shart on purpose though."

Zach chuckles. "All right then. The next weekend you're with your daddio, it's on. We'll have a big, huge slumber party. Me, you, Delia, and the S'mores brothers. Deal?"

"Deal," Xavie replies enthusiastically, then promptly goes back to playing his video game like we didn't just have an entire conversation revolving around him sharting.

I exchange a look with Zach.

"Your kid," he mumbles, picking up his own controller and getting back into the game.

I shake my head and check the message waiting on my phone.

> Monty: I think that's something we could do.

> Me: You think? Or you're sure?

> Monty: Are you asking if I'm sure I'll still want to bang you once I get to know you? No. That I have no darned clue about.

> Monty: But if you're asking if I'm sure I want to get to know you, then yes.

> Monty: You seem interesting enough and I don't have any friends here, so why not?

> Me: "Interesting enough." My ego thanks you.

> Monty: I'm certain it could use the blow.

> Me: I know of something else that could use a blow…

> Monty: YOU ARE SO PERVERTED!

Me: Guilty as charged.

Me: But you like it.

Monty: You think you're so smooth.

Me: I have something that's smooth. 😉

Monty: ARE YOU FINISHED?

Me: Give me five minutes and I can be. 😉

Monty: ROBERT CROSS!

Me: Stop calling me Robert. It's not even my name.

Monty: Your name is just Robbie?

Me: Yes. Was actually one of the things Zach and I bonded over. He's just Zach, not Zachary or some other shit. I'm JUST Robbie.

Monty: Goodness. I am so embarrassed right now. Why didn't you correct me earlier?

Me: I was too focused on your weird name to pay attention.

Monty: My name isn't THAT weird.

Me: You're named after a state. That's not exactly normal.

Me: You said you have a sister, right? Does she have a weird name too? Any other siblings?

Monty: I have two siblings. My sister's name is Denver, but we call her Denny, and my younger brother's name is Charleston, but we call him Chuck.

Monty: And I've just realized why you said our names are weird. *facepalm* Thanks, Mom and Dad!

Me: It's kind of cute though. Except Charleston. That's just weird.

Monty: We thought so too, that's why he's just Chuck.

Me: Why those names?

Monty: Dad's from Charleston. Mom's from Denver. We lived in Montana.

Me: Be honest, Monty—how much did you get picked on for being named after your home state?

Monty: Ugh. SO much. They all thought Denny's name was cute though.

Me: *cue eye roll*

Monty: LOL thanks for being on my side, ROBBIE.

Me: Much better.

Monty: So, FRIEND, what are you doing right now?

Me: Oh hell. This is going to sound so nerdy and not sexy.

Monty: Good. You need to be knocked down a few sexy pegs.

Me: Do not.

Me: Anyway, I'm sitting in a basement playing video games.

Monty: NERD!

Monty: KIDDING! Maybe.

Me: I mean, I kind of AM a nerd, though.

Monty: Because you play video games? I play a mean Mario Kart and I'm not a nerd.

Me: You're totally a nerd, Monty. You're a buttoned-up, study until you die kind of nerd though.

Me: And it's sexy as hell.

Monty: You're really going to give me a complex here.

Me: I doubt that.

Monty: Why are you a nerd though?

Me: I, uh, I code for a living.

Monty: Right. And was that code for something else?

Me: Ha! No. I mean, I write codes. I develop apps.

Monty: I thought you worked with kids?

Me: I do, but in a roundabout way. I helped develop an app called Embody Positivity (go ahead and Google that shit...we're legit) and we run a "safe house" of sorts.

"You guys still talking?"

"Yeah."

He pokes my cheek. "You're blushing and it's cute as hell."

"Please go away."

"Uh, bro, you're in *my* house—you go away." He gasps. "Holy crap! I just realized I can kick you out because you don't live here anymore. This is the best news I've heard all day."

"Someone's exaggerating."

"He does that a lot," Delia says as she makes her way down the stairs. She looks from me to Xavie. "Are you boys staying for dinner?"

"What are you having?" my son asks.

"Dude! Not cool. Thought I was raising you better than that."

He shrugs. "It's an important question."

"He's not wrong," Zach adds.

"If it's pizza, we're in," Xavie answers for us.

I grin, because, like Zach said, he's not wrong.

Delia laughs and shakes her head. "Pizza is fine. Zach, put in our order, please?"

"You got it, babe."

"*You got it, babe,*" I mock. "Disgusting."

"You just wish I'd call you babe." Zach smacks a kiss to my cheek and dodges my fist before running up the stairs to go place the pizza order.

Delia takes his spot on the couch and shrugs. "He's your best friend."

"He's your boyfriend!"

She sighs. "Don't remind me."

"Xavie thinks Zach hung the moon. Maybe we should let him claim the doof."

"I'm pretty sure your son still eats his own boogers, Robbie—is he really the best judge of character?"

"Hey! I don't eat my boogers!" He slides his eyes sideways, which is his tell. Kid will probably dig one out on the car ride home and stick it to the seat or some shit. "Anymore."

Delia curls her lip and mimics Raven-Symoné's character from *That's So Raven*. "Ya nasty."

He giggles, and they launch into some sort of who can do the better "ya nasty" voice competition.

> Monty: I Googled.

> Me: Yeah? Was wondering where you disappeared to.

> Monty: Boobie, I'm in awe right now.

> Monty: Oh crows. I meant ROBBIE.

> Monty: But you knew that...

> Monty: Still embarrassing.

> Monty: As you can tell, I'm not so great with technology.

> Me: Did they not have any in Montana?

> Monty: HUSH IT, MISTER!

> Monty: They have technology. WE just didn't have it in my house. My parents weren't fond of it, so we didn't have computers or cell phones, and we had tube TVs. MIND BLOWN, HUH?

Me: Fuck yes it is! That's...that's... PREPOSTEROUS! How is that even possible?

Monty: It was my norm.

Me: What if you were stuck somewhere and needed a ride? What if something happened? If your car broke down? What if the world was ending and the aliens were coming for you AND YOU COULDN'T PHONE HOME?!

Monty: First, very clever. Second, I didn't have a car. Third, we'd just make do? That's what my parents always said. I didn't get a cell phone until I went away to college. That's when I got my first computer too. I wasn't allowed to even buy anything when I got my first paycheck.

Me: This is seriously blowing my mind right now.

Me: My parents made me work hard as shit for everything I got, and cell phones weren't even cool for kids to have until I was a junior/senior, but still.

Me: So what'd you do for fun?

Monty: Read.

Me: See? Nerd. So hot.

Monty: Stop it.

Me: What are you gonna do? Call me Boobie again?

Monty: I don't think I wanna be your friend anymore.

Me: We can still bang though, right?

Monty: We'll see.

CHAPTER 5

MONTY

Python: So, I was thinking about the night we met...

Me: You're still horny, you want to bang —yes, I get it, Robbie. *eye roll*

Python: Well, little miss THANG, I wasn't going to say anything about how I still wake up nearly every day with morning wood courtesy of a certain redhead, or how I've spent a stupid amount of time taking cold showers, or hot showers with extra soap, BUT, I digress...

Me: Get on with it already.

Python: Ooooh. Someone's testy today. Get your Cheerios peed in?

Me: Basically.

Me: Just frustrated by a coworker.

Python: I thought you hadn't started work yet.

Me: I haven't. I'm here decorating.

Me: Anyway, he keeps asking me out for drinks and stuff. Normally, I'd go but...

Python: But you're busy making banging plans with a hot-as-fuck, tattooed single dad, right?

Me: Whatever helps you sleep at night.

Me: No. I'd love to make a friend, but he doesn't want to be just friends. He wants more and I'm not into that...not into him.

Python: Then tell him that.

Me: I have! Several times!

Python: How? Men are real fucking stupid and sometimes we need shit SPELLED THE FUCK OUT for us.

Me: I've turned him down every single time.

Python: Something tells me that while that may be true, it's only partially true.

Me: Wait, what?

Python: Listen, Monty, you're a sweet girl, super fucking sexy in a girl-next-door kinda way, but that's just it—you're sweet. I bet when you turn him down you say, "Not tonight. Maybe next time." Huh? That's what you say, right?

Me: Oh cats. Yes, it is.

Me: Is this all my fault then?

Python: First, "Oh cats"? Really? You don't even say hell?

Python: Second, no. The dude is a fucking idiot for not taking the hint, but next time be firm.

Python: Tell him about the hot, VERY muscled, big-cocked guy you're gonna be banging soon. That'll chase him away.

Python: Still there, Monty?

Me: Is it possible to die from rolling your eyes so hard?

Python: You texted back, so apparently not.

Me: You know what I just realized? You never elaborated on the whole "the night we met" story of yours.

Python: Because you just had to go and make it all about you.

Python: Kidding. And no, I didn't, huh?

Me: Well?

Python: I was wondering why it was ME you went into the bathroom with. I mean, out of all the dudes in Lola's, why me? And don't say I was the first to approach you. That's bullshit, and if it isn't bullshit, your standards are extremely low and we need to have a chat about that.

Me: No, you weren't the first to approach me. You just had the best opening.

Python: I think you're the one with the best opening. 😉

Me: What??

Me: Oh. EW! ROBBIE!

Python: Sorry, sorry. Keep going.

Me: ANYWAY, your, um, for lack of a better word, pickup line was the best I'd heard.

Python: THAT was the best one? There is literally no way.

Me: It's true. One guy asked if I wanted to see his "holy grail" and another said he "farts in my general direction." A third said something about going the "full Monty" with me, and I had no clue what that meant until I Googled it later.

Python: Oh. No wonder you picked me, huh?

Me: Stop saying "picked" like I planned to make out with a stranger in the bathroom.

Python: That's not all we did.

Me: Don't start.

Python: Fine, I'll finish—oh wait, you already did...

Me: And you didn't. Who's the real winner here?

Python: Fuck. FOILED AGAIN!

Me: It's, "Curses! Foiled again!"

Python: Well, I said fuck.

Python: Did that turn you on, Monty?

Python: FUUUUUUUUUUUUUUCK

Python: Did I lose you again?

Me: No, I was driving back to my apartment. My phone just read that out loud and I almost swerved off the road from laughing so hard. SO, THANKS FOR THAT.

Python: But did you die?

Python: Guess what I'm doing right now.

Me: Not working even though you should be?

Python: Damn, you're good.

Python: I finished all my work already and have an hour to kill.

Me: Can't you just go home?

Python: And miss an entire hour's worth of pay? Hell no. I have bills and a kid to take care of.

Me: Good point. I didn't think of that.

Me: I can't wait until I'm collecting a steady paycheck again. I feel like such a freeloader.

Python: Aren't you though?

Python: Kidding, by the way.

Python: What are you doing while you're waiting to start work?

Me: Prepping for it, mostly.

Me: Or do you mean how am I contributing to society?

Me: Because the answer to that is napping.

Python: I miss naps so much. I regret not taking every single nap I was told to when I was a kid. If I could turn back time...

Me: IF I COULD FIND A WAY

Me: Cher break. Sorry, continue.

Python: You a Cher fan?

Me: I feel like I need to know if you're going to judge me or not before I answer this.

Python: Of course I'm going to judge you.

Me: There's that honesty...

Python: That wasn't an answer.

Me: Remember how I told you I was kinda sorta sheltered?

Python: I believe "kinda sorta" is putting it lightly, but continue.

Me: We didn't listen to "modern" music. Classics only.

Python: You're shitting me.

Me: Nope.

Python: You poor, poor soul.

Me: Hey, it's not bad when it's all you have.

Me: So, yes, I'm a Cher fan. Don't judge.

Python: You kidding me? I'd never judge. That woman has to be a goddamn vampire or some shit though. Doesn't look like she's aged a day.

Me: I've thought that myself a time or two.

Python: I knew I liked you for a reason.

Me: Guess what I'm doing right now.

Python: That's my line.

Python: But whatever it is, please tell me you're doing it naked.

Me: No! Stop picturing me naked, Robbie!

Python: Um...no.

Python: What are you doing?

Me: I'm downloading a music app so I can "get with the times".

Python: No shit, huh? Let me link you to my playlist.

Me: ARE YOU TRYING TO MAKE MY EARS BLEED?

Me: That just blasted through my speakers so loud I peed a little!

Python: First, I'm trying so hard not to laugh right now.

Me: I AM AT MY PLACE OF WORK, ROBERT.

Python: You are not!

Me: Fine. No, I'm not. I'm on the couch. But I DID have to go change my panties.

Python: I tend to have that effect on women.

Me: *glares*

Python: What?

Me: You know what!

Me: Now, please, send good music.

Python: What? That music IS good!

Me: It's LOUD!

Python: Okay, okay. Calm down, grandma.

Me: I am not a grandma!

Python: You're basically a grandma. I bet you play bingo for fun, don't ya?

Me: No.

Python: Why do I have a feeling you're lying?

Me: Shush! Now send me GOOD music.

Python: I repeat…that WAS good music.

Python: Give it another try. Listen to the lyrics.

Me: You want me to go deaf?

Python: Stop being so dramatic. Go listen and report back once you've given it a fair chance.

Me: UGH!

Me: But fine. Just know I'm going to moan and groan the entire time.

Python: Aw, I love it when you moan.

Me: Hate you.

Me: I have a confession to make.

Python: Please tell me you've been texting me while naked this entire time.

Me: You think I've been naked for DAYS?

Python: A man can dream, Monty. A man can dream.

Me: You finished?

Python: Dreaming of you naked? Never.

Python: But please, do tell me this juicy confession.

Python: P.S. I'm still holding out hope for it to be that you're naked.

Me: *rolls eyes*

Me: ANYWAY. I've been listening to your playlist.

Python: Yeah? Good shit, huh?

Me: It's not as bad as I originally thought it was. It's actually quite good...once you get past all that noise they make. The lyrics and message are beautiful.

Python: That's not noise, Monty. That's a fucking beautiful, chaotic symphony.

Me: That was...kind of lovely.

Python: Even with fuck thrown in there?

Me: Especially with it thrown in.

Python: You're loving my dirty mouth, aren't you?

Me: Yes.

Me: But don't tell people I said that!

Python: Too late. I just put it up on every social media platform.

Python: After our convo last night, I tried very hard to internet stalk you.

Me: Let me guess, you didn't get very far.

Python: I did not.

Python: You're going to tell me you're some unicorn and don't have a single social media account, aren't you?

Me: Yes.

Python: HOW IS THAT EVEN POSSIBLE?

Me: I didn't grow up with access, remember?

Python: I know, I know, but you're a grown-ass woman. You can do what you want now.

Me: Like choose not to use any social media?

Python: Ooooo. Robbie 0, Monty 1.

Me: More like Monty 13548.

Python: Someone's exaggerating.

Me: Am I really, though?

Python: It makes me feel better if I believe you are.

Me: So you're admitting that I'm winning by A LOT?

Python: Let's just move back to what we were talking about before.

Me: Uh huh. *chants* Monty, Monty, Monty!

Python: ANYWAY. I have to admit, I kind of like that you don't do the whole social media thing. It's...refreshing. Most people are so busy looking for that picture or counting the likes on their latest update that they forget to live.

Me: I feel the exact same way.

Python: Plus, without being attached to your phone, you get to miss all the Game of Thrones spoilers.

Me: SEE? Maybe I'm not so crazy after all.

Python: Whoa, calm down. I wouldn't go that far.

Python: Kidding.

Python: Kind of.

Python: Also, Robbie 1, Monty 13548.

Me: YOU ADMIT IT! *screenshot*

Python: Are you going out to Lola's tonight?

Python: Asking for a friend...

Me: No. Me being at Lola's last weekend was a once-in-a-lifetime thing.

Me: Are you going to Lola's?

Me: Not asking for a friend. I'm curious is all.

Python: My friend was going to go if you were going be there but now he's just gonna stay in, catch up on sleep. Kids are exhausting.

Me: Tell me about it.

Me: How is that, by the way—being a single dad and all?

Python: Hard. Rewarding. Exhausting. Fulfilling.

Python: He wasn't planned, in case you were wondering. I've never been married, so he's not from a previous marriage. People always ask that.

Me: Oh. Well, that's good to know, I guess.

Python: And his mom and I are on good terms too. No drama there. We co-parent the shit out of this kid, so you don't have to worry about our banging encroaching on "her" space or whatever.

Me: Um, also good to know...I think.

Me: I love how you can always throw your banging plans into any conversation.

Python: Just keeping the idea fresh in your mind.

Python: Also, hold up a second, MY plans? I thought you wanted to bang too?

Me: I have remained safely on the "we'll cross that bridge when and IF we get there" side of things since the beginning.

Python: That's not a no.

Me: Not a solid yes, either.

Python: Same-same dif.

Me: What?

Python: Nothing. Something Zach says.

Me: This Zach guy sounds interesting...

Python: But not more interesting than me, right?

Python: RIGHT, MONTY?

Python: Monty...?

CHAPTER 6

MONTY

Python: I just wanted to clear the air here—I'm never going to forgive you.

Me: Give it a rest, Robbie! It's been two days!

Python: NEVERRRRR!

Python: You fell asleep on me. AT 6PM. ON A SATURDAY! You practically called me boring.

Me: I did not.

Me: And don't you dare do that same-same dif thing again.

Python: *smirks*

Me: *rolls eyes*

Python: But my smirk was hot, right?

Me: Go work!

Python: Fine.

Me: I'm bored. I want to chat and you're my only friend.

Python: You know, the way to my heart is telling me how much you missed me.

Me: Fine. I missed you.

Python: DOWNLOAD ATTACHMENT

Me: Gee, thank you for the picture of your face.

Python: What? You said you missed me.

Me: Ugh.

Me: Also, are you still at work?

Python: Yeah. The youth center stays open late on Wednesdays. We're trying to get an all-nighter thing going on for anyone who really needs it, but right now all the kids just have our personal numbers in case they need any help or need to talk to someone.

Me: That's awesome.

Python: That's what I am, awesome.

Me: What time do you get off?

Python: Why? You want me to swing by?

Me: Don't you have to go be a dad or something?

Python: First, I'm ALWAYS a father, not just when I'm at home. Second, no. He's at his mom's this week.

Me: This week?

Python: Yep. We do an every-other-week thing, that way we aren't rushed for time with him.

Python: We'll trade random days here and there too. Like Saturday, for example—I should have had him, but there was something his mom wanted to take him to, so she got him. We're lax about it.

Me: It's great you two have such a solid relationship.

Python: It wasn't always this way, but yeah. I'm glad we're in a good place now.

Me: Were you together long?

Python: We were never really together.

Me: Explain that, please.

Me: Then I'll tell you all my juicy relationship drama.

Python: See, what had happened was...

Python: That was funny. Laugh.

Me: HAHA

Python: Good. It was a one-night stand...or at least it was supposed to be. She got pregnant and we tried hard to give things a go, but nothing stuck. I won't lie, we've been together several times over the years, always trying to make something work for our spawn, but it never has. So, we finally called it what it is and decided it was over. She has a new boyfriend now who I really like and he's good with the kid, so I'm happy for her.

Me: That's really mature of you, Robbie. I like that.

Me: Also, you made me laugh really hard when you called him your spawn.

Python: That's my favorite comic book hero, so I've called him that since birth.

Me: Er, spawn is a comic book hero?

Python: Get on Amazon. Right now. Download all the comics. Buy the movie. NOW.

Python: NO WAIT. I'll just come over. I'll read you the comics, touch your butt, watch the movie, do some heavy petting, and then we can discuss and bask in the glory that is Spawn, the greatest antihero ever.

Me: Very subtle on the butt-touching.

Python: What? Me? *blinks innocently*

Me: I'll get on Amazon now if it'll make you happy.

Python: Immensely.

Python: Don't forget to text me your address.

Me: MONTY ANDREWS HAS SIGNED OFF

Python: Get your technology right at least!

Python: Now, what about your drama?

Me: Well, now I don't want to tell you. It doesn't end up all hopeful and positive like yours. It's sad.

Python: A deal's a deal, Monty.

Me: Fine. Girl meets guy. Girl falls for guy. Girl won't, uh, give it up, so guy sleeps with everyone who isn't her. She doesn't find this out until AFTER they're engaged. It's tragic and heartbreaking, so she packs her bags and moves across the country.

Python: Holy fuck. That IS sad.

Python: Also, I want to punch that asshole.

Python: I'm sorry you had to go through that. But, hey, bright side to all this... YOU MET ME!

Me: So you keep reminding me with the incessant texting.

Python: You love it.

Me: I plead the fifth.

Python: That's always code for yes.

Me: He asked again.

Python: No fucking way.

Python: Show him this...

Python: DOWNLOAD ATTACHMENT

Me: Really? A picture of you flexing?

Python: What? I want him to see his competition.

Me: *sighs*

Me: I told him I had to go pick up tampons and left.

Python: You're never going to get your place decorated at this point.

Me: Probably not.

Python: So...did you save the pic or what?

Me: *glares*

Python: What do you think about a kid having a pet?

Me: This is extremely random.

Me: It's fine as long as they take responsibility for it. We had a farm in Montana, so we spent a lot of time with animals at an early age and learned how to care for them.

Python: You're a farmer too?

Python: This just keeps getting better and better.

Me: It was a very small farm. We only had a few goats and horses.

Python: Goats? Oh man, you'd really love Zach then.

Me: He has goats?!

Me: You should just go ahead and give me his number now. Might as well give up on us. Goats are my weakness.

Python: You are literally never meeting him. Ever.

Me: We'll see.

Me: (Also, I'm teasing. He's in a relationship, and I'm not trying to step on any toes.)

Python: I love that you felt the need to clarify all that. You're so...sweet. It's cute.

Python: But, yes, I know you only have eyes for me.

Me: That is NOT what I said.

Me: Let me guess, "SAME-SAME DIF?"

Python: *zips lips shut*

Me: Ughhhh.

Me: Why'd you ask me about pets?

Python: Because my son wants one and I'm considering it.

Python: I really just wanted an excuse to text you again, not gonna lie.

Me: Oooh! What does he want? A cat? A dog?

Python: A bunny.

Me: No way! Bunnies are SO cute! DO IT!

Python: But they poop.

Me: Everybody poops. Except girls. We don't do that.

Python: Riiiiight.

Python: I'll take him to look, maybe. I have a friend who has a rabbit rescue habitat. Maybe he'll be able to help us decide.

Me: You have a friend with goats AND a friend with bunnies? Please, please, please give me a number here!

Python: Watch it, missy. I'll start taking your begging for numbers seriously soon.

Me: Oh, you weren't already? Oops. 😉

Python: Ah, and another point to Montana Andrews.

Me: Nothin' but net.

Python: You know what I just realized? Our two-week anniversary is coming up.

Me: That's not a real thing.

Python: No, no, it totally is, and to celebrate, we should recreate our special moment in the bathroom, only this time we'll both be naked.

Me: I'm sorry, you want to bang me in a bathroom? A BATHROOM?

Python: What? We all have fantasies. Don't judge me.

Python: And don't act like YOU haven't thought of it either.

Me: Have I thought of us naked in a public restroom? No, I haven't. That's disgusting.

Python: You specifically said public... hmmm, noted. A private bathroom can be arranged.

Python: Come on, Monty. You looked so fucking hot up on that countertop, and you enjoyed every moment of it just like I did.

Me: You also bruised my bum!

Python: I'm sorry, what? I didn't even touch your ass.

Python: Well, I mean I did, but not in the really fun kind of way.

Me: What's the "really fun" kind of way?

Python: Oh, you know. YOU KNOW.

Me: Like...anal sex?

Python: My, Monty, did you just ask me to have ANAL sex with you? We haven't even had REGULAR sex yet. You dirty little thing you.

Me: And we never will if you keep this up.

Python: Okay, I'm done.

Python: Butt maybe we can talk about anal later?

Python: I see you're ignoring me. Just tell me how I bruised your ass.

Me: It was how I was...pinned against the counter.

Python: Are you being serious right now? Did you really bruise?

Me: Yes. Had a nice little reminder of our encounter for DAYS.

Python: Shit. I'm so sorry. I had no idea I was holding you up there at such a horrible angle for you. I feel terrible.

Python: And also a little sad I didn't get to tend to the bruise.

Me: You don't tend to bruises. You just want to see my butt.

Python: True.

Python: I really am sorry, though, and I do feel bad.

Me: Eh, it's no big deal. I bruise easily, and it's not like I was shoving you away.

Python: Because you want me.

Me: I'm deleting your number.

Python: Deleting it doesn't mean I can't still text you.

Me: Oh, right. BLOCKED!

Python: Suuuuure.

Me: MONTY ANDREWS HAS SIGNED OFF

Python: Nope, still not right.

Me: UGH

CHAPTER 7

MONTY

ALL I CAN THINK about is Robbie.

Scratch that, all I can think about is *giving in* to Robbie.

We've been texting nearly non-stop for almost two weeks now, and every time he brings up our "plan", I want to ask him for his address and drive over to his house... throw open the door, wrap my legs around his waist, demand he carry me to the nearest bedroom.

And finally lose my virginity.

All because of him. He's crass and sweet and so unlike any guy I've ever met.

It's really beginning to get to me.

Other than my ex, I've had approximately one boyfriend...if you count holding hands with a boy in the sixth grade as having a boyfriend. It isn't a lot to base my whole "unlike any guy I've ever met" thing off of, but it's enough.

I shouldn't still be thinking about him though...right?

"Pardon me."

"Oh, I'm so sorry," I apologize quickly.

It's official—I've lost it. Robbie is so stuck in my mind that I was just seconds away from running over an elderly woman.

"It's no problem, sweets. You look like you've got your head in the clouds. Thinking about a man?"

My face heats up and she chuckles when she sees the blush.

She's a little old lady, no more than five foot two, decked out in a bright pink suit and no shoes.

Which makes sense, because I did wander into a shoe store at the mall. The thought of that makes me giddy. The mall is a place every young girl loves to spend her time. It's also a place I wasn't allowed to go.

Since moving out east, I've been here no less than ten times, and I've only been here since the beginning of the summer.

"Aha!" She snaps her fingers together. "I caught ya!"

"How'd you know?"

"You had that whimsical look about you and almost plowed over an eighty-three-year-old woman. A man has to be on your mind for that to happen." She waves her hand. "When you're my age, you can spot young love from across the room."

"Love?" I balk. "No, it's definitely not love. I hardly know the guy."

"Oh." Her eyes light up. "You're thinking about having sex with him then." She nods like she understands completely. "I see. Well, that makes even more sense."

I choke on air and she's beating on my back with all her might within seconds. She sure does pack a punch for an octogenarian.

"I was not expecting that."

"Come on, now. What's a little sex talk between gals, huh? No harm in wanting some lovin'."

I blink twice. I cannot believe this is happening.

"I suppose that's true."

"So, what's this hunk look like?"

"He's, uh, he's tall and tan." She nods, hanging on to my every word. "Very muscled." Another nod. "Tattoos."

She fans herself. "Oh, my. I do love tattoos. It's not something us old folks grew up with, but it's one new trend this lady can appreciate."

"It was never something I was much into either until..."

"I hear you, sweetie." She grabs my hand in hers. "Well, he sounds like a catch, and if he has you all wrapped inside your head like that, you hold on to him."

"There's nothing to hold on to. We're just friends."

She winks. "With benefits, though."

My cheeks heat up again and she pats my hand before walking off.

What in the world...

I shake my head and continue on my way, only to

come to a complete stop when I round the corner to go to the next aisle.

"You said tall, tan, muscled, and full of tattoos, right? Didn't even bother mentioning my sexy grin and charm?" He tsks. "I'm disappointed, Monty."

I'm struck silent.

There's no way he's standing in front of me right now. It's impossible. I have to be hallucinating.

"Cat got your tongue?"

"W-What are you doing here?" I manage to sputter.

He lifts a broad shoulder. "Shoe shopping."

I roll my eyes. "I know that, Robbie. I mean...how'd you know I was here?"

He takes a step my way and leans down close.

Too close.

A woodsy scent wraps around me and I find myself leaning toward him without wanting to. The smell...it's too enticing, too warm, too *man*.

"What cologne are you wearing?"

His chest heaves with laughter. "No cologne. That's probably my deodorant."

"That's the best smelling deodorant that's ever existed."

Robbie gets even closer, his grinning face now just an inch from mine. He reaches out his hand and I can feel my heart begin to beat faster and faster, already anticipating his touch—only he drops his hand at the last moment, thinking better of it.

I try not to feel defeated.

"It's good to see you, Monty."

"I'm not sure how I feel about seeing you, Robbie," I admit.

"Why is that?"

"It's a little weird."

"Weird? How so?"

I hold up two fingers. "Two reasons. One, I'm out shoe shopping and here you are, popping up out of nowhere."

"I already told you I'm shoe shopping too. It's not *that* out of nowhere."

"Right, so you say, yet you're not holding any shoes."

He glances down at my hands. "Neither are you."

I roll my eyes and continue, "And two, I haven't seen you since you had me pinned to a counter in a public restroom with your tongue in my mouth. It's weird."

His grin grows. "Don't forget where my fingers were, Monty."

My body lights up and I wish I were back in that bathroom with him.

I wish his lips were on mine, his hands on my body, his warm skin under my palms—

"You're thinking about it, aren't you?"

I am. I'm thinking about how confident and sexy I felt with his hard body pressed against mine, how perfectly my legs wrapped around his waist, the way his hands tangled in my hair and pulled with the right mixture of sting and pleasure.

I'm thinking about the way he made me quake with desire and fall apart under him, how freeing it was, how good it felt, and how badly I want to do it again.

I want *him*.

"Stop it," I say out loud, partially to myself and partially to Robbie.

He chuckles, because he knows he's right, and I stick my tongue out.

"Real mature, Monty."

I push past him and mosey down the aisle. He follows.

"What are you doing at the mall in the middle of the work day?" I ask.

"Oh, you know, just stalkin' ya."

I turn around to glare at him, and he holds his hands up in surrender.

"Fine, fine. I'm getting shoes for Embody Positivity. We try to keep a few pairs at the center for anyone who needs them."

Tears spring to my eyes and I try to look away before he catches it.

"Stop it. You're making me out to be a hero or some shit."

"You're their hero, Robbie."

He snorts. "Am not."

"Accept it."

"Whatever. What are *you* doing here in the middle of the day?"

"Trying to find something classy, cute, and sensible for

work." I grab a box off the rack and show him. He shakes his head no, so I put them back and keep moving. "Besides, middle of the day is the best time to shop. No one's around to bother me." I raise a brow. "At least, no one is *supposed* to be around to bother me."

He smirks. "Sorry, not sorry."

"I'm shocked," I deadpan.

"Ah, that sarcasm—I've missed it."

"You have not."

I grab another box of shoes—this one a pair of practical flats—grab the pantyhose socks they provide, and find a seat, leaving Robbie standing there.

I'm sliding the second shoe on when he eventually saunters my way. I stand, checking the shoes out in the floor-length mirror.

"Wrong. It's my..." He holds his hand up, counting on his fingers and mouthing I don't even know what. "Fourth —fourth favorite thing about you."

"What are the other three things?"

"Well, for starters, your hair."

I bark out a laugh and spin his way, deciding this pair isn't for me. "That is *not* number one," I say as I slide past him and head toward the bench to take them off.

"Is too."

"Is not, Robbie. It can't be."

"And why not?"

"Because it's *ugly*. It's—"

He grabs my hand and tugs me his way without much

effort, effectively cutting off everything I was going to say next. I let out a gasp as I crash into him, and the memories of the last time we were this close slam into me.

I can't breathe. He's too close, feels too good.

He drags me back over to the mirror, turning me until I'm looking at our reflection.

We look ridiculous standing here together, his arm curled around my waist, my hand clutching his.

I'm so pale compared to him, my skin untouched and pristine. He's a walking wall of artwork. He towers over me, and that's saying something because I'm tall for a girl. The top of my head barely brushes his chin. I'm wearing another knee-length skirt, a pale blue t-shirt to match, and a short-sleeved button-up cardigan over top. He's in jeans and a polo.

There's nothing about us that's alike. We don't have a thing in common.

Yet, I can't deny how good it feels to be in his embrace.

"There is nothing ugly about you, Monty."

"I have—"

"Nothing," he insists. "Don't argue. Just accept it."

I close my eyes and we stand here. He doesn't let me go, and I don't try to leave.

I can feel his gaze raking over me and I love how it makes me feel. If there's one thing I've learned about Robbie in the past few weeks, it's that he doesn't hold back, and he's not doing so right now either. His gaze slides over every single inch of me, slow and leisurely.

I'm eager to open my eyes, wondering what he sees, but I don't. I'm enjoying the wait too much. The anticipation is making me antsy, and good things come to those who wait.

"God, Monty, I wanna touch you again, so bad."

I want you to touch me too.

"I haven't been able to get you out of my head since we met. You don't know how many times I've stopped myself from asking for your address, from calling you just so I could hear that rasp of yours again."

"My voice isn't raspy."

His lips collide with my ear as he whispers, "It is when I'm making you come."

I nearly drop to my knees, not expecting those words.

His grip tightens around me, and the hard length of him presses into me from behind. Brazenly, I swivel my hips, pushing against him...against *it*.

"Fuck," he mutters.

Then we're moving.

My eyes fly open as he tugs me down the aisle. The heat from the summer air licks at my skin when he pushes open the door and navigates us outside.

I don't say a word the entire time. I'm too curious...too excited.

He's speed walking and I'm uncertain where he's leading us until we round the corner and the loading bay comes into view.

He tucks us into the shade, my back resting against the

brick wall as his arms come up to cage me in. His eyes drop to my parted lips and he watches me with rapt attention.

His breathing is labored, and mine is no better. His eyes are wide, pupils dilated, and his tongue snakes out to wet his lips.

Finally, our eyes lock. The connection is so intense I want to look away. I *need* to look away, but I don't. I can't.

Because I know what's coming next, and I don't want to miss it.

"I'm going to kiss you, Monty. Fair warning."

He waits for my protests, but he's not going to get any.

He smashes his mouth to mine, and it's just as good as it was before.

No, it's *better*.

I'm not sure how it's possible, but it's true.

Robbie's hands slide into my hair as he draws me closer and pushes me away all at once. I don't even care that my favorite sweater is rubbing against the dirty building or that there will probably be pilling from it.

In this moment, the only thing that matters is Robbie's lips on mine, how soft and hard they are, how perfectly they fit my own, how stupid amazing it feels when he sucks my lower lip between his and bites down just the slightest bit.

I need more—more kisses, more contact, more of everything.

Somehow, he knows it. His hands are suddenly under

my bottom and he's lifting me into his arms. My legs lock around his waist.

"That better for you, Monty?"

I gasp at the contact and nod. I can now feel every inch of his arousal against me.

He chuckles. "That's what I thought."

He trails kisses from my collarbone to just under my ear as he thrusts his hips into me. His...*python* rubs against all the right spots, and I do my best not to moan.

Me—moaning as a man presses me against the wall of some building at one in the afternoon, his mouth on my neck, my legs wrapped around his waist, his erection teasing my clit.

Who have I turned into?

"Goddammit, Monty." He exhales against me. His hands grip my ass tighter and I can tell it's taking everything he has to not take this any further. "You're killing me."

"You're the dying one? Are you serious right now? You've been rubbing against all my favorite places for the past several minutes and I'm completely tied up in knots over here."

I pull back and he grins at me. "You really going to complain about that?"

I roll my eyes and pull his head closer. "Shut up and kiss me again."

And so he does.

This time he's swift to sweep his tongue into my

mouth and I'm lost...lost in this kiss, his touch, and the dirty words he keeps muttering.

There's this soft patter taking over, and I swear it's my heart trying to hammer out of my chest.

"Ahem."

That sounds out of place.

I'm too lost to care.

"Ahem. Excuse me."

Excuse you, sir.

Wait...

I wrench my mouth from Robbie's, whipping my head to the side to find a man standing there, arms crossed over his chest and eyebrows raised into his hairline. He looks pissed.

Robbie's still peppering kisses down my neck, my fingers are still threaded in his hair, and I'm just now thinking I should push him away.

"Robbie..."

"You're right, we should go back to my place. I agree."

"No, *Robbie.*"

Finally, he lifts his head from my neck and locks eyes with the stranger.

His stare turns cold and he gives the man a sinister grin. "Enjoying the show?"

You can see the guy's confidence begin to waiver with the way Robbie's looking at him, and I can't say I blame him. It's scary, and Robbie's massive.

"I don't want to cause any trouble. I'm just here for the girl."

Robbie unhooks my legs from around his waist and sets me on my feet. The movement is swift and easy, like my weight is nothing to him.

"Want to try that sentence again?"

The guy gulps and plucks at the lanyard around his neck. "I, uh, I'm from Shoe World. I'm going to need you to come with me, ma'am."

"W-What? Why?"

His eyes slide down to the flats on my feet.

The shoes I was trying on.

The ones I didn't take off before Robbie dragged me from the store for an impromptu make-out session.

I stole.

I stole.

"Oh my cats!" I smack my forehead a few times. "I can't believe I'd be so stupid. I-I...I have *never* stolen anything in my life. I'm *so* sorry. Please don't arrest me. I'll pay for them. I..."

Robbie's laughter breaks through my plea and I spin his way with a glare.

"You! This is all *your* fault!"

"My fault?" he argues. "How could this possibly be my fault?"

"Because you...you...y-you..."

"I, I, I what?"

He stands there with his cocky grin, hands on his hips, waiting for me to give him a good reason.

"That! Right there. Just...*you*."

He laughs again and I know I'm being stupid, but now he's being annoying and that's irritating me even more.

"Stop it, Robbie! You did this with your charm and good looks and spouting all that 'you're so beautiful, Monty' mumbo jumbo and then kissing me...*again!*"

"First off, that wasn't 'mumbo jumbo'," he says, air quotes and all. "You *are* beautiful. Right?" he asks the Shoe World employee who's still standing there, looking rather confused.

"Very much so."

The blush steals over my cheeks. "Th-Thank you."

"Second, are you telling me I've finally won you over with my charm and we can move forward with our plan?" He waggles his brows, like I needed a clarification that he's talking about banging.

"Robbie!"

"Monty!"

"You are insufferable!"

"Right, that's why you can't stop kissing me."

"I can't stop because *you* keep starting it," I insist.

"Uh, excuse me..."

"You can't stop kissing me because you *like* it—big difference."

"I do not!"

His grin grows because he knows that's a lie. "You

dirty, dirty liar."

"Um, miss?"

"Robert!"

"Montana!"

"Ma'am?"

"What?" I screech at the interruption.

The moment I realize what I've done—yelled at this poor man who's just trying to do his job—I'm pressing my skirt straight and patting my hair down. I clasp my hands in front of me and give the mall employee my best smile, despite being annoyed with myself for letting Robbie and his stupid charm get the best of me—again.

"I'm sorry, sir. I didn't mean to yell. Obviously, I'm out of my mind right now." I wave my hand Robbie's way. "This is not normal behavior for me, but that's no excuse. If you'd be so kind as to escort me inside, I'll hold my head high and take my punishment without any complaints."

"I just need you to pay for the shoes, ma'am."

"Oh." I will myself not to blush. "I-I...I can do that."

With one last glance at Robbie, the employee nods. "If you'll come with me, please."

I fall in step behind him, only sparing Robbie one last look before I'm carted off to buy the most uncomfortable shoes in the world because he just *had* to drag me outside in them.

"Fine. We'll call it a draw...for now," Robbie says with a wink.

Stupid charm.

CHAPTER 8

MONTY

Python: I'm not sorry about kissing you again.

Me: I don't want you to be sorry.

Me: But, I mean, you DID ditch me at the store after YOU made me STEAL. You can be sorry for that.

Python: I'm not sorry for that either. It was funny.

Me: You're oozing charm right now.

Python: It's a gift.

Python: I also feel like I should say that I wasn't stalking you...that much.

Me: I know...I think.

Python: So we agree then? I wasn't stalking you?

Me: What kind of question is that?

Python: I don't know. Ignore me. I'm tired. I've had a long day.

Me: I saw you three hours ago!

Python: Hey, a lot can happen in three hours!

Me: And what happened that has made you so tired?

Python: I was attacked.

Me: WHAT? When?!

Python: Earlier today. I was minding my own business, just trying to get some work done, and BOOM, attacked.

Me: Attacked how? One of the kids at EP?

Python: No, it wasn't one of them.

Me: Then who? A parent? TELL ME, ROBBIE. I'm worried!

Python: It was at this store. I was there to pick up a few supplies for EP and I ran into someone who's...let's say dangerous to me. Makes me lose my mind and do things I'm not usually prone to doing.

Me: ARE YOU SERIOUS RIGHT NOW?

Me: UGH.

Python: Yeah. Dead serious. I was attacked by some redhead who was dressed like she was from the prairie.

Me: I DO NOT DRESS LIKE THAT!

Me: Okay, maybe a little bit.

Python: Stop interrupting! I'm telling a story here.

Python: ANYWAY. There I was, just strolling through the shoe store, doing my thang. Then BAM! She's talking about how incredibly sexy I am, how much my muscles and tattoos turn her on. I was so stricken by this. I'd never even properly met her before and here she is, lamenting on and on to some poor old woman about my gorgeous body. Talk about awkward.

Me: ROBERT!

Python: SHH! And then, she FORCED me around the store while she tried on shoes. But wait, there's more! She then DRAGGED me out of the store, using me as a DECOY while she STOLE! GASP!

Me: I hate you.

Python: Oh, it gets better, because she then just threw her legs around my waist and KISSED ME. It got extra awkward when she was caught stealing. I hightailed it outta there as fast as I could.

Me: I'm never texting you again.

Me: Like, ever.

Me: NEVER EVER.

Python: You adore me.

Me: Not even a little bit.

Python: You still mad at me for yesterday?

Me: Yes.

Python: Liar.

Python: Also, I want to see you again.

Me: You JUST saw me yesterday.

Python: I know, but I wasn't properly prepared for that. I wasn't on my A game.

Me: THAT wasn't your A game?

Python: Fuck no. That was like B minus game at best.

Me: Is it sad to admit I'm now a little afraid to see what your A game is?

Python: There's no reason to be afraid of the python, Monty. 😉

Me: I swear, you have the biggest ego of anyone ever.

Python: Not true. Zach is 100 times worse than I am.

Me: I don't even know how that's possible.

Python: Trust me, it is.

Me: I'll take your word for it.

Me: Though now I REALLY feel like I need to meet this Zach character. He has goats, a giant ego, and says weird things—seems like an interesting guy.

Python: He's not. Horrible. Worst best friend ever. And ugly to boot.

Me: So you're madly in love with him then?

Python: Obviously.

Python: He's kind of amazing. He's the reason I didn't completely fall on my ass when I got Holly pregnant. We'd only been friends for a short amount of time, but he was right there with me for everything. Now I can't get rid of the guy.

Me: I can feel the love through your words.

Me: I promise to never tell him how much you love him.

Python: Good, good. We don't want rumors flying around that I have feelings and stuff. That's gross.

Me: Oh stop it. I have a feeling you're one of those guys who just looks huge and scary but you're really the biggest teddy bear there is.

Me: I feel like I should change your name in my phone now.

Python: To what? Teddy bear?

Python: WAIT! What do you have my name as now?

Me: Umm...no comment.

Python: No, no, no. You HAVE to tell me now. Them's the rules.

Me: Are you going to laugh at me?

Python: Yes.

Me: It's Python.

Python: ARE YOU SHITTING ME?

Python: Proof. I need proof.

Me: DOWNLOAD ATTACHMENT

Python: HOLY SHIT. It really is!

Me: Why would I lie about that?

Python: I don't know. I just didn't expect that outta you.

Me: What? It was a very clever joke. I mean, it did get me to make out with you and all.

Python: I'm so smooth.

Me: You have something that's smooth.

Python: God, I wanna kiss you so hard right now for that.

Me: Stop it.

Python: Stop what?

Me: Making me WANT you to kiss me again.

Python: Dammit, Monty.

Me: What?

Python: That didn't help. At all.

Me: Sorry.

Python: But not sorry, right?

Me: *grins*

Me: Hey, Robbie?

Python: Yeah?

Me: Happy two weeks.

Python: Happy two weeks, Monty.

Python: P.S. I told you it was a real thing.

Me: I take it back.

Python: Too late. No take-backs.

Me: What are these, kindergarten rules?

Python: I'll trade you my pudding for your cookie.

Python: Oh man. If you're sick and twisted that could be a really gross joke.

Python: I'm sick and twisted enough as it is.

Me: EW! ROBBIE!

Python: Did you get it? Pudding = love juice and cookie = love canal.

Me: Did you just call my vagina a love canal?

Python: Um, possibly.

Me: Remind me why I still talk to you?

Python: It's because I'm a good kisser.

Me: Ah, it's all coming back to me now.

Python: And because you're secretly turned on by all my perverted comments and my dirty mouth.

Me: I didn't say that.

Python: You didn't have to, Monts. I know you.

Me: You can't possibly know me. We've only been texting for like two weeks.

Me: No, wait—LESS than two weeks.

Python: It IS possible to get to know someone via text, you know. Zach and Delia are proof.

Me: How so?

Python: It's a long story that involves a wrong number, a baby goat, and the nerd who got the girl.

Me: That sounds...odd, but also kind of romantic.

Python: Sure. We'll go with that.

Me: I bet you're a closet romantic. You loooooove love and want to fall madly and deeply in love one day.

Python: I'm already madly and deeply in love.

Me: With whom?

Python: It's...complicated.

Me: How so?

Python: Because this relationship turns me into someone I don't want to be, makes me become someone I'm ashamed of, and that's not how relationships should be. It's forbidden. WE'RE forbidden.

Python: But I guess that adds to the romance, huh?

Me: Okay, so, this started out all cute and fun but now I'm kind of worried.

Python: No, no, don't be. There's still plenty of room in my life for you, Monty. Don't get scared on me now.

Me: *waits impatiently for the punchline*

Python: No punchline. I'm being serious. This forbidden relationship of mine is something I take very seriously. If I don't, I'll give in to the temptation, and it never ends in my favor.

Python: You know what, here—I'll send you a picture of us together.

Python: DOWNLOAD ATTACHMENT

Me: ROBERT CROSS. I HATE YOU.

Python: Keep telling me that and I might actually never start believing you.

Me: You are the literal worst.

Python: Nah, I'm too cute for that.

Me: DONUTS? Donuts are your "forbidden love"?

Python: It's a very toxic relationship, Monty. TAKE THIS SERIOUSLY!

Me: Seriously going to delete your number.

Python: Doubt it. You're in too deep with me now.

Me: Am not.

Python: Are too.

Python: Hey, Monty?

Me: Ugh. What?

Python: You at least chuckled, right?

Python: Monty? MONTY?

Python: Pft. You totally did.

CHAPTER 9

MONTY

Me: What's your favorite color?

Python: Royal blue. Why?

Python: Oooh! Are you buying me a present? I love presents! Do you need my clothing size? Shoe size? Dick length? Any other favorites?

Me: Why on earth would I need your wiener length?

Python: Holy shit. Say wiener again, Monty. PLEASE.

Me: No.

Python: I'm going to make you say it next time I see you.

Me: You act like there's going to be a next time.

Python: Oh, there is. You can only resist me for so long.

Me: We'll see about that.

Python: Why'd you wanna know my favorite color?

Me: I don't know. Sometimes it feels like I know too much and nothing about you all at once.

Python: Hey, I told you I sent that picture of me on the toilet by ACCIDENT. It was supposed to go to Zach.

Me: Right, and why do you two send each other bathroom shots again?

Python: It's a dude thing. You wouldn't understand.

Me: Sure. Whatever you say.

Python: Do you wanna know some of my other favorites?

Me: Yes! Tell me everything!

Python: Well, you already know my favorite color, food, and comic book hero (or antihero).

Me: Royal blue, donuts, and some dude named Spanky or something. Continue.

Python: I'm going to pretend you didn't just call him Spanky.

Python: My favorite movie is Waiting. Song is Bohemian Rhapsody. Book is Green Eggs and Ham. TV show is Buffy the Vampire Slayer. Favorite sport to watch is hockey. Favorite animal is French bulldog.

Python: Go ahead. Judge me.

Me: I have so many comments I'm not sure where to start.

Me: One, I don't know what Waiting is, but it sounds like a romantic comedy.

Python: No. It's disgusting and hilarious. There is a little love shit but not enough to make it a gross girl movie.

Me: My bad. How is a Queen song your favorite? I thought you liked that loud, obnoxious music?

Python: Excuse me, Queen is CLASSIC, and the music I like, which I know you enjoyed too, is based on TALENT. Freddie Mercury is the epitome of talent. Queen is lucky to have had him.

Me: I'll give you that.

Me: I'm not even touching the Dr. Seuss thing.

Python: IT'S A CLASSIC, DAMMIT!

Me: Fine. Explain the Buffy love.

Python: How can you NOT love it? It has everything: a badass crusader who's a woman, a kickass cast, VAMPIRES, romancy shit, and all kinds of cheesy lines.

Me: I've never watched it.

Python: Sometimes, not often, but sometimes, I question why I'm still texting you.

Python: Then I think of how hot you are and it all comes back to me.

Me: You like me for more than my "hotness."

Python: First, knock that quotes shit off and just own it. Second, yes, obviously.

Me: Favorite hockey team?

Python: Do you watch hockey?

Me: Yes. My family was big on sports.

Python: Red Wings.

Me: Seriously? No! Bruins are where it's at!

Python: Did we just get divorced before we even got married?

Me: Did you just propose before we've even dated?

Python: Hmm...depends on if you're saying yes or not.

Me: I'm not.

Python: Yikes. Awkward.

Python: Then no.

Python: Aren't you gonna hate on my favorite animal now? That's what you've been doing, hating on all my favorites.

Me: No. French bulldogs are adorable.

Python: So you're telling me the way to your heart is through a dog?

Me: No. But also maybe yes. We'll see.

Me: Also, why don't you just get one as a pet for your son if you love them so much?

Python: Because I'm a baller on a budget, baby, and those little shits are expensive as fuck.

Me: Well, baller, you better find a bigger budget if you wanna get to my heart.

Me: Oh my gosh! I'm kidding. That felt so dirty to write.

Me: Forgive me.

Python: You're adorable, Monty. Slightly awkward, but abso-fucking-lutely adorable.

Python: P.S. I'm not buying you a puppy.

Me: It was worth a shot.

Python: So, I did something and now I can't get rid of it.

Me: What kind of something?

Me: Wait...it? IT?

Me: YOU BOUGHT ME A PUPPY, DIDN'T YOU?

Python: DOWNLOAD ATTACHMENT

Me: Seriously? ARE YOU BEING SERIOUS, ROBBIE? I need to know!!!

Me: He is so cute!

Python: Oh, sorry. Wrong picture. That's just a photo of the pet I WANTED to get.

Me: ...

Me: So you didn't buy me a puppy?

Python: What? No. I hardly know you. That'd be dumb.

Me: *cries*

Python: Brush it off, Monts. I have something BIG to tell you.

Me: And now I'm scared.

Python: I can't say I blame you.

Me: Ugh. Stop leaving me in suspense and just get to it already!

Python: I...

Python: Gosh. I just...I don't even know how to tell you this.

Python: It's going to change the course of everything.

Me: You're stalling.

Python: Fine. I...I have crabs.

Me: ...

Python: I'm being serious, Monty. I HAVE CRABS.

Python: DOWNLOAD ATTACHMENT

Me: You know what? You really ARE a dad. You've got those dad jokes down to a science.

Me: What happened to the bunny?

Python: The bunny "doesn't have a cool color-changing option, Dad. What if I get bored and don't want it anymore?"

Python: So, hermit crabs it is!

Python: DOWNLOAD ATTACHMENT

Me: How many shells did you buy?!

Python: Quite a few. I never in my life thought I'd be a grandparent to crabs, but here I am.

Me: Congrats...I think.

Me: I'm also slightly sad you didn't get a bunny.

Python: Wellllll...

Python: DOWNLOAD ATTACHMENT

Me: YOU BOUGHT A BUNNY TOO?!

Python: I RESCUED a bunny.

Me: What's its name?

Me: Can I name him/her?!

Python: No. I don't trust you.

Me: Well, you should. I have a great name suggestion.

Python: For some reason, I doubt that.

Me: Is it a boy or a girl?

Python: A girl.

Me: Thumbelina Bruce Wayne Cross

Python: You're kidding.

Me: ...

Python: Oh wow. You're NOT kidding.

Python: No. HELL NO.

Python: Also, what in the actual fuck kind of name is that?

Me: I don't know. Thumbelina is cute and Bruce Wayne is Batman. Why wouldn't you want to name your pet after Batman? He's Batman!

Me: Come on, Robbie. Just do it.

Python: No!

Me: What were you going to name her?

Python: Sure as hell not Thumbelina Bruce Wayne!

Me: Spoilsport.

Python: I regret nothing.

Python: I think it's my turn to hate you.

Me: You named her Thumbelina Bruce Wayne, didn't you?

Python: Yes.

Python: It just fits her so well.

Me: Someone just took one step closer to making our "bang plan" happen.

Python: For real? Shit. I'll go buy ten bunnies and you can name them anything you want! Spanky, Sparky, Spidey, Tinker Bell! Whatever!

Python: Can I just say I enjoy the fact that a bunny is what's caused this? We'll be banging like rabbits in no time.

Me: And just like that, one step back. Don't be a creeper, Robbie.

Python: I take it back!

Me: Weird. As I recall, we're operating firmly under the "no take-backs" rule.

Python: I hate my mouth sometimes. It just runs and runs and I forget that the things it says can come back to bite me in the ass.

Python: Fine. You win this round.

Me: We can call it a draw. 😊

Python: You're my favorite.

Me: I know.

Python: I don't get it.

Me: Hello random conversation.

Python: Huh?

Me: Sometimes I feel like you text me in the middle of a conversation you're having with yourself. It's endearing at times, but also very confusing.

Python: We're supposed to be all in sync by now, Monty. Get with the program.

Me: Sorry. You're right. Let's start over.

Python: I don't get it.

Me: OMG!!! I KNOW!!! ME EITHER!!!

Python: Wow. Nice overkill.

Me: How rude.

Me: What don't you get?

Me: And if it's a math problem, I can't help you there. I'm not a good mather.

Python: Or speaker of English. Mather isn't a word.

Me: Is now.

Me: Now, what don't you get?

Python: Ah, yes. I don't get why we can't just hang out. We've been texting for three weeks now.

Me: We're still getting to know each other.

Python: You named my damn bunny, Monty. We're practically dating by now.

Me: Then why haven't you taken me on a proper date yet?

Python: BECAUSE YOU WON'T LET ME!

Me: Oh. Yeah. Right.

Python: Is that what you want? A date?

Me: No. I don't think I do.

Python: So just bang?

Me: That was the plan, right? We just have to bang each other out of our systems.

Python: Yes, that's the plan.

Me: Then we'll stick to that—getting to know each other, then work it out of our systems and going our separate ways.

Python: Yes. Yes, I'm liking this plan.

Me: If you don't fall in love with me first, that is.

Me: (I've always wanted to say that. I've seen it in so many movies, which is dumb because then the guy does fall in love...obviously.)

Python: Yeah, that won't happen. We don't have to worry about that.

Me: Right. We're good to go then.

Python: Yeah, totally.

Python: Right.

Python: I'm gonna go away now. This has gotten awkward.

Me: Your fault, not mine.

Python: Totally your fault, but whatever is gonna help you sleep at night, Monts.

CHAPTER 10

MONTY

"WHAT IS up with you lately? You're always attached to your phone."

I glance up from the screen to find Denny giving me that same exasperated look Mom would give her. Funny how that works.

"What do you mean?"

I ask it to save face because I know exactly what she means. I *have* been attached to my phone as of late.

Like, the last three weeks kind of late.

It's not non-stop, but it's enough to take note of. Sure, he's the first person my mind wanders to in the mornings and usually the last on my mind at night, but that's because we're still all keyed up from our tryst at Lola's...right?

"I mean, you're obsessed with it. You take it to the bathroom with you, and that's super gross because there are floating poop particles in there." She wrinkles her nose in disgust. "If girls pooped, that is."

I try not to laugh. You can leave home all you want, but sometimes things are just so ingrained in you that you don't even realize it.

Mom used to always tell us that talking about our "bodily functions" was the epitome of unladylike, so it's something we always avoid.

Which I find absurd because it's *natural*, for goodness sake.

But, that's how we were raised—to be good and proper, to follow directions and walk a very narrow path in life.

A path we couldn't choose.

Everything we did was decided for us: our clothing, our haircuts, colleges, majors. *No* was not in the Andrews children's vocabulary, nor were *I don't want to* and *I don't like that.* You liked what Martha and Clark said you liked, and that was that.

Denny rebelled against all of it. I embraced the struc-ture...until they took it too far and made me accept the proposal from my ex.

"Anyway, who are you talking to all the time?" she asks.

My body stiffens, and I'm suddenly highly annoyed by the fact that I can't lie to Denny, not even a little white lie like *Oh, nobody.* I can't do it. She'll know. I don't know if it's a twin thing or what, but she can *always* spot my lies.

"Robbie."

She frowns. "Who?"

"Robbie."

This time she rolls her eyes. "Yes, my hearing is perfectly fine, Montana."

"Well, Denver, all you did was ask me who, so I told you."

"Where do you know him from? You haven't been anywhere but..." She trails off and her eyes light up. "No way!"

I nod, knowing she's connected the dots.

"That guy from Lola's? You've been texting with that guy from Lola's? Are you serious right now?"

"Yes."

She claps her hands together and bounces around on the couch. "How's it going? Show me all the dirty pictures he's sent. I want to see that dick!"

I roll my eyes at her. "No."

"But he has sent dick pics, right?"

"Um, no. We don't do that."

She pretends to yawn and smacks her hand over her open mouth. "Boring."

"Denny, please tell me you do *not* send naked pictures to strangers."

"I don't." A smile forms on her lips. "I post them on Snapchat."

My mouth drops open. "You're insane."

"I'm having fun." She shrugs like it's no big deal, and

to her it's not, but me doing something like that? Never. *Ever.*

Sometimes the stark differences between me and my twin amaze me. We're polar opposites in everything. It's so weird how you can share the womb with someone for nine months, be as close as two people possibly can be, and yet have nothing in common.

Denver is wild and carefree; I'm reserved and care*ful.* She's a boy magnet, and I'm certain I put off some sort of repellant. She's "experienced", and I'm virtually untouched compared to her.

Even the way we look is different.

Denver has shoulder-length dark brown hair and skin that doesn't burn after she's in the sun for five minutes, while I'm stuck with red locks that come down to just above my butt and a complexion so pale Casper thinks I'm his doppelgänger.

"If you're not sending dirty pictures, then what are you guys doing?"

"We're talking."

She sighs and throws herself back into the cushions, pointing the remote at the TV and looking bored. To be fair, she does have some reality TV show on, and that stuff isn't even remotely interesting. "Classic Monty."

"What exactly does that mean?"

"It means you're playing it safe like you always do."

"I don't always play it safe," I argue. I shake my phone

her way. "I'm talking to the last person I didn't play it safe with."

"You made out with one man in a bar—not that big of a deal."

"To you, maybe, but it is for me."

She purses her lips. "Fair point, but you need more adventure, more fun. You need to—"

"Just go for it. Yeah, I heard you before, but I'm fine with what Robbie and I are doing. We're getting to know one another, taking things slow."

"This guy isn't leading you on, is he?"

"How could he possibly be leading me on via text?"

She shakes her head. "You know nothing about men. Hiding behind flirty messages is typical guy behavior— pretending to be someone else, someone you like, but in person he's different. Basically, he's just trying to get into your pants with his sweet, fake words. Then once you finally sleep with him, he'll never talk to you again."

I lift a brow at her. "Sounds like someone's talking from experience."

She shoots me a glare but doesn't say anything else. I don't push my luck.

"Besides, that's not him. Robbie is sweet. He's *kind.*" *And so very dirty.*

"And how do you know that's who he really is?"

"Because—" The rest dies on my lips because I realize I need to tread carefully. I still haven't told Denny about what happened at the shoe store. She has no idea I've seen

Robbie again since Lola's, and I need to keep it that way. She'll make this *huge* deal out of it, and that's not something I need right now.

Besides, I kind of like having Robbie and whatever it is that's going on between us...well, just between us. It's none of Denver's business.

"Because I just know," I finally say.

"From the texting, right. You can't *truly* get to know someone via text, Monty."

I want to argue with her, but I don't have the energy right now.

I've gotten to know Robbie better via text than I have any person I've met in my life thus far. Sure, I know a lot of that is because we have the screen to hide behind, but I also like to think it's because there's something there, some sort of chemistry between us.

Or I'm just making all this up to make myself feel better about maybe kind of sort of falling for a guy I barely know.

I'm a mess.

"Do you want me to step out of my comfort zone or not?" I shake the phone her way. "Because what I'm doing right now—carrying on a conversation with a virtual stranger—is *way* out of my comfort zone and we both know it."

"It's a good start, but you need more. You *know* you need more."

I do. I need to see Robbie again, but I know that's not what she's talking about.

"I'm not going to hook up with some random guy at a bar, Denny. I'm not..."

Her eyes fall to slits. "Go on. Say it."

I don't.

"Me, huh, Monty? You're not me. That's what you were going to say, right?" She laughs, but it's laced with malice, not humor. "I knew this would happen if you moved here. You'd spend your days judging me instead of realizing what a stuck-up goody-two-shoes you can be."

If there's one thing I've learned while living with Denny since the beginning of summer, it's that discussing her "extracurricular activities" is strictly off limits. The first week I was here she brought home two different guys —which, hey, that's her thing and whatever—and when I asked her about it, she jumped down my throat about how I was "judging her life".

It was a knockdown fight, and I'd like to not have a repeat of it.

"I didn't mean anything by it, Denny," I say, trying to calm her.

"Good." She crosses her arms over her chest and turns her nose in the air. "Good."

She stomps into the kitchen where she begins rummaging around in the cabinets. I hear a familiar crinkle and then the click of the microwave door opening, and I know she's making popcorn.

Popcorn is my weakness, and this is her apology for freaking out on me just now.

I know she didn't mean the cruel words she hurled my way, but it doesn't mean they don't hurt. She knows I'm upset, but she also knows I won't call her out on it.

"How about we go out tonight? Maybe we can find you someone else to talk to, not some stranger from three weeks ago who isn't even sending dirty pics."

"I'm perfectly fine with what Robbie and I are chatting about."

"Probably bunnies and puppies," she says with annoyance, and I can't help but laugh.

"Close, so close," I mutter.

"What was that?"

"Nothing!"

"Right." The microwave beeps and she pops the door open. "Ow, ow! Fucking fuck. That shit is hot!"

She empties the contents into a bowl, just like I like, and comes back into the living room.

"Anyway," she says as she takes a seat on the couch and passes me the bowl after taking a handful for herself. She doesn't actually *say* sorry, but I know that's what this is. "Tonight, you and me, Lola's. Let's go get our dance on."

"Do I have to?"

She eyes me and then the popcorn.

Maybe she wasn't apologizing. Maybe she was just buttering me up for a favor.

Ha. Buttering—because popcorn.

"Yes, you have to. It's a Saturday—we are not sitting around in our jammies all night, *and* you have to put your phone away while we're out. No Rob. This is a girls *only* night. You're spending way too much time on this one guy. You need to get out there and explore your options—you know, with a *real* guy."

"Robbie," I correct, even though she doesn't care. "I thought this was a 'girls only night'—doesn't that mean no bringing guys home?"

She scrunches her nose. "Don't get crazy, Monty. We'll see where the night leads us."

"I STILL CAN'T BELIEVE you wouldn't change."

I glance down at my outfit and shrug. "Why would I?"

"Because you look like you're going to church, not a bar."

"I'm wearing the shortest skirt I own!" I hiss. "I would never wear this to church."

"And yet it still comes down to your knees."

"I'll have you know this is *at least* two inches above my knees."

"Prude," she retorts with a grin. "Let's go grab a table."

Her words have me reeling, and I find myself studying

the vast differences between our outfits as we make our way through the crowded bar.

Denny is wearing a pair of skintight jeans and a top I'm certain is more of a swimsuit cover-up than a garment meant to be worn in public.

I *am* wearing my shortest skirt, and it feels as if everything is hanging out even though it does nearly come to my knees. My top isn't anything to glance twice at, just a plain white t-shirt, and I'm wearing a sensible pair of canvas shoes. I let Denny do my makeup and curl my long, red locks, and it's the most dressed up part of me.

We do an entire lap around the bar before she finally settles down at one of the few empty tables.

"Guess this one will have to do," she says on a sigh before waving a waiter over our way.

A guy who looks like he just stepped off the Jersey shore saunters our way, and there's an instant spark in Denver's eyes.

Looks like she's found her prey for the night.

"What can I get for you two beautiful bombshells tonight?"

Denny falls for his false charm in the blink of an eye. I know he just wants a good tip.

"I'll take a shot of your top-shelf tequila and a vodka tonic."

"Sure thing, babe." He turns his attention to me. "And for you, Red?"

I cringe at the nickname. It's so overused and so...typical.

"I'll take an iced tea, please. Unsweet," I think to add, nearly forgetting I'm in the south now and these restaurants constantly try to poison me with all that sugar.

Denver lets out an annoyed huff. "You're not drinking?"

"After last time, no. Besides, one of us needs to stay sober."

"You're the DD? I dig that," the waiter says with a grin. "I'll be right back, ladies."

"How?"

"Huh?"

"I said, *how*? How in the hell are we here for five freakin' minutes and you already have the waiter drooling over you!"

"The shortness of my skirt," I deadpan.

She laughs and flips her hair over her shoulder. "You look so sweet, but that tongue of yours can be so sharp, Monty. I love it."

I wave a hand. "Trust me, he doesn't care about me. He couldn't take his eyes off your cleavage."

"My, my—did you just say cleavage? I don't think I've ever heard such a profane word leave your clean little mouth."

"I can come up with a few profane words right now."

She laughs my comment off because she knows it's not

true. "Come on, scan the room with me. Tell me who you're calling dibs on."

"Um, none of them?"

"No, none of that bullshit, Monty. We're having *fun*. You're going to have *fun*."

"I can have fun sitting at the table," I argue. "I'm sure they'll bring me some sweetener with my tea. I can count the packets."

Denny fake yawns. "No. Not happening."

A tall Latino man with the most interesting brown eyes I've ever seen struts up to the table. His hair is cut close to his scalp and his lips are full, kissable.

"I saw that." He flashes a white smile at Denver. "There's no yawning this early on a Saturday night. How about we get you on the dance floor, wake you up a bit?"

She purses her lips and looks him up and down. "Hmm...tell me your name first."

"Right, of course." He stretches his hand toward her. "I'm Jarred."

"Jarred." She tests his name on her lips. "I like that. I'm Denver. Show me your moves, Jarred."

She places her hand in his outstretched one and he pulls her off the stool with little effort. As he leads her away, she grins back at me.

"You're next!"

I shake my head vehemently and her loud cackle mixes with the music, fading away as she gets lost in the crowd.

The waiter arrives at the table holding our drinks and frowns when he sees Denny is missing.

"Your girl left already?"

I nod toward the crowd. "Nah, just found new prey. You're off the hook."

He laughs and shakes his head. "That's a relief. I don't play for her team anyway." He winks. "You ladies just wave or holler when you need a refill. I'm Kayden, by the way."

"We will. Thank you, Kayden."

He hurries off to his next table and I'm left alone.

Most people would be uncomfortable sitting by themselves in a crowded bar; not me though. I'm...at ease, solitary but comfortable. I'm in the middle of all the chaos but no one's paying attention to me. It's the best of both worlds.

I scan the bar, people watching like it's my lifeline.

There's a couple making out in the corner of the bar, another arguing, a few other lonesome patrons, and several groups of people who are obviously together celebrating something fun.

I look toward the bar, eyeing the customers on the stools, and I nearly fall off my own when my line of sight crosses over familiar tattoos.

His back might be facing me, but I know exactly who it is.

Robbie.

His head is bent toward a caramel-haired woman,

her face full of laughter. She's stunning, leggy, and tanned with wild, curly hair. She's the exact opposite of me.

My heart sinks.

It's not that Robbie's "mine" or anything—he's free to do what he wants—but I thought we had *something* going on.

You're jumping to conclusions, Monty.

I'm right. Of course I'm right. I don't know her. He might not even know her. It doesn't *have* to be a date. She could be a friend. She could be...

Perfect for him.

He throws his head back and laughs. She laughs harder, leaning toward him.

They look so good together, so happy.

I want to run and cry and bury myself in my bed until I stop thinking of him.

Instead, I rise from my seat and begin walking toward the bar.

I don't make it far before Denny's sliding in front of me, sweaty from the dancing.

"Hey," she says, grabbing my hand and pulling me back to the table. "Rule number one of being at a bar: never leave your drink unattended. You could get drugged. Where ya headed?"

"I was going to the bar."

She eyes my full glass then grins. "You were so gonna sneak some booze, weren't you?"

"Do you even know me at all? I thought twins were supposed to be all-knowing about one another."

"A girl can dream, Monty. Give me that at least. If you weren't getting booze, what were you doing?"

"I..."

Ugh. I don't know if I should tell Denny that Robbie's here. She'll embarrass me, approach him, probably berate him *and* me for being right about him playing me through texts.

I don't want to deal with that.

My eyes flick toward the bar out of curiosity.

He's still there. She's still there. They're looking awfully chummy together.

"Who is that? Do you know her?" She's craning her neck, trying to get a good look at mystery girl. "Is she someone you work with? She's ridiculously gorgeous. I need to ask how she gets her hair to stay that curly because *damn.*"

"I don't know her," I say quietly.

Denny's still looking at them. "Why are you being a creeper then? You and that people watching of yours, so weir—"

Slowly, she faces me, her eyes wide, mouth slack.

"Monty, is that Robbie?"

"Y-Yes."

"Is that Robbie with *another* girl? That same Robbie I said was playing you?"

Here we go. "Yes."

"That son of a bitch!"

She leaps off her seat and marches their way before the shock wears off and I rush after her, though not before grabbing her drinks, leaving mine behind in my haste.

Denny's mouth is moving fast, no doubt giving Robbie the business as I make my way toward them as fast as I can.

I arrive just in time to hear Robbie say, "You're not Monty."

"No shit, Sherlock. I'm her twin."

Robbie's hazel eyes slide my way, the corner of his mouth tilting up in a grin.

"You never told me you have a twin."

I shrug. "You never asked."

"Oh, excuse me. My bad. I'll add that to my list of questions to ask everyone I meet. 'Hi, great to meet you. By the way, do you have a twin? I need to know just in case I get accosted in public. I have to make sure it's not you. You get it, I'm sure.'" Robbie's grin grows. "What is it with you Andrews gals attacking me?"

"What? We have *not* attacked you," Denny argues.

"I beg to differ."

"Beg to differ all you want, bucko. We haven't done shit."

His lips thin as he tries to hold his laughter back. To me, he says, "You didn't tell her?"

"Shush, Robert."

"She calls you Robert?" the woman, who I almost

forgot about with all of Robbie's sexiness so close, interjects.

"We'll get to that later," he says casually. "I'm dying to hear Monty tell Denver this story."

"How do you know my name?" Denny snaps. She gets so protective of me when she thinks I've been done wrong. "How does he know my name, Monty?"

"Because I told him."

"What's this 'attack' he's blabbering about?"

"He's delusional."

"He is not," Robbie says. "He is, however, very curious to hear how you're going to explain this one."

"Robert!" I hiss at him.

"Montana!" He laughs back.

"I am two seconds away from throwing this drink on you."

His eyes darken, but not in a menacing way—no, it's *sexual.* "You don't even want to know the thoughts that just ran through my mind."

I gulp and take a step back—not because I'm afraid of Robbie but because I'm afraid of what I'll do if I stand too close with him looking at me the way he is.

Denver lets out a low growl. "Would someone just explain things, please? I'm getting annoyed and I want to slap this asshat already."

"Why am I getting slapped?" Robbie asks. Then he shakes his head and waves his hand. "No, no. We'll come back to that. Monty first."

"I hate you," I grumble.

He snickers. "Liar."

"Monty." Denver says my name with fire in her tone, and I know she's reaching her last nerve.

"I'm with her," the girl says, pointing at my sister. "I have no idea what's going on right now and I want to know."

"Fine!" The single word nearly explodes out of me. I point at Robbie. "This guy stalked me at the mall last week and dragged me out of a store to *kiss* me while I was wearing a pair of shoes I stole. *He* made me steal!"

Robbie sits there with a satisfied grin on his face and the girl laughs, slapping him on the back.

"You're incorrigible, Robbie. Reminds me of something Caleb would do."

"Who's Caleb?" I ask.

The girl stands and extends her hand my way with a smile. "Hi, I'm Zoe, one of Robbie's best friends. Though Robbie never told me he made you into a thief, he has told me a lot about you. It's great to finally meet you, Monty."

"I...I..."

"Thought this was a date or something? No, gross. Robbie's like a brother, *and* he's a dad." She shakes like she's disgusted. "As cute as his spawn is, I don't do kids."

"Well, it's nice to meet you, Zoe."

Denny makes a noise and scrunches her face. "So, you're not a ho?"

Zoe barks out a laugh. "Not anymore."

"So I don't get to slap you?"

Robbie crosses his arms over his chest, brow arched, lips turned down. "Afraid not. Maybe next time though?"

A smile stretches across my sister's lips. She likes that answer, and she's so falling for all of Robbie's charms. "Sounds like a good time to me." She grabs her shot and vodka tonic. "I'll be taking my leave then, let you two catch up."

As she turns, Zoe says, "Care if I join?"

"Not at all. I need the secrets on how you get your hair like that."

"Birth, girl. It was birth."

"Shut up! I love it. I want mine..."

The rest of their conversation is swallowed by the crowd as they find another table to take over.

It's just me and Robbie now.

His hand slips into mine and he pulls me until I'm standing between his thick legs. His fingers graze my jawline and he tilts my flushed face his way. His touch is gentle, yet demanding, and I love it so much.

"Hi," he says once our eyes connect.

"Hi," I whisper.

"Did you really think I was here with another girl?"

"I...I didn't know what to think, Robbie. We haven't exactly talked about seeing other people while we're doing whatever it is we're doing. All we've discussed is the plan."

"Do you think I'm the kind of man to have multiple women in my bed at a time?"

"Did you just ask me if I think you're the kind of man to do threesomes? Because those are so out of the question."

He laughs and tugs me closer. His hands are on my hips, and the spots where he's touching me are on fire. "No, not at once—unless that rule can be twisted a bit."

I glare at him as he laughs.

"No, I don't think that about you. I was just... confused. I had no idea Denver would march over here like she did. I'm sorry about that."

He lifts a heavy shoulder. "It's no big deal. I'd probably have done the same thing if I saw you with another guy."

"Yeah? You a jealous guy?"

"Not at all, which makes me want to start asking myself a lot of questions, but I'll leave those for later. Right now I want to know if you're stalking me. I mean, first the shoe store, and now Lola's again." He *tsks* and shakes his head. "I can't seem to escape you, Monty."

"Oh, please. Like you'd want to."

"You're not wrong." His hands tighten, not enough to hurt, just as his tongue rolls over his lips, wetting them with an inviting glisten. "I'm glad you're here, stalking and all."

"I'm glad I'm here too."

"I'm sorry you thought you had something to worry about with Zoe. She's just a good friend, I promise."

His eyes plead with me to believe him, but there's no pleading needed.

"I believe you. You have nothing to worry about."

"Good. I was worried I'd messed this up before we even got started."

"Oh, we haven't started yet?"

"Baby, what you've been getting is *just* the beginning."

I laugh and push away from him, walking around to take the seat Zoe was previously occupying.

"So, if you're not following me, what *does* bring you here?"

"You, actually."

He raises a brow and signals to the bartender without looking away from me. "Color me intrigued."

"Denny was complaining that we text too much. She also thinks you're playing me."

"So *that's* why I'm getting slapped."

"Yes. She's insane. Ignore her."

"That I can do, but I have to ask...why does she think I'm playing you? What could possibly give her that idea?"

"Because she's been burned too many times and she's taking it out on me." I shrug. "She thinks you're just going to sleep with me and bail."

"That's a dick move. However, she's not wrong—I mean, that is our plan, isn't it? To get to know each other and do our thang to get this out of our systems, bring that first night here full circle, and then move on?"

When he puts it like that... "Yes. I suppose you're right."

"But you didn't explain that, did you?"

I shake my head. "I did not."

"Didn't think so. Can I ask... Why? Are you embarrassed of me?"

"What? No! Not at all. It's just... That's not me, and Denny knows that. If you think she freaked out this time, her knowing our plan would make it even worse."

He twists his lips and scratches at his stubble. "I can see that. Fine, I accept your answer."

"Gee, thanks."

The bartender finally slides in front of us.

"What can I get you?"

"I'll have another Corona, and an unsweet tea for the lady."

The guy behind the bar nods and goes to grab our order.

"How'd you know I wanted that?"

"Because you're safe, Monty, and you're already sweet, so you don't need more sugar. Plus, you've told me about your tea obsession before." He winks and turns back to the bartender, who's already back with our beverages.

My stomach drops at his words, not because I told him my drink and he remembered, but because he's right.

I *am* safe, and I don't want to be known as safe to Robbie. Safe sounds boring, and I want to be anything but boring.

I want to be that girl who has fun at the bar, who meets a new guy, who isn't afraid to take a leap and do something daring.

I want to be free.

"Dance with me," I say suddenly.

Bottle raised to his lips, Robbie looks surprised. "You dance?"

"No, but I can learn."

"And you want *me* to teach you? All I can do is bump and grind."

"Bump and what?" I roll my eyes and take a sip of my drink. "Never mind. Let's just go. If I think about it too much, I won't do it, and I want to do it."

"What a coincidence—I want to do it too."

I give him a hard stare. "Pretty sure your *it* and mine are two different things."

"Two can become one."

"Did you just backward quote Spice Girls to me?"

His mouth drops open. "You know the Spice Girls?"

I shrug. "What? Denny stole the CD when it came out."

"Good to know petty theft runs in the family."

"Robert!"

"Fine, fine." He drops down off his stool and stands tall above me. "Let's dance."

I place my hand in his and he leads us out onto the floor.

A fast song, one I don't recognize, blasts through the

speakers. Robbie grabs hold of my hips and pulls me into him. "You sure about this?"

"Yes. Why? Should I be afraid?"

He chuckles at the panic in my voice. "No, but I will laugh if you're terrible."

"You're so mean."

"I have a feeling you like it."

We fall into a rhythm and move together. It's easy and fun and I'm horrible at it. I'm sure I look like a moron to everyone in the bar. Robbie wasn't kidding when he said he'd laugh at me, but I don't care. I'm enjoying myself.

Flailing arms and all.

We're three songs in when he drops his hands to his knees, still laughing at me.

"Okay, no. I'm done. I can't take this anymore. You suck *so* bad. It's too awkward to watch."

"Then teach me, you meanie!"

"Oooh, meanie—good one."

"Come on, Robbie. I want to do this!" I shout over the music.

The song ends and shifts seamlessly into a slower one.

"Okay, now this I can do," I insist, stepping toward him and positioning our arms where they need to be.

"What in the hell are you doing, woman? You do *not* ballroom dance in the middle of a bar."

"But this is how you slow dance. We're slow dancing, right?"

"This isn't a damn Disney movie. Get over here."

He grips my waist and hauls me close to him so fast I let out a *hmph* when we collide.

The music sways to life around us as Robbie drags my arms up around his neck before gripping my hips and lining them up with his. He starts moving us to the beat, and it's unlike anything I've ever done before. We're rubbing against one another in ways meant for behind closed doors.

It's so sensual, so *sexy*.

"This isn't your traditional slow dance song, is it?" I ask, our foreheads resting against one another.

"*This* is bumping and grinding, Monty."

He pushes his hips into me, and there's no missing the erection he's sporting.

"Okay, I believe you," I whisper, squeezing my eyes shut at the contact.

"This is killing me, you know."

I swallow the lump in my throat. "Me too."

"You've been driving me nuts for weeks now. I can't stop thinking about you, can't stop wondering what it would be like to kiss you again."

"Stop wondering then."

He pulls away, smirking. "Was that your way of asking me to kiss you again?"

"What if I say yes?"

His eyes swirl with heat, darken with desire. "You better say something, Monty. You better say something right *now*."

"What do you want me to say?"

"I want you to ask me to kiss you."

I stare up at him. He's so...Robbie.

There's just no other way to describe it. We look so silly right now, wrapped up in one another in the middle of the floor... His tanned, toned skin next to mine... His strong, massive build overtaking my small frame.

We make no sense, but I'm tired of trying to figure it out.

I want that night of passion he's promised, want to know if us rolling around in the sheets is going to feel as good as this.

I want him, and I'm done trying to tell myself otherwise.

"What if I want to say more than that?"

His nostrils flare as he tries to hold himself together.

"Monty..." His voice is hoarse and raw. "Don't say things you don't mean."

"And if I mean them?"

He groans as his head falls back onto mine, our foreheads connecting again, noses rubbing together. "Fuck," he mutters.

Another prayer—one I'll answer.

I push onto my tiptoes until my lips are brushing against the shell of his ear.

"Take me home, Robbie."

CHAPTER 11

MONTY

"I SHOULD TEXT DENNY."

"Already did."

"How?"

"Technically, I texted Zoe, who then told Denny. We're good." He tugs on my hand. "Come on. Cab is almost here."

"Cab? But I drove—we can just take my car."

He stops short and I nearly crash into him. Spinning my way, he grabs my arms and pushes me against the nearest wall.

I'm starting to find that I like being pressed between Robbie and a wall...or a sink...any hard surface will do, really.

Without warning, he dips down and captures my lips between his. The kiss is hard and urgent, like he's not sure if he'll ever be able to do this again, which is so silly because we're going to do *far* more than just kissing.

He wrenches his mouth from mine. "Because I can't not kiss you the entire way to my house."

"You think I'm going to make out with you in a cab in front of a stranger?"

"Yes." His answer is sure, strong, like he knows that's exactly what will happen.

Thing is, he's not wrong.

Every time Robbie presses his lips to mine, I'm lost—lost like I never want to be found, no matter the audience we have.

His phone pings and he tugs it from his pocket, checking the screen. It must be good news judging from the way his eyes light up.

"Cab is here. Let's go."

He takes my hand and rushes us toward the front of Lola's.

We slide into the back and Robbie gives the driver his address. The cabbie takes off and we're silent. Though I know he's staring at me, I don't look over at him.

It's partly because I know I'll start kissing him as soon as I do, and partly because I'm starting to get nervous. This all feels so...*real*.

I'm about to have sex. With Robbie.

A man I met three weeks ago. A man who makes me think of him non-stop, who sets me ablaze with a stupid grin.

I just need to figure out how to tell him I'm a virgin before we reach his house.

How exactly do you explain something like that to someone? I never talked about it with my ex-fiancé. He was told by my parents I was to save myself for marriage, and he respected that—if sleeping with everyone but me means respect, that is.

But Robbie...he has no idea. We've never discussed it. There aren't many twenty-something-year-old virgins out there, so it's not something that comes up naturally.

How am I supposed to bring it up now?

I can still feel his gaze on me, and it makes me shift uncomfortably.

I hear his hand slide across the seat. He strokes my finger with his own and I shiver from the touch...which is *so* stupid.

If one simple collision of skin can cause this reaction, what will it feel like when we're naked in his bed? When his body is pressed against mine, all our delicious places lining up?

How am I going to survive any of this?

"Monty."

It's not a question, not really a statement either. He says my name like he can't help himself.

"Yeah?"

"I want to kiss you again."

I'm on the other side of the car before I can stop myself.

I press against him, my lips finding his with ease despite the darkness of the cab. We cling to each other, but it's not enough. I don't think it'll ever be enough. His hands are on my waist, fingers flexing against me over and over again until he lifts me and hauls me onto his lap.

I sigh in relief the moment we connect.

This is what I've been missing.

"You'll need to buckle in if you'd like to continue this ride," the cabbie says with laughter in his voice.

Robbie yanks his mouth from mine and sighs dramatically. His eyes are glazed over, and I can tell he's regretting not letting me drive my own car in this moment.

He nods toward the other side of the car. "Better get back over there. We're still miles away and unless you want our first time to be behind some bush in the park, scoot."

With reluctance, I slide away.

Speaking of first times...

"Ro—"

"I remember being in love like you two—best five minutes of my life." The old man laughs again.

Robbie and I exchange a look.

"It's not love, sir. We're just...uh..."

"Relieving some tension," Robbie supplies.

The cabbie turns around just long enough to wink at us. "That's why I said five minutes."

I politely laugh and then tune out as Robbie directs him the best way through his apartment complex.

My heart is beating so fast.

In just moments, I'll be inside Robbie's home. Then inside his bedroom. Then under his sheets.

Is this happening too fast? Am I insane for doing this? Will I regret this? Will I—

"Here we are!" the driver announces. "That'll be twenty-two fifty, please."

Robbie pays the man and slides out of the car then sticks his hand back in to help me out.

"You two have fun. Don't do anything I wouldn't do," the cabbie says before speeding off once we're clear of the vehicle.

We're quiet as Robbie grabs my hand and leads me up the walkway.

For a Saturday night, it's rather noiseless outside. All that can be heard is the cars passing on the street and the chirping of the crickets.

We come to a stop in front of a door, and he pulls a set of keys from his pocket.

As he pushes the key into the slot, he turns my way, eyes searching and questioning.

"Are you sure about this, Monty?"

I chew on my bottom lip as I stare up at him.

I haven't known him long, and I might be crazy for doing this, but every inch of me is screaming to say yes.

"Open the door, Robbie."

Without another word, he obeys my command.

I'm met with the smell of something sweet, which surprises me because I know Robbie lives here alone.

"It smells amazing in here."

"Lavender. It's an essential oil diffuser."

"I'm not going to lie, I was kind of expecting the smell of dirty socks or something equally disgusting."

"Nah, I'm kind of a neat freak now. I used to be a mess, but now that I have my own place, I'm trying to keep it as together as possible."

"So you'll trash your buddy's pad but not your own?"

He blushes. "Now I sound like an ass."

"If the shoe fits..." I shrug with a grin as I walk past him and farther into the room.

The apartment is small but cozy. The walls are bare, but the overstuffed navy couch is full of vibrant throw pillows, enough to give the room some life. On top of a sleek stand, there's a TV against the wall opposite the couch. It's massive, taking up most of the space in the room.

"Sure you can see that thing?"

He laughs. "It might be a *bit* big."

"You think?"

"Hey, a man's gotta have his toys."

"Fair enough. I like this apartment. It's cute, *warm.*"

"It's a little boring, but we manage."

"We? Ah, yes. I almost forgot about your spawn. Where is he tonight?"

"He *should* be here—it is my weekend after all—but he's at Zach and Delia's. I promised him two weekends ago he could stay the night soon. Good thing, too, or we might not be where we are right now."

"Delia...that's the girl Zach met via wrong number, right?"

He nods. "A situation not too different from ours."

"Right."

You can literally *feel* the sexual tension in the air, but I'm still scared, still nervous...and I still haven't told him about that pesky virginity thing.

"Where's that cute bunny of yours?" I ask as a distraction.

"You want to see Thumbelina? *Now*?"

"Yes, Robbie, now. It's not like we have to go bang right this second. We have all night, don't we?"

"We also have all night to see the bunny."

I smirk at him. "What? You're not going to tire me out so much that I won't be able to get out of bed? What a shame."

He steps toward me, towering over me with his massive frame. "Don't think I don't have special plans, Monty. I'm *very* prepared to spend the entire night in bed with you."

My body sings at his promises, legs quaking in anticipation.

Tonight is going to be the best night of my life.

"Where's Thumbelina?"

He laughs and leads us into the small kitchen. Much like the living room, there's not much to it, and it's exceptionally clean, not even any appliances out on the counters. I'm impressed.

Sitting in a small space near the back door, there's a wire cage taking up every inch. Curled up inside is a cinnamon ball of fluff, my new favorite obsession.

"She is *so* cute! I love her already. Can I hold her?"

"Sure, but just so you know, she's a little skittish. She might try to wiggle away."

"I just want to touch her. I bet she's soft."

"The softest. I keep finding myself holding her and petting her for stupid long amounts of time. It's a little embarrassing how she's managed to wrap me around her finger already."

"Nah, you're a father—being that way is just ingrained in you now."

"Good point." He lowers down onto his haunches and unlocks her cage. "Hey, girl. How you doing?" he coos, scooping her up with his hands.

The bunny panics for only a moment before realizing who has a hold of her.

"Ah, there she is." She curls into his arms and snuggles close. "How was your night?"

Thumbelina makes a noise in return and it's so cute, like they're having their own private conversation.

"You want to hold her?" he asks.

"Actually, maybe another time. She looks really comfortable and I don't want to freak her out."

"Are you sure? She'll calm down after a few minutes."

"I'm sure," I tell him, though my fingers are itching to reach out and touch her fur.

Robbie smirks. "You can pet her."

I blow out a relieved breath. "Thank you. I was dying."

With caution, I run my fingers through her fluff, and she's just as soft as I was hoping she'd be.

"How big will she get?"

"Not very. She's a Mini Plush Lop, so only about three or so pounds max."

"I think she can fit in my purse," I comment.

"I think you're on crack cocaine if you think I'm giving her up."

"Can't we share her? Please?" I beg. "I'll come over and walk her and change her litter box, whatever you need."

"First, you don't *walk* bunnies. Second, having someone to help with the litter box might not be a bad idea... Third, are you planning for our *future*, Monty?"

Robbie's flirty grin has me blushing and fighting the urge to duck my head and hide behind my hair. Instead, I laugh off his comment. "I'm planning my future with Thumbelina. You'd just be a bonus."

I can tell he likes my answer. *I* like my answer, no matter how much it scares me.

"Fucking hell," he mutters, bending down again to lock the bunny back in her cage. "You're going to be the death of me."

"You shouldn't put that on Thumbelina's shoulders, Robbie. So rude."

He side-eyes me. "I meant you."

"I know." I grin back. I point toward the sink. "Mind if I wash up?"

I quickly wash and dry my hands, then begin roaming around the small kitchen, opening and closing cupboards as I go.

"You're so...minimal."

"Is that your polite way of saying I'm severely lacking in decorating skills?"

"No. It means you're... Well, okay, yes, I suppose it is. Either way, I like it."

I walk over to the fridge and pull open the doors. Robbie leans against the counter, watching me and letting me explore.

"Checking out my fridge too? Damn."

"I had to check for severed heads."

"I keep those in the basement."

I tap the side of my head. "Smart thinking."

"I know. You gonna let all my food spoil?"

"Huh?" He nods toward the still open fridge. "Oh rats. Sorry."

I take a quick peek inside and am surprised to find so much healthy food.

"Not what you were expecting, huh?"

"Not at all. I thought for sure it would be takeout box

after takeout box. That's what our fridge looks like. Denny isn't much of a cook, and cooking for one isn't very fun."

"You cook?" he asks, flabbergasted.

"I dabble."

"Nice. I make meals at home as often as I can. Makes the dad life easier sometimes too."

"Oh, I'm sure."

We fall silent, and the reality of the situation lands on me. I'm in Robbie's apartment, in his space. I'm looking through his cabinets, his fridge, acquainting myself with his pet. I'm in his life now, and it's so weird that I didn't even know him a month ago.

If we do this tonight, if we follow through with our plan, it'll all be over.

I'm not sure I want that, but I am sure I don't want tonight to *not* happen.

The sexual tension rises with each step I take toward him. I don't stop until our toes are touching. With a much-needed breath of confidence, I look up into his searching eyes.

"I'm ready."

CHAPTER 12

ROBBIE

I'M READY.

With two words, my cock is throbbing painfully against my jeans.

I haul her to me, dropping my mouth to hers in an instant. The way she feels against me...*fuck*. It's like she was made for me, which feels so fucking foreign.

She's pliant and soft beneath me, begging for more with her body.

I want more. I want it *bad*.

I slide my hands down her sides and grip her ass, lifting her until she's wrapped her legs around my waist. I spin us until she's sitting atop the counter.

"You missed this, didn't you, Monty?"

She lets out the softest sigh when I say her name.

"You know you sigh when I say your name?"

As predicted, her cheeks turn a bright red, possibly the

brightest I've seen yet. She smacks my chest and laughs nervously. "I do not!"

"You so do." She ducks her head, another signature move of hers. I grab her chin, pulling her attention back to me. "You do, Monty, and it's the sexiest fucking thing I've ever heard."

"It is not. It's stupid."

"My very hard dick says otherwise."

Her sea green eyes blaze to life with need.

"You like hearing that, don't you? You love it when those dirty words drop from my lips. They turn you on, make you feel alive." She nods. "Yeah, that's what I thought."

I take her mouth again, this time being less gentle than I was before, which is just the way she likes it.

It's not long before she's scooting forward on the counter, her body reaching for mine, pleading for the contact.

She moans when she finally connects with me, her hips working to get the friction her body desires so much.

I can feel my legs beginning to give out, and I don't know how much longer I'll be able to endure this.

I need to be inside her—*now*.

"Bedroom," I mutter as I lift her off the counter and carry her down the hallway, though not before pressing my lips to hers over and over again.

I don't think I'll ever get tired of kissing her.

I push my bedroom door open and walk us to the bed.

Depositing her on the mattress with a bounce, I step back and slip my shoes off.

Monty sits there, panting and staring up at me with pure want.

"You should take your shirt off too," she says.

I can't help but laugh, which again causes her to blush. "As you wish," I reply, stripping the material from my body.

Barefoot and jean-clad, I stand here for a moment, hers for the taking.

She rises from the bed, standing so close that my chest brushes against her with every breath I take. Her hands land on my bare chest, and the touch burns my skin.

"I wondered if you had more."

I give her a singular nod, not trusting myself to speak.

"Robbie...this is the most beautiful thing I've ever seen. Why the phoenix and the dragon?"

"I like what it represents: strength and courage and rebirth and second chances. I was kind of thrown for a loop when Xavie was born. That moment changed my life, and it was like I got a whole new one." I shrug. "It fits."

"And it wraps up here and..." Her fingers skate softly over my chest and shoulder, tracing the tattoo as it continues. "Keeps going."

I turn slowly, letting her take it in. The piece is colossal, taking up nearly my entire front half, both shoulders, and wrapping around to my back. I spent many hours in the chair and way too much money it, but it was worth it. The dragon and phoenix wrapped together—it's me.

Her hands roam all over and I can hardly breathe as she touches every inch of the tattoo.

When I'm finally facing her again, she gives me a shy smile.

"You're gorgeous, Robbie. A true, actual work of art. It's amazing."

"Keep saying things like that and I'm going to have my way with you."

"I wouldn't argue, but first, I want to know if you have other tattoos."

Without breaking eye contact with her, I unbutton my jeans. The zipper making its way down the track reverberates around the room with the most delicious sound.

Monty's skin begins to flush, telling me she wasn't expecting this.

"Down there?"

I nod.

"On your wiener?"

I burst into laughter, the moment officially ruined.

"Good God, woman. No. *Hell* no. I would never let a needle near my cock." She shivers at the word, and said cock jumps at the reaction.

I shove my jeans down my legs, kicking them off to the side and standing before Monty in nothing but tented boxer briefs.

"My thigh."

Her eyes make a slow perusal, and don't think I don't notice how much time she spends staring at my hard dick.

She bends down to see better and of course my little man jumps at the movement, thinking she's coming down to play.

Chill, junior.

"Poseidon."

"Why?"

"You ask a lot of questions."

"I've been told that before."

"Because he's god of the sea, and there's nothing as alluring or terrifying as the sea. I love it."

She glances up at me. "You're a complicated man, Robert Cross."

"I've been told that before," I echo.

Her attention drifts to my other leg, and I can see she's having a hard time making out what exactly it is she's looking at.

"What was the first thing I said to you?"

"You asked me if I..." Her voice trails as she continues her perusal. "No way."

I put two fingers under her chin and bring her stare to mine. "Hi Monty. Wanna see my python?"

She bursts into laughter, and I love watching as she throws her head back.

"I thought you meant your wiener."

I shrug. "Can't help that you're a perv."

"Oh, you *totally* meant your penis."

"Did I? I mean, that's a pretty crass thing to say to a stranger."

Her eyes fall into slits but she's not mad, not with that grin on her lips.

"How is it?"

"Huh?"

"My python—how is it?"

"Did you just ask me how your wiener is?"

I tsk. "There you go again, being a perv."

"Robbie!"

"Robbie Junior, actually."

"You named him?" She rolls her eyes and mutters, "Of course you did." I see her bite at her lip, trying hard not to laugh. "Your python is very beautiful, Robbie—long, thick, and just as big as I thought it'd be."

"You're totally talking about my cock right now."

She scoffs. "Your tattoo!"

"Whatever helps you sleep at night, babe." I laugh at the look of disbelief on her face. "I'm teasing. I know you meant both of my pythons."

"Actually, I haven't really gotten a good look at one of them. I think I'll need to look again..."

Monty drops to her knees, and I about fall to mine. A loud groan escapes me as she reaches for the waistband of my underwear.

"What are you doing, Monts?"

"I'm exploring."

"You're *killing* me."

She chuckles softly as she drags my last piece of clothing down my legs. "I know."

Leaning back, she just sits there.

And sits and sits and sits.

Staring.

"It's not going to suck itself," I say softly.

She slams her eyes closed and traps her plump bottom lip between her teeth. "I really hate how much I loved hearing you say that. I should be really annoyed, but with you standing before me like this, staring at me like you are, I can't be."

Without another word, she curls her hair around her hand, pushing it to the side as she drags her tongue along the side of my cock.

I hiss as soon as she makes contact. She hasn't even properly put her mouth on me and it's already too fucking much.

Another long, slow lick.

I want to fucking scream.

And come. I'm dying to come.

It seems like days before she finally takes my length into her mouth, swallowing as much of me as she can. She hasn't even completely taken me in yet, but I can't handle another second of this. It's been too long, and she feels too fucking good.

"Holy shit," I mutter. "Monty, stop. You *have* to stop. I'm gonna blow."

But she doesn't stop. She keeps going, taking more and

more of me with each stroke. I gather her hair in my hand and guide her, helping her find that rhythm I love. She's receptive to my touch, and her eagerness only adds to the fire burning inside me.

I'm close to the edge when her lips fall from my dick and she replaces them with her hand, stroking me with just the right amount of pressure and speed, enough to keep up the building momentum.

She grins up at me. "You said to suck."

"I did." I stroke two fingers over her chin. "So move your hand and use your mouth."

Her eyes spark and I guide her back to my dick. I believe I've just discovered that Monty *loves* dirty talk, especially with the way she's sucking on me. It's like a whole new fire was lit under her ass and her sole purpose is to see me explode.

She's getting her way too, because I'm on the brink of the best kind of high.

I gently pull at her hair. "Shirt—hand me that shirt."

She pops off of my cock and the material is barely in my hand before I'm unloading. Monty stays kneeled, fully clothed and staring at me with pure lust.

I reach out, run my fingers along her jaw, and beckon her to stand.

"My turn," I say once she's standing before me, her breathing ragged like she's the one who just came undone.

Watching her, I'm surprised yet again by how undeniably attracted I am to her.

She's so...*plain*, yet so much more.

Right now, with a thin sheen of sweat and a glow that can only be caused by sexual gratification, she's stunning.

I latch onto the hem of her plain white shirt—see, there's that word again, *plain*—and pull her toward me. Her breath hitches as I pull the material up past her thin waist and over her breasts. She lifts her arms and I toss the shirt aside.

Unsurprisingly, she's wearing a white cotton bra—nothing sexy about it at all, but somehow, it's the hottest fucking bra I've seen in my lifetime. There's a light dusting of freckles over her shoulders and across the tops of her tits.

I want to lick every single fucking one.

But first, I want to lick somewhere else.

I reach for the top of her skirt and lift my eyes to hers. She's watching me with rapt attention, standing so pin straight and still, waiting.

"I'm taking your skirt off, Monty. Then I'm going to lay you down on this bed. I'll kiss every sexy fucking freckle across your chest, admire every inch of those gorgeous damn legs. When I'm done, I'm going to devour you until *I'm* done. Then I'll start all over again."

Her throat works double-time as she tries to swallow my words, her lips trembling with anticipation.

"If you don't want any of that, tell me now."

"I want it."

I pull her skirt from her body, guide her down on the

bed, and then crawl on top.

As promised, I kiss all her freckles as she writhes beneath me with each touch. Her full breasts are threatening to spill from the cups and I run a hand along her back, arching her off the bed as best I can until I can unhook the contraption stopping me from sucking on her nipples.

She helps me free her from the bra and I fling it to the side, hearing something crash to the floor but not giving a shit what it is.

Her pert nipples are the exact same shade as her lips, and they're begging to be kissed. I wrap my mouth around the erect tip and she cries out. I can't help but chuckle at her desperation and am pleased when she shivers.

She slaps at my back but doesn't make a move to push me away. No, she's enjoying this too much, just as I am. She wants this.

I want it more.

Switching my attention to her other breast, I'm hyperaware when she slides her hands into my hair and holds me to her chest like she never wants me to leave.

I don't want to either.

Testing the waters, I gently nip, and she about flies off the bed.

"*Oh...*" she sighs. "Oh my stars."

I laugh again.

"More."

Another nip, another sigh.

I could do this all night, but I have other plans.

"Who knew you'd be so responsive?" I say to her when I lift my head, moving until our foreheads rest against one another.

She's panting again, and I love the sound. "Honestly, I had no idea, but I'm not surprised. You drive me nuts, Robbie."

"You drive me crazy too, Monty."

I capture her lips again and lead us into a searing kiss.

Before I can get too lost, I pull away, trailing kisses down her chin, neck, in the valley between her breasts. I kiss and kiss and kiss until I reach the top of her plain, pale pink briefs.

Nothing lacy for her. All cotton, all plain. All Monty.

I hook my fingers in the band and pull the material down her legs.

She instantly clamps them together and I eye her.

"You ever had this done before?"

"Y-Yes."

"Did you like it?"

"Not particularly. He wasn't really...into it. It made me uncomfortable, so it's not my favorite thing ever."

"Do you mind if I try to change your mind?"

"I..." She goes quiet.

There's a fight in her eyes, one telling me she *does* want this, but she's nervous. I don't want her to be nervous with me. I want her to know how mind-blowing this can be—for both of us.

I want to fucking blow her mind.

"If you don't want me to, I won't, but I'm dying to taste you, Monty—seriously fucking *dying.*"

Her gaze doesn't leave mine for what feels like forever, until finally, she gives me a single nod and parts her legs just the slightest bit.

I rest my hands on her knees and spread her wide enough for me to fit, not once breaking eye contact in case she changes her mind.

She doesn't.

"I promise to make this good."

"You bett—ahhhh!"

Her words die on her tongue as I put my mouth on her.

"That's...*oh!*"

I lick her, stroking all the right spots, alternating the pressure when I know she's right there on the edge. She's itching for a release, and I'm right there with her again.

"Please, Robbie," she begs.

I lift my mouth from her center and work a finger inside of her. She clenches around me, begging for more with her body, so I add another finger and rub small circles over her clit with my thumb.

Her hips begin to move in a rhythmic pattern. She's so fucking close.

"Please what?" I say, watching her ride my hand.

Eyes clenched closed, she swallows—or tries to. Her mouth is dry as the Sahara, I'm sure. *"Please."*

"Say it, Monty. Say the words."

"Let me come."

I bury my face between her legs and don't move until she's unraveling beneath me.

Her jagged breaths fill the room, but I don't give her a moment to rest.

My cock is leaking and if I don't get inside her now, I'm going to come all over the bed and that'll just be goddamn embarrassing.

I reach over to the nightstand beside my bed, fish out a condom, and suit the fuck up.

I slide between Monty's legs and wrap them around me.

"Last chance," I say. "We can't go back after this."

"Stop trying to talk me out of this."

"Trust me, that's the last thing I want to do. You have no idea how close I am to blowing my load again. You've got me so fucking hard, Monty. I can still feel the hum of the last orgasm you gave me, can still fucking taste you on my lips, and all I want to do right now is bury my cock deep inside you."

She moans at my words and yanks my head down, pressing a hard kiss against my lips before releasing me and grinning up at me. "Then stop talking and do it."

I'm not going to argue with that invitation.

I line my dick up and slowly push inside her, not wanting to plow in full steam ahead. I want this to last too much to do that.

Her pussy grips me, and it's hot and wet and tight.

It's almost *too* tight, like she's never been stretched like this before, like she's...

No. There's no fucking way.

I stop moving and stare down at her. She's holding her breath and trying not to make a sound, but tears roll down her cheeks into her hair, revealing the horrible pain she's in.

This isn't happening.

"Monty, open your eyes."

She shakes her head.

"Open your fucking eyes," I growl.

Her tear-filled green gaze meets mine and my heart stops beating for only a second. She's in pain, and I hate that I'm the cause of it.

I'm also really fucking pissed right now.

"How? Why? Why didn't you tell me?"

"It's not like it's something you just tell a stranger, Robbie."

"I'm not a goddamn stranger. We've been talking about sex for weeks, Monty—*weeks*—and you didn't find it important to mention you're a virgin?"

"I was going to, tonight...but I forgot."

"You *forgot?*"

"You made me forget. I wasn't thinking about it, about my inexperience. All I was thinking about was you. I was lost in the moment."

"Dammit, Monty," I bite out angrily.

Her eyes fall shut against the harshness of my words and she whispers, "I'm sorry. Are you mad?"

"That you're a virgin? No, I would never be mad about that, but you not telling me? You're fucking right I'm pissed."

She lets out a soft cry and I don't know if it's because I'm still inside her or because I know the truth. "It hurts so bad."

Softly, I say, "This is kind of a big deal. If I'd have known, I would have been gentler, worshipped you more, lit some fucking candles or some other girly shit. I would have made this something special for you."

"If I wanted something like that, I would have told you, but I don't want those things. I just want you."

"That's the lust talking."

"Probably," she agrees. "But it's still the truth."

"I don't want you to regret this. I don't want you to look back and count this as a mistake. All those comments about banging...they were just jokes. You know that, right?"

"Yes, I know. I would never put myself in this position if I didn't want this. You should know I'm a pretty calculating kind of gal, and this is a very calculated decision. I want this. I want *you*."

"Were you saving yourself for marriage? Because I'll do it. I'll whisk you off right now and marry the shit out of you."

She laughs through her tears and I love the sound.

"You would not. You're just saying that to make me feel better."

"Yeah, you're right, but you didn't answer my question."

"I wasn't waiting for anything special. I was just...waiting."

I sigh and drop my head until it rests on her forehead.

We lie here for several heartbeats. I'm still halfway inside her, still hard as ever, still wanting to make her scream my name again.

"You should have told me," I say quietly.

"I know, and I'm sorry, but Robbie?"

"Yeah?"

"Move—*please*. It hurts and I need you to move. I need to get it over with."

I know she doesn't mean the act, she means burying myself inside of her. For the first time tonight, it's me who's following the instructions as I slowly push myself forward until I'm fully in.

"I can't fucking breathe."

"Me either," she says.

She's still crying, and I know this is hurting her.

"It'll get better," I promise, taking the shortest, slowest stroke of my life. "It'll get so much fucking better. The pain will turn into a pinch." Another stroke. "The pinch into pleasure." Another. "And soon you're going to be on fire in the best way possible. You'll be begging for a release." Another. "Begging for more."

I press my lips to hers, kissing away the pain she's feeling, kissing away the doubts I'm sure she's having. I kiss her until my lips are numb.

And then I kiss her some more.

She begins to move with me, her body settling into the invasion, the pleasure taking over.

"Are you okay?"

"Yes," she moans. "You were right."

"I know." I laugh before kissing her again.

I pick up my pace, driving into her with more force. Monty digs her heels into my ass, spurring me on, her way of asking for more.

But I can't let her off that easy.

I slide out of her nearly all the way, leaving just the tip of my cock nestled inside her as a tease. She cries out in frustration and my chest rumbles with laughter.

"Say it," I murmur.

"You are seriously the worst." Using her heels, she tries to pull me into her, but I'm too strong. "Robbie!"

"Say it."

She swallows thickly, her tongue darting out to wet her lips.

"Why do you want to hear me say it so bad?"

"Because I *need* to hear it. I need to hear that you want this, that you *need* this. You're always so wound up. Let loose. Give in to your desires, Monty."

After another failed attempt to pull me toward her, she sighs. "I'm trying to, but you won't let me."

"Just say it."

Her eyes fly open and she looks at me. They're a swirling mess of a deep blue and green and want and lust. She *wants* to beg for release. She likes it.

It gives her the power.

"I need more, Robbie." Her voice has dropped an octave, that husk creeping in. It does things to me I can't even explain. "*Please.*"

I slam into her and her body begins to tremor with her impending release. I lean back just far enough to be able to watch her unravel.

Eyes squeezed shut, neck strained, body taut.

She comes undone.

And I love every moment of it.

I quicken my pace, driving myself deeper and deeper until I'm tipping over the edge right along with her.

I collapse on top of her in exhaustion, my breaths coming in stuttered succession.

I lie here, doing my best to hold my weight up and waiting for the moment to come.

We achieved our goal. I've fulfilled my fantasy from three weeks ago. I should feel a sense of...relief.

Only I don't.

I've had a taste, and now I want more.

What in the hell did we just do?

CHAPTER 13

MONTY

"SON OF A BISCUIT EATER..." I mutter as I try to wrap the sheet around my upper body and hold it in place while peeing at the same time.

What a time to be modest, Monty.

It feels like there's so much pressure sitting on my bladder that I can't pee—either that, or it's because I know Robbie's on the other side of that door.

Naked.

Waiting.

We just had sex. I'm not a virgin anymore.

What did we just do? What did I just do?

That was the most un-Monty-esque thing I've ever done, and I loved every single moment of it. My body's still buzzing from the orgasms. I'm so greedy that I want more—*a lot* more.

With Robbie.

The thought causes me to pause. Other than the small

stinging sensation when I pee, the slight pinch of pain between my thighs, and muscle soreness like I've just run a 5K, I don't feel any different. All the tension I've been harboring since I met Robbie hasn't subsided in the least. In fact, it's worse.

There's no way I could possibly walk out his front door right now and never want to look back.

"You okay in there?" he asks through the bathroom door.

"Y-Yeah," I tell him. "I'll be out in just a sec."

"Good, because it's fucking cold as tits and you took all the blankets."

Smiling, I listen as he pads back across the bedroom, the creaking of the mattress telling me when he crawls back onto the bed.

The one we just made love on.

A sigh slips out and I slap my hands to my cheeks, feeling so giddy and silly and high-school-ish.

I just had sex!

With a ridiculously hot guy, at that.

A guy who's waiting for me to get back out there and—

My stomach sinks.

Does he want me to leave? Is this it? We've done what we set out to do. Does that mean we're done? Because I don't want to be done.

I also don't know how to tell Robbie that without sounding like a clingy moron.

Ugh.

I finish up my business—finally—and use a washrag from under the sink to clean myself up as best I can.

Wrapping the blanket around myself again, I inhale a steadying breath and walk back into Robbie's room.

I try not to frown when I notice he's slipped on a pair of boxer briefs.

"I was going to sexily lounge naked on the bed, but I really am fucking cold," he tells me like he can read my thoughts. "Get over here."

"Why didn't you just use the other blankets?" The last of the words fall into a mutter as my eyes land on the pile of material crowding the corner.

"You're a messy gal, Monty."

I want to run back into the bathroom and hide as the embarrassment floods through me. "Right, the blood."

"Yeah, the blood—you know, from your hymen, that pesky little thing you failed to mention was still intact."

I roll my eyes and scoot onto the bed next to him, though I don't share the warmth of the sheet. "You're still upset."

He makes a noncommittal noise before running a hand through his dark locks and blowing out a breath. "Yes and no. I'm just... I wish I had known, you know?"

"Would that have changed anything?"

"Fuck yeah it would have!" he exclaims.

"Would we not have done this?"

"I... We..." He can't seem to find the words he wants to say. "I think we'd have ended up here anyway. Would our path have been a little different? Perhaps, but there's no way I wouldn't have had you in my bed. We're too...*us* for that not to happen."

"Us?"

"Yeah. You know...compatible and shit. We click sexually."

Right. *Sexually*. Of course.

"Can you forgive me then?"

He grins, and it's wolfish. "I can think of a few ways you could make it up to me."

"You just want me to put your wiener in my mouth again."

He bursts into laughter, the entire bed shaking with each loud guffaw that leaves him. "I swear, I'm going to call you every single day and demand you say wiener." He snaps his fingers. "Wait, no—I'll record you saying it and make it my text tone."

"You wouldn't."

"If you honestly don't think I would, you don't know me at all."

"You might be the most interesting man I've ever met."

He leans toward me, our mouths mere inches apart. "Yeah? Good."

Then he rips the sheet from my body and wraps himself in it.

"Mean!" I shriek, trying to pull the fabric back with no real results to show for it. It's no use; he's too strong for me.

I groan loudly and fold my arms across my chest.

My chest.

"Robbie! I'm naked!"

"I'm aware." He grins, eyeing me like I'm his next meal. "So what though? I'm naked too."

"You at least have undies on."

He reaches under the blanket and wiggles around a bit before whipping his underwear around his index finger like a lasso and slinging them off into some unknown corner of the room.

"See? Told ya I'm naked." He flings open the sheet. "Get in here."

"I am *not* getting under that blanket with you when we're both naked as jaybirds."

His brows shoot into his hairline. "You're joking, right? Monty, we just had sex—actual *sex*. We were all kinds of naked and wrapped together." He leans in close. "Get. In. Here."

I both loathe and love the way my body responds to his commands.

There have been many times tonight where he's used that dominating tone with me, and every single time I've felt a tingle run up my spine.

Robbie bossing me around in the bedroom is *hot*, and I wouldn't object to hearing him do it over and over and over again.

I slide under the blanket with him and he rolls to his side to face me.

"Hey," he says quietly. He gently glides his fingers up my cheek as he tucks a few loose hairs behind my ear.

"Hi," I murmur back.

We don't say anything else for a long time. We simply lie here. The only contact we have is Robbie running his thumb back and forth over my cheek. I close my eyes against the touch, reveling in it.

Slumber is begging to take over, but I fight it. If these moments are going to be my last with this man, I don't want to miss them.

"Can I say something without it sounding really fucking corny and you revoking my man card?"

I smile at his words but don't open my eyes. "No promises."

"Brat." He places a soft kiss on the tip of my nose. "Thank you for trusting me with your body, Monty. Thank you for choosing me, for allowing me to be the one who will always have that part of you, for..." His voice trails off, and it's clear he's doing the best he can to hold his emotions at bay. "Yeah, just thank you. It really means a lot to me."

My eyes flutter open, and I'm surprised to find his glistening with unshed tears.

"It means a lot to me too, Robbie, and don't worry—you still have your man card."

He laughs and takes my mouth with a kiss that surprises me.

It's slow, unhurried. It's sensual and soft.

Until it's not and it turns into something so much more.

The soreness between my legs is long forgotten, replaced by the need to have Robbie inside me again. It already feels like it's been too long.

I push at him until he's flat on his back and crawl on top. His erection brushes against me in all the right spots and I can't stop my hips from circling on their own, searching for the connection.

He pulls his mouth from mine, beaming up at me. "Oooh, you on top—me likey."

"I've never done this before. No promises it'll be good."

"Trust me," he says, sliding his arms up until they're resting behind his head. "I'm going to enjoy it no matter what."

"Don't be so sure."

Before I can understand what's happening, he's sitting up and wrapping his arms around my waist, holding me tightly to him as he moves us until his back is resting against the headboard.

He stares up at me with eyes so filled with determination and lust it knocks the breath out of me.

"Get a condom, Monty."

I reach into the drawer he pulled open earlier and produce a foil packet. He snatches it from my hand and rips it open. His hand collides with my rear, and I know he's doing it because he wants me to lift up so he has room, but I can't help the moan that escapes me.

Robbie's eyes snap my way and he grins. "Noted."

"Shut up and hurry," I hiss.

He slides the condom over his length and grabs my hips, positioning me until his erection is resting at my opening.

"Lead."

"Huh?" I question.

"You lead."

One hand is splayed across my left cheek while the other finds its way to my clit. He works his thumb over the bundle of nerves, my orgasm already starting to build.

His eyes don't leave my body as he says, "I want to watch."

Slowly, I lower myself over him. I wince at the pinch but keep pushing through, his thumb on my clit helping to keep the pain at bay.

I sigh when he's fully inside me, the feeling of being stretched one of the most delicious sensations I've ever felt.

He squeezes my butt. "Move, Monty. Ride me."

And I do. I move on top of him, trying to find an angle and tempo that's comfortable. Robbie's eyes never leave where we're connected and the glow in them tells me he's enjoying this, no matter how green I am at it.

My thighs are on fire, my entire body begging for release, yet too tired to find it.

I whine when he abandons my clit, and he laughs.

"Hush. You'll like this more. Put your hands on the headboard."

I do as he says and he grins up at me again, a glint of mischief in his gaze.

"Hold on tight."

"Hu—*oh*!"

He pistons into me and I don't understand how he's keeping the pace he's moving at, but I'm not going to argue.

It's magic, and he has me firmly under his spell.

He lets out a string of curse words and without warning, I combust. Robbie isn't far behind.

His pace dies into short, slow strokes as we both come down from our highs.

I crumple against him, satiated and drained.

"Fuck, I'm screwed," he mumbles.

"Literally," I mutter.

He laughs and presses a kiss to my temple. "Just sleep, Monty. We'll figure this out later."

# CHAPTER 14

ROBBIE

"TWO THINGS. One, your feet are stupid fucking cold. Two, I'm gonna need you to move because I *really* have to pee."

She laughs and burrows herself closer to my side, sliding her feet between my legs.

"Nope. I'm comfy."

An hour or so after we drifted off to sleep, she awoke, complaining about the needy ache between her legs. I was more than happy to help her ease it...again and again and again.

We finally fell asleep around four AM, which—I peek over at the alarm clock glowing on the bedside table—was only two hours ago.

"Why are you awake?"

"Sun's up, I'm up," I answer.

She groans. "Robbie, I can't. No more sex."

Laughing, I reach down and brush the hair out of her face. "I didn't mean my dick, Monty."

"Oh."

"Why do you sound disappointed?"

She peers over me. "Do I?" I nod. "Well, I didn't mean to. I meant what I said—I'm exhausted. No more banging."

"Ever?"

"Don't get crazy," she says, rolling away and stretching out. The blanket slips down her chest, exposing her bare breasts.

Prior to our first tryst last night, she would have freaked about this. Hell, she might have even freaked *after* the first time. She'd have snatched the blanket back up so fast I'd have missed it if I blinked.

But something's changed in Monty in the past several hours.

She's more comfortable. Confident. *Sexy.*

Not that she wasn't sexy before, because the buttoned-up goody-two-shoes look she has going on totally gets my cock hard, but her newfound self-esteem boost is making her even more irresistible.

Which is real fucking inconvenient for my libido.

She almost reminds me of that teacher every dude secretly had a crush on in high school, the one who was all business and no fun but looked fucking hot in those cardigans you're pretty sure your grandmother also owned. There was no reason behind your attraction other than the fact that she was guarded, something you couldn't touch.

That was Monty...until last night.

"What?" she asks, grinning up at me with sleepy eyes.

"Huh?"

"You're staring at me...what is it?"

"You're beautiful, Monty. So fucking beautiful."

She brings her hands up over her face, covering her smile. "Stop it."

I yank at her hands, grabbing hold of them and rolling until I'm on top of her. I fit right between her legs like that's the place I was always meant to be. My dick brushes against her pussy and I laugh when she seeks more contact.

No more banging, my ass.

I press her hands overtop her head, holding them there as I stare down at her.

"Never. You're fucking gorgeous and I'll never stop telling you that."

"It makes me blush, and I look ridiculous when I blush."

"*Sexy*—you look sexy when you blush."

"Robbie."

"Nope." I pepper kisses along her cheek, trailing a path to her lips. "You're not talking me out of this. I'm right."

"You're annoying first thing in the morning."

"I take much offense to that." I grind my hips into hers, my cock sliding effortlessly over her clit. "But I'll go ahead and let you make it up to me now."

She groans. "No more sex."

"I didn't mean that, but since you mentioned it..."

She gives me a hard stare. "No."

I laugh. "Fine. How about you join me for a quick shower then?"

"No shower sex either. Shower sex is still sex."

"Shower sex is the most overrated sex there is. It's cold and wet and hard to keep balanced—not worth it. I just meant for a quick wash. Then we gotta get going 'cause I have to pick Xavie up at seven thirty."

I hate saying the words, and I can tell she hates it too.

Goodbye.

It's coming and we both know it.

Our plan from the beginning was to work each other out of our systems and move on. I've always been the type of man to honor plans, but now? Now I want to break them more than I've ever wanted to break anything in my life.

But, I have Monty to consider. Is that what she wants? Taking on something other than a meaningless fling with a single dad is hard.

Is that something *I* even want to do? I'm finally in a good place with Holly and Xavie. We're doing good; would adding someone new to the mix be a good thing right now?

Fuck. I don't know. I hate that this is so hard.

She still hasn't answered, and I can see the wheels spinning in her head. She's considering if she should say no, and I can pinpoint the exact moment when she decides.

"I'd, uh, I'd rather not," she lies. "I'm going to head home and shower there. No offense or anything, just not into showering in a stranger's bathroom."

There she goes using that word again.

Stranger.

I'm no stranger and she knows it.

But, I get it; it's her way of separating things.

"Totally understand. Wait for me while I shower? I'll be out in less than five minutes."

She nods. "Sure. I'll be here."

Giving her one last kiss, I roll away and climb off the bed. When I peek over my shoulder, I'm not surprised to find her pushed up on her elbows, checking me out.

"You just wanted to stare at my ass."

"Guilty." She grins back at me.

Her eyes scan my body, her gaze landing on my junk, which has been standing at full attention for far too long. She takes the time to peruse my body, her lip between her teeth as she looks over my tattoos for the millionth time like she can't get enough of them.

The way she looks at me...*shit*, it just does something I can't explain. I can *feel* it, all over the place. It's like she's grazing over my skin with her fingers, not her eyes.

Despite what she said earlier, she wants me again, and I want her too. I want to stride back over to the bed and use my hands to give her the same appreciation she's giving me right now.

"It's weird," she murmurs, still staring. "You say I'm beautiful, but then I look at you and I think there's no way that's possible. The gods sculpted you themselves, Robbie."

"Nah, baby. I was sculpted by hard work, dedication, and my hard-ass trainer at Platinum Gym, not the gods." I wink. "But I'll take the compliment."

She tosses her head back and laughs, her long red hair spilling across the bed, the light from the morning rays of sun shining across her pale skin in the most alluring way.

Time stands still.

She looks stunning, free, and confident, and it's my favorite moment I've had with her thus far.

I charge toward the bed, capturing her face between my hands and slam my lips down on hers for a hard, fast kiss.

Our mouths fuse together with such finesse you'd think we'd been doing this for decades, not hours.

Something feels different about this kiss. It feels so...final.

Though I'm sure that's just my mind playing tricks on me.

When I finally pull away and let her loose, she's gasping for breath, and I love the sounds of the sharp inhales echoing around the room.

"I'll be five minutes, tops," I say, backing away from the bed.

"I'll be here," she promises.

Good.

Because I know one night with her won't be enough.

"LEMME GET THIS STRAIGHT: you took her virginity, made sweet, sweet love to her all night long, and she *bailed* while you were in the shower?"

"Yep. Cleaned house. Beat feet. Scrammed. Vanished right the fuck into thin air."

"Wow." Zach shakes his head. "I never pegged you as a bad lay."

I scowl. "You've thought about my bedroom skills?"

"With those biceps, can you blame me?" He sends me a teasing wink. "No, man. I've just always thought you were this Casanova-type guy. You've always been the brawn to my brains, the Fonzie to my Richie, the Jason to my Tommy."

"Did you just compare us to Power Rangers?"

"Yes," he says, completely serious. "But that's not the point. Point is, I'm surprised she left. I thought you two really hit it off."

"We did, but...we kind of had this deal."

"Deal? What kind of deal?"

"A 'bang plan'."

"Shut the fuck up. No you didn't."

"It was your idea!"

"What?" he shouts incredulously. "How?"

"You said we needed to bang to 'get it out of our system'. So, we did."

"I didn't mean like a wham-bam sort of thing. I was thinking of a relationship, you taking the first steps to forming a real, healthy relationship with someone new."

"I... Well, shit. I did not take your advice that way. We made plans to hit it and quit it to scratch the itch, then move on with our lives."

Zach raises one of his bushy brows. "Am I that type of guy? No? Didn't think so. Why would I *ever* hand out that kind of advice?"

"Because *I'm* one of those guys," I argue.

"No, you're not. You think you are, but you're not. You're not built for it, not truly. Sure, you're a bit of a make-out slut, but there's a reason you kept going back to Holly, and it wasn't because of your son. It was because you're not the type to go out and sleep with someone random, not after what happened with getting Holly knocked up and all that. You're too careful, so you always go the safe route." He taps on the side of his head. "Think about it, man."

I hate to admit that he's right about anything, but he's right. I *did* keep going back to Holly because she was safe.

Sure, our son had something to do with it, but his part was a lot smaller than I let myself acknowledge.

Holly was safe. I knew what I was getting myself into each and every time with her.

Monty, on the other hand...I have no fucking clue. She's been a surprise at every turn.

Including this morning when she left me there, wet and naked and fresh out of the shower after a night full of sex.

Who does that?

Was she embarrassed? Ashamed? *Hurt?*

"Yeah, you're right," I tell him. "I don't want your dumb ass to be, but you are."

"Gee, thanks."

"You know I love you, Zach."

"You love me so damn much that you went out and bought a bunny so I'd stop making unannounced visits to your place, right?"

"First, who in their right mind is actually *afraid* of bunnies? Bunnies! The most innocent creatures ever."

"Hey, Marshy resents that remark!"

I roll my eyes. "Second, you leave Thumbelina Bruce Wayne out of this. She's done nothing wrong."

"Except plot my demise. I can see it in her beady little eyes. She's out to get me."

"You're deranged."

"I tell him that *all* the time." Delia lets out a yawn as she slides into the kitchen. "Good morning, boys. I heard you exchanging 'I love yous', by the way." She shakes her phone at Zach. "I recorded it for future blackmail."

I blink at my best friend. "You're dating the devil, you know that, right?"

He wraps his arms around her waist, resting his head on her shoulder. "I know. Aren't her horns so cute?"

"I swear, fate couldn't have brought together two better suited weirdos."

"That wasn't fate, Robbie, that was you. Don't forget, this is all your fault," Delia says.

"I hate myself."

"But you love us." She shakes her phone again. "I have proof."

I groan, smacking my palm over my face. "Where's my kid?"

"Outside with the other kids."

"Wow. You just went there, huh?"

"You expected it." He plants a kiss on Delia's cheek and heads toward the coffee pot. "Coffee, babe?"

"Does a bear shit in the woods?"

"Excellent point. One coffee coming right up." He pours her a cup like the good boyfriend he is and shakes the pot my way. "More?"

I push my mug away. "No. I've already had three cups. Any more and I won't be able to sleep tonight."

Zach snorts. "Like you'll be able to anyway—not after last night and this morning."

"Oooh." Delia rubs her hands together and rests her

elbows on the counter, leaning toward me. "What happened? I want *all* the juicy details."

"Yeah, Robbie, tell her how bad you are in the sack."

"I am *not* bad in the sack."

Delia frowns. "That's a bummer. I always thought you'd be amazing."

"That's what I said!" Zach agrees before furrowing his brows. "Wait a damn minute—you think of him in the sack?"

"With biceps like those, can you blame a girl?"

"Holy shit," I mutter, laughing. "I'm getting my child and leaving. I can't handle any more of you two today."

"What?" Delia inquires innocently. "What'd I say?"

Zach grins, proud of his girl. "Exactly what I did."

She falls into a fit of laughter. "I love us."

"Me too, and you know what else I love?"

"Pizza? Me too. I'll make us some."

She pulls open the fridge and slides out a box of pizza then retrieves a skillet from the cabinet right next to her. She flips the stove on and turns back toward me.

"Wanna see some cool shit I learned on the Facebook?"

"*The* Facebook, huh?" I tease. "Sure. Show me your magic pizza skills, D."

"After you heat up the pan you..."

She starts going through all the steps and Zach pays attention like he hasn't heard all this before, though I'm certain he has.

Me...I tune her out after the first step.

I adore Delia, love her like my own sister, but right now all I can think about is Monty.

Monty who abandoned me.

Monty who fled.

Monty who bailed on me the morning after I took her virginity.

Who the fuck does that?

My first instinct this morning was to call her, chase her ass down, and demand she give me answers. I *needed* answers—deserved them.

Then the anger set in. I was *pissed*, absolutely fuming. How could she just leave? After the night we had?

She gave no sign this morning that she was going to flee. It surprised me, because it's unlike her. Hell, she even left me her number after Lola's. I one hundred percent expected her to be lying on the bed when I stepped out of the shower, but there was nothing but an empty apartment and this unfamiliar, aching hole forming in my chest. I can feel it now, thinking about her. I cannot leave things as we did; it's just not who I am. If she thinks we're done, she's wrong.

"...and that's it—the perfect reheated pizza," Delia says, sliding the plate my way.

I missed *all* of what she said, but I'm not about to tell her that.

I grab the slice and take a bite. "Damn, girl. This shit is good."

"Right? Better give me credit when you steal my genius shit."

"You mean Facebook's genius shit."

She lifts a shoulder. "Same-same dif."

I nearly choke on my pizza laughing. "Can't believe you've got her saying that now."

"Blame our new assistant, Will. It was all his fault."

"Fucking Will," I mutter.

"Kid's a hoot. Not one single filter."

"Filters are overrated," Delia says through a mouthful of bread and cheese.

I point at her, nodding in agreement. Finishing off the last of my pizza, I push away from the counter, standing.

"Okay, I'm outta here," I announce. "I'll grab my kid and scram. Need to get a few hours with him before he ditches me for the week."

I cross the kitchen and swoop Delia into my arms.

"Delia, it's been a pleasure."

She greets the hug with affection, wrapping her arms around my waist. Then she stiffens and, in a deadpan voice, says, "You're rubbing your greasy pizza fingers all over my shirt, aren't you?"

"Me? Nooooo."

"Robbie!" she hollers.

I pull away, smacking a big kiss to her cheek and dodge the tiny fists flying my way.

She whirls on her boyfriend. "You owe me a new shirt!"

"Me, why?"

"Because that's your friend!"

"I'm going to go ahead and not complain about you not calling me your friend right now because I don't want to go buy you a new shirt." Delia's eyes flare at the comment, and I try my best to hold in my laugh as she realizes she's caught in her own trap. "Gotta go, bye!"

I wave to them, grab Xavie's overnight bag from the back of my chair, and duck out the back door.

Xavie's sitting outside the hut Zach built for his goats, sliding treats inside one by one.

"Yo, spawn of mine, you ready?"

"Can I take Marshy with me?"

"I have two words for you: hell and no."

He sighs, gives the goat one more treat, and sluggishly makes his way over to me. "Lame."

"I know you are, but what am I?"

"Real funny, Dad."

I laugh at the sulky little shit who I love so dearly and steer him toward the car. As much fun as I had last night, I missed the kid, and I only have a few hours left with him today; I plan to make the best of them.

I realize now that, to do that, I'm going to do the one thing I've been fighting to do all damn morning.

As Xavie climbs into the car and buckles himself in, I slide my phone from my pocket.

> Me: I have two things to say to you, Monts. You ready?

Me: #1, it didn't work. Whatever we did last night, it didn't fucking work. I'm still thinking about you, and I'm gonna need more—a whole hell of a lot more.

Me: #2, you can run, but we're not done. THIS isn't done. We clear?

Monty: We're clear.

CHAPTER 15

MONTY

Python: I've given you a day. I can't wait any more. I was going to call but I had a feeling this might be easier for you.

Me: You're probably right.

Me: Not because I'm a chicken though. I'm having a girls' night with my sister and we're watching a movie. Our only rule is no phone calls.

Python: But you can text?

Me: No. I'm just being a rebel.

Python: I'll allow it.

Me: THIS IS GIRLS' NIGHT. PUT YOUR MAGIC DADDY DICK AWAY. WE'RE HAVING A DICK-FREE NIGHT.

Python: Denny, hi. Great to meet you again.

Python: Loving the new nickname. Magic Daddy Dick. I can get behind that.

Me: And my sister wants to get ON that. NOW SHUT UP.

Python: Right. My bad.

Python: Psst...Monty. Is it safe? Is she gone?

Me: NO BITCH.

Python: I won't lie, I'm imagining all these dirty words coming from Monty's mouth and it's making me laugh really fucking hard. Thank you for that.

Me: Okay, first, I would NEVER speak like that, so don't even THINK about it. Second, sorry. She's the worst.

Python: I don't know...that totally turned my shitty day into something much better.

Me: Well...you're welcome...I think.

Me: Though I think the reason you had a bad day might have to do with me, so maybe you're not so welcome.

Python: Correct.

Python: Why'd you bail, Monty?

Me: Wow. We're going to just jump right into this, huh?

Python: If you want me to maintain my sanity, then yes. We need to.

Me: Fine.

Me: I got scared.

Python: I need more.

Me: I knew it wouldn't be enough either.

Python: And why is that a bad thing?

Me: It's not, at least logically I know it's not, but it's scary, Robbie. You're...so much more than I am. You scare me.

Python: I don't feel like it's in a bad way though.

Me: It's really not, and that's also something that scares me.

Python: I don't scare you, Monty—I push you out of your comfort zone.

Python: Something you crave and equally hate.

Me: I know.

Me: I just...I don't know what we're doing here.

Python: Banging.

Me: Robbie...

Python: What? That's what we're doing. We're sleeping together, having fun, enjoying just being.

Python: Can't we just be, Monty? We don't have to make this anything serious. We can just enjoy each other.

Python: And bang—lots and lots of banging.

Me: I did rather like that part.

Python: Trust me, baby, I know. I've got the scratches to prove it.

Me: I did not scratch you!

Python: No, but you should. It's hot.

Me: You're so annoying.

Python: Admit it, it's one of your favorite qualities of mine.

Me: Totally not.

Python: Monty?

Me: Yes?

Python: We're cool, right? We're good to just keep this light and fun and let it happen how it happens?

Me: I'm scared.

Python: Then walk away.

Me: I can't.

Python: Then there's your answer.

Me: There it is.

Python: DOWNLOAD ATTACHMENT

Me: THUMBELINA!

Me: Can I confess something?

Python: You tried to steal my rabbit, didn't you?

Me: ...

Me: Yes.

Me: HOW DID YOU KNOW?!

Python: Because she's adorable as shit.

Me: There is nothing adorable about human excrement.

Python: Keep going, Monty. I love it when you talk dirty to me.

Me: Gross. Stop it.

Me: So what's next for us? It's been two days since...you know.

Python: I'm sorry, are you asking to jump on my Magic Daddy Dick again? My, my, I didn't realize you'd be such a little horndog.

Me: I AM NOT ASKING THAT.

Me: But if you're offering...

Me: IGNORE, IGNORE, IGNORE. Stupid voice to text. OMC

Python: OMC?

Python: Oh. Cats. Duh.

Python: Just for the record, I am ALWAYS offering.

Me: I'll keep that in mind.

Me: Remember how I was all, "I'll keep that in mind", trying to play it cool about, you know, us.

Python: You mean yesterday? Yes. Continue.

Me: Well…

Me: I'll be there in twenty.

Me: WAIT. Can I…can I bring food? I get hungry afterward.

Python: Monty, I am hungry right now, but not for food. Make it quick.

Me: I'm coming, I'm coming.

Python: You will be.

Python: DOWNLOAD ATTACHMENT

Me: Are those what I think they are?

Python: You tell me. They came off your ass.

Python: Which, by the way, is my favorite ass in all the land.

Me: *rolls eyes* You're just saying that to try to get lucky again.

Python: Geez, all about the sex with you, huh, Monts?

Me: Robert...

Python: What? *blinks innocently*

Me: Innocent my butt.

Python: Mmm, dat ass though.

Me: Did you just "mmm" my butt?

Python: Yes, I did, AND I AM NOT ASHAMED.

Me: OH NO. I just realized something. What if Thumbelina was running around and accidentally ate my panties? That would have been HORRIBLE!

Python: I got you one better: what if MY SON had found them?

Me: Oh. OH. Oh my. I feel sick.

Python: You should, you sex-crazed vixen.

Me: ROBBIE! I AM SERIOUS!

Python: I AM TOO!

Python: Seriously, though, it's okay. He won't be here for another few days so he wouldn't have found them. I DO clean my apartment, you know.

Me: I know, I know. I just worry.

Me: Wait, your son...OMC, you're a father!

Python: Yes, yes. We've established that.

Me: No! I mean, what are we going to do about that?

Python: Oh. Um...well, fuck. I don't know, actually. I've never had to introduce him to anyone before.

Python: I mean, not to jump ahead or anything, because we're just banging... but, you know, just in case. We should probably discuss this further. Over drinks. And sex. Lots and lots of sex.

Me: Who's the crazed sex vixen now?

Python: Still you. Your title is safe.

Me: You're so mean.

Python: But you like it when I'm mean.

Me: Are you working tonight?

Python: There she goes again...

Me: UGH

Python: Yes, I'm working the late shift.
Sorry.

Me: Darn. I was wanting that magic
daddy wiener.

Python: God. I wanna kiss you so
fucking bad right now that I hate myself
for it because you saying wiener is
absolutely goddamn ridiculous and I
hate that I love it.

Me: I just want to kiss you because I like
kissing you.

Python: I'm screenshotting that.

CHAPTER 16

MONTY

Me: I'm at a bar.

Python: Looking for your next victim already?

Me: Yes. You're boring and a terrible lay.

Python: That's it, I'm spanking you tonight.

Me: I'M KIDDING.

Me: You are, however, the best I've ever had.

Python: Don't you threaten me with winning by default because it still counts.

Python: Why are you at a bar?

Me: Well, it's more like I'm sitting at the bar of a restaurant. Still counts, right?

Python: You are so badass with your day drinking.

Me: Oh, hush. I'm having an iced tea and you know it. I'm out with my coworkers. We're doing our weekly luncheon before I start work next week and before parent-teacher meetings tonight.

Python: Are you nervous?

Me: Completely. It's my first big-girl job.

Python: You're going to do great.

Me: Or the kids are going to hate me.

Python: They won't. Promise. Might have a crush on you, but they won't hate you.

Me: How do you get the kids at the center to adore you?

Python: Candy. Lots and lots of candy.

Me: Of course.

Python: And my charm. I have a lot of it.

Me: Yes, I've noticed.

> Me: Go ahead and screenshot that too.

> Python: Oh, I did.

"YOU HAVE A BEAUTIFUL SMILE, MONTY."

Brandon slides onto the stool next to me and I quickly tuck my phone back into my purse sitting on my lap.

"Um, thank you, Mr. Donahue."

He grins, and it pales in comparison to Robbie's.

Robbie.

My mind begins to drift to him and I have to redirect myself before I let my imagination run too wild, something that's easy when it comes to the sexy-as-sin single father whose bed I've been occupying night after night.

"I've told you, call me Brandon outside of school."

"Right. Sorry. Just feels weird to not maintain the same level of professionalism outside the classroom as we should inside the classroom."

My words are a dig at him and his inappropriate comments.

He doesn't catch it.

Which isn't surprising. Maybe I should ease up on him some. I mean, all he did was compliment my smile. That's not too bad, right? Robbie says *way* worse stuff to me daily.

But Brandon isn't Robbie.

"We're friends outside the classroom, not coworkers. We have to let loose and have fun some time."

"Very true."

He nods toward my half-empty glass. "Need another drink?"

"No, I—"

"I'll get you one," he interrupts, heading down the bar to the bartender.

I pull my phone from my purse once he's turned his back.

> Python: Why are you texting me if you're supposed to be at lunch?

> Me: Oh crud. Am I bothering you?

> Python: You never bother me, Monty. I was just curious why you weren't enjoying hanging with your coworkers.

> Python: Wait, is Mr. Can't Take a Hint there?

> Me: Yes. He's why I'm hiding—keeps scooting closer and closer to my chair and into my space. Well, he's why I was trying to hide. He decided to follow me to the bar. He's buying me a drink right now.

"Here you go. I got you that sweet tea you've been drinking."

"Thank you," I say politely, pretending to take a sip through the straw as he watches me the entire time. I *hate* sweet tea.

"Are you nervous for tonight?"

"A little," I say honestly. "Mostly worried the parents are going to look at me like I'm stupid or something."

"They won't. Besides, even if things go south, you get to do it all again next Wednesday for the other half of the parents."

"Ah, yes. Very considerate of the district to do, but also twice as nerve-racking."

He laughs. "Very true."

Tonight is night one of parent-teacher meetings, and night two is next Wednesday. The district is very aware of how many working and two-household families there are these days and want to ensure every parent can meet with the teacher, hence us having two separate events and me having to endure speaking in front of a room of adults twice.

I'm so nervous about it that I wasn't even able to eat all my lunch, and I *love* chicken fingers.

"You're going to be a great first-year teacher, Monty. I just know it. You have this...certain air about you, like this was meant to be your thing."

"I...wow. Thank you, Brandon. That means a lot coming from you."

I want to eat my words the moment I say them, especially when his cheeks flush.

I go to tell him I didn't mean them in any way other than friendly when my phone buzzes against the counter, interrupting me.

"Python?" Brandon asks, glancing at the screen. "Is that a code name for someone?"

I snatch my cell from the counter and quickly stash it in my purse. "It's...uh...kind of, yes."

"A boyfriend?"

The question takes me off guard.

One, it feels so personal, and he shouldn't be asking me questions like that.

Two, *is* Robbie my boyfriend? How do I explain what he is to me? *I let him do dirty things to me every now and again but he's not my boyfriend* does *not* sound like the appropriate answer...at all.

I rack my brain, trying to find a better, simpler answer.

"You know what? That's none of my business. Sorry I asked."

I blow out a relieved breath. "He's not my boyfriend. It's complicated."

"Complicated? Ah, I've had one of those—many of those, actually. Want to know something interesting about me?" He waves his hand, beckoning me closer like he's going to tell me a secret. "I used to be engaged."

I sit back at his statement, surprised.

"Yep," he says, taking another sip of his soda. "We were two months shy of getting married, invitations sent, venues booked, RSVPs noted—all that fun stuff. Then I caught her in bed...with our former gym teacher."

I gasp at his reveal, and the sadness sinks into his eyes.

It's a sadness I am all too familiar with.

"I'm sorry, Brandon. I can relate to that on many levels," I admit.

Our eyes connect, and we share a moment of understanding.

Maybe all his advances aren't so much advances as a pursuit of friendship. Maybe I'm reading this whole thing wrong.

I hope I am.

"Yeah?" He lifts his drink and clinks it with mine. "I'm sorry too, Montana." He clears the emotion building in his throat. "Well, now that I've made this extremely awkward, I'm going to head back to the table. I'll let you get back to whoever you were texting."

"I'll be back over there in a few minutes."

I watch him walk off, his shoulders resting a bit lower than before, and I feel bad for him.

I want to race after him and give him a hug, because that's just who I am, but I don't want to give him the wrong impression...again.

Maybe I can set him up with someone? Just to help get his mind off his bad breakup. Denny maybe?

No. That girl would eat him alive. They're total opposites.

Like me and Robbie.

Speaking of...

I pull my phone from my purse and check for more messages. There are two waiting for me.

Python: He still bugging you?

Python: DOWNLOAD ATTACHMENT

I gasp so loudly three patrons at the bar look my way.
I don't care, not even a little bit.
My face is on fire as I stare down at the screen.

Me: ROBERT CROSS. WHAT IN THE...

Me: I think I may faint.

Me: THAT IS YOUR WIENER!

Python: I know. You're welcome. Show
him his competition.

Me: I am not showing anyone that!

Python: It's okay to brag sometimes,
Monty.

Me: It's not MY wiener—what do I have
to brag about?

Python: Um, that you're totally hitting
this.

Me: Oh. Well, I guess I could brag about
that.

Me: But not with your dirty picture!

Python: Because you're keeping it all to yourself, right?

Me: YES!

Python: *waggles brows*

My thighs tighten as I realize what he's suggested. *Pleasuring myself.*

Me: Not like that, you pervert!

Python: Riiiiiiight.

Me: Okay, maybe a little bit like that.

Python: I knew it. You're totally gonna flick your bean to that tonight.

Yes.

The thought makes me heat with embarrassment.

Me: No comment.

Python: SCREENSHOT

CHAPTER 17

ROBBIE

Me: So…last night was fun.

Monty: It was okay.

Me: OKAY? What about when I did that thing with my tongue? You were SCREAMING.

Monty: You mean when you greeted me at your door by LICKING THE SIDE OF MY FACE?

Me: Yes, and then you spent twenty minutes ignoring me and only playing with my bunny.

Monty: Because you licked me, and it was gross!

Me: You loved it.

Monty: I hated it. HATED IT.

Me: Liar.

Monty: Go work or something.

Me: Nah.

Me: I like bothering you more.

Monty: Well, I'M trying to work, so go away.

Me: DOWNLOAD ATTACHMENT

Me: Shh...don't tell anyone.

Monty: Tell me you didn't...

Me: Oh, I did.

Monty: At work? Really?

Me: What? She's cute and lonely!

Monty: Robbie, you have a bunny in your desk drawer. A BUNNY!

Me: Stop judging me.

Monty: I'm not.

Monty: Fine, I am, but only a little.

Monty: I am also very jealous because she's the best little snuggle bunny ever.

Me: I see what you did there.

Monty: Good. Now go work.

Me: Yes, ma'am.

Me: Oooh, I kind of liked saying that.

Monty: We are NOT adding that to our bedroom happenings.

Me: We'll see.

Monty: DOWNLOAD ATTACHMENT

Monty: Does this outfit say "authoritative but fun"?

Me: Pretty sure that one says, "Fuck me".

Monty: It does not! It's a floor-length skirt and a blazer!

Me: What? I have a problem when it comes to you and your old granny clothes. They're so hot!

Monty: Stop hitting on me and help! I need an outfit for my first day.

Me: Just so we're clear, I will never NOT hit on you.

Me: But, yes, that's a good first day outfit.

Me: Now stop freaking out. You're going to do great.

Monty: Just a few more days.

Me: Want me to give you a good dicking? That could help calm you down.

Monty: I cannot believe I'm going to say this but...YES, PLEASE!

Monty: When? Your lunch break? You get one of those, right?

Me: What have I turned you into?

Monty: YES. THAT. This is all your fault!

Me: I'll gladly take the blame.

Me: You're more than welcome to come to my place of employment, Monts. You can meet Zach.

Me: Wait, no—you'll totally fall for him. I lied.

Monty: Darn! That was my plan all along: get you to invite me to your office so I can meet this swoony fella and fall for him instead.

Me: Delia would never let someone steal her main squeeze...most days.

Monty: So you're saying there's a chance?

Me: Not even a tiny one. Thank god.

Monty: BOOOO!

Monty: And we can't meet on your lunch break. I was only teasing. I have too much work to do.

Me: Maybe tonight?

Monty: Can't. I have plans with Denny.

Me: *cries like Padmé* YOU'RE BREAKING MY HEART!

Monty: Um, who?

Me: ...

Monty: KIDDING, KIDDING! I've seen Titanic.

Me: That's it. We're breaking up.

Monty: I WAS KIDDING.

Monty: Also, can we "break up" if we're just friends with benefits?

Me: Oh totally. Me denying you dick would be us breaking up.

Me: Actually, I don't know...I just really like dangling the D in your face.

Monty: Robbie...

Me: *blinks innocently* What?

Monty: You're making me want a nap.

Me: A naked nap, right?

Monty: No!

Me: *yes

Me: It's been days since our last tryst.

Monty: I knew I was just a booty call.

Me: Oh, did you think this was something more? My bad.

Me: Seriously, though, I'm kinda missing you.

Me: And by kinda, I mean I really fucking miss you, and not just for the extra-amazing sex either.

Monty: Extra amazing? Someone's buttering me up for something.

Monty: I'm not doing any weird positions.

Me: We'll come back to that later.

Me: But do you want to get together tonight? Just to hang?

Monty: I can't. I need to prep my schedule for the first week. It's just days away.

Me: You're killing me.

Monty: You'll live.

Me: Not if I'm dead I won't.

Monty: So dramatic.

Me: *cries a thousand tears*

Monty: If I'd have known you were going to be such a handful…

Me: I am way more than a handful and we both know it. 😏

Me: We're meeting tonight. I'm not taking no for an answer.

Monty: Yes, you are. I can't.

Me: Can.

Me: Be prepared.

Me: It's happening.

Monty: I'm too tired for sex.

Me: If you think you're tired now, just wait.

CHAPTER 18

MONTY

"GOOD MORNING, class. I'm Miss Andrews."

I slap my hand against my forehead.

"Nope. That's dumb. Let's try again."

Squaring my shoulders, I hold my head high and try one more time. "Good morning, class. I am Miss Andrews and today..."

I stop myself because I sound ridiculous...again.

I've been standing in front of this mirror for the past thirty minutes trying to nail my opening for my first day, and everything I say sounds robotic or asinine—there is no in between.

It was the same way on Wednesday when I had my first set of parent-teacher meetings. I sounded so stupid in front of all the smiling parents, and I could have sworn I saw a few cringes when my voice squeaked mid "good evening". My stomach rolls at the thought of having to do it again this Wednesday.

Good thing I have time to practice. Hopefully, the kids will be more forgiving than the parents.

I clear my throat and try again.

"Good—"

There's a loud knock on the door and I nearly jump out of my skin at the sudden noise.

I bet Denny forgot her keys again.

I slide my robe over my pajamas and make my way to the front door.

Another loud knock.

"I'm coming, you hairbrained goof!"

The moment I pull the door open, I regret not looking through the peephole first, because the person standing on the other side isn't who I'm expecting.

Not at all.

He's leaned against the doorframe, big arms crossed, a smirk gracing his lips.

"Hairbrained goof? Is that the best insult you could come up with?" He holds his hand up and shakes his head. "Wait, wait, wait—never mind, totally is."

"I could absolutely come up with something better. I could say...um...I could call her...."

"Go on. I'll wait."

"I can't think with all this pressure!" I draw my robe tighter around my body. "Why are you here? Better yet, how did you get here?"

"Gee, it's so great to see you too, Monty. Nice outfit,

by the way—very sexy. As for how I got here, I traveled by this amazing modern invention called *transportation*."

My hair is piled on top of my head in a messy bun and I'm wearing my tiniest pair of sleep shorts, a tank top, and no bra.

I look like a mess as I glare at him from my doorway. "I meant, how do you know where I live?"

"Oh, that's easy—Denny."

"Denny? How?"

"Remember Zoe?" he asks.

"You mean that insanely beautiful girl from the bar? Yes, quite well."

"Was that jealously I just heard in your voice?"

Yes, I want to scream, which is ridiculous because deep down I know I have nothing to worry about, but sometimes our emotions get the best of us and we react to certain situations in ways we normally wouldn't.

Hence my voice going an octave higher as I shake my head and say, "No."

"Because you have nothing to be jealous of. One, she has a boyfriend. Two, she's like a sister to me. Three, you're my main squeeze, Monts."

He winks, and I hate that it makes me want to reach out and pull him closer, then sear my lips to his.

"Anyway," he continues, "she and Denny have become good friends since then. Zoe, being one of my very best friends, was kind enough to give me Denny's number, who was more than happy to give me your address."

"Was she now?"

He nods. "Definitely. She said—and I quote—'My sister needs a good dick'. Then she proceeded to give me your address, holler something about not bothering her at work, and hang up." He holds his arms out. "And, well, here I am."

"Why?"

"Why what?"

I sigh and fold my arms over my chest. "Why are you here, Robbie?"

"Oh, someone is cranky tonight." He shakes his junk my way. "You need some lovin'?"

"I *will* close this door," I threaten.

"You won't. You've missed me too much."

"False."

His smirk grows. "You're a terrible liar. Now, go get dressed. We're going out."

"We most certainly are not. I told you, I need to work on my lesson plans tonight."

"What you need is a night out, to relax. You have all day tomorrow and all night because I'm certain you won't be able to sleep with first day jitters."

He's right, and it annoys me that he's right.

I've always been horrible when it comes to that.

The night before the first day of school? I can't sleep. The night before a big trip? I'll be lucky if I get an hour's worth of sleep. Before a doctor's appointment? Forget it.

I am way too much of a worrywart to relax.

Hence why I've been running around like an insane woman, barely squeezing in any time for myself this past week.

"Robbie, no. I need to get stuff done."

"Please, Monty, just tonight. I'm doing this for you, not for me. You *need* this."

"I need this, or *you* do?"

"Fine, I admit I'm being a little selfish because I miss the shit outta you, but also because what I said is true—you have got to relax or you're going to scare those kids on Monday with all your crazy."

"I..." *Crud. He's right.* "Just tonight, and you have to promise you will not bug me at all on Sunday."

He holds his hand up. "Scout's honor."

I side-eye him, waiting for him to squirm under my scrutiny, but he never does.

He means it. He'll leave me alone tomorrow.

"Fine," I agree.

"Good!" He pushes off the doorframe and stalks my way, forcing me to back into the apartment. "Now go put your tits in a sling and let's get outta here."

"How do you know I'm not wearing a bra?"

He shrugs, closing the door behind him. "I'm just good like that."

"You mean you were staring at my breasts?"

"Fine, you caught me." He reaches out like he's going to grab them but I slap his hand away. He laughs and begins wandering around the very tiny apartment. "I like looking at your boobs—sue me," he says over his shoulder.

He inspects the place, which doesn't take long because all we can afford is a very small two-bedroom apartment.

"This is cute."

"It's smaller than your place," I comment. "I wish we had more room, but it's all we can afford."

"I'm not judging you on how big your apartment is or isn't, Monty. If you think I'm rolling in dough, you're wrong."

"Good. Wait, no," I backtrack. "Not about you not rolling in dough, about you not judging me. I mean, not that I thought you would or anything like that, I just mean I—"

I gasp as his hands cup my face and his lips cut my words off. He moves his mouth over mine with such mastery, giving me a soft, chaste kiss that leaves me wanting more.

"I've missed you," he says quietly when he pulls away.

"I know."

"And..."

"I guess I missed you too."

He laughs and gives me another quick kiss before pushing me an arm's length away.

"If you don't go away now, this night is going to take a turn it's not supposed to...yet."

"And that would be a bad thing...why?"

"Because we have plans. Now get them boobs in a holder before I do something stupid."

With reluctance, I drag myself back to my bedroom and strip as quickly as possible. Out of habit, I reach for one of my skirts, but my hand freezes over the garment.

Robbie can surprise me, so I can surprise him too.

I grab a change of clothes and dart across the hall to the bathroom. I pull my outfit on and stare into the mirror, trying to figure out what I'm going to do with this mess of hair.

"I'm totally judging your 'Continue Watching' list on Netflix!" Robbie yells through the apartment.

"You snoop!"

"You bore!" he teases, poking fun at all the documentaries and cooking shows I'm sure are listed on the screen.

It takes me another five minutes to get my red mane under control and swipe some lip gloss on. I zip back over to my room, grabbing my favorite mantra-stamped necklace and slide it on before taking a steadying breath and meeting Robbie in the living room.

"You seriously watch this shit? It's s—"

Whatever he was going to say dies on his lips when he sees me. His jaw hangs open, eyes wide with disbelief.

"Holy fucking shit. I never in my entire life thought a pair of jeans would be the hottest thing on a chick, but damn, woman. You wear those *well*." He twirls his finger in a circle. "Let's see that ass."

"Robbie! I am not a piece of food. Stop drooling."

"I could eat you like a piece of food." He grins wolfishly and winks. "But you know that."

My face flames and I shake my head. "Let's go before I change my mind about going out in public with you."

He clicks off the TV and stands to meet me. "You love going out with me."

"Actually, this is our first time going out."

"Is not. There was Lola's." He holds up his index and middle fingers. "Twice, mind you."

"That doesn't count. Both times we were there together were on accident. This is our first date."

"There is no way! We..."

He trails off and his eyes widen as he realizes I'm right.

We've been texting for over a month now, he took my virginity, and we've gotten dirty between the sheets several times since then—but we haven't been out on a date yet.

How backward is that?

"Fuck, Monty. I feel like such a dirty asshole right now. I didn't mean to not properly take you out. It's just that we've known each other for weeks now and talk every day, and I guess I never realized we hadn't actually been out together." He shakes his head, disappointed in himself. "I'm sorry."

"It's okay. It's not like we're actually dating. We're just having fun, doing the light and fluffy thing, not taking anything too seriously. I guess it doesn't surprise me that we haven't been on a real date yet."

"But does it sadden you?"

I twist my lips up, thinking. "I think if you weren't so fun and we didn't have such a good time texting, it might. I might feel like we were missing something, but I don't."

"Good. That's good. Makes me feel a bit better."

"But..."

"Always with the butts. You're such an ass girl."

I glare at him. "But that doesn't mean I wouldn't want to go out on dates. I think that would be nice. Nothing over the top, but dinner or a movie together every now and then would be fun."

"Well, we're not doing dinner and a movie tonight, sorry. I'm planning something else that's a lot more fun."

"Then lead the way," I tell him. "Let's go have some fun."

"No, no. After you." He holds his hand out. "Ladies first."

I push past him, and not until I hear him suck air in through his teeth do I realize what he just did.

I peek back over my shoulder to find him standing in the middle of the apartment, knuckles tucked between his teeth as he stares at my behind.

"*Damn.*"

"Ugh!"

I pull the door closed, right in his laughing face.

"That ass is what dreams are made of, baby!" he hollers from inside.

I roll my eyes but can't stop the smile spreading across my face.

What have I gotten myself into with this guy?

"OKAY, okay, so you were right: metal isn't bad, especially that Parkway Drive band. Did you know they're from Australia and are surfers too?"

Robbie grins at this information. "I did. How do *you* know that?"

"I looked them up. That lead singer is mighty cute."

"You bone one bad boy with tattoos and suddenly that's all you want," he teases.

"Stop it." I shove at him playfully as he puts the car into park.

"We're here. Stay. Let me get the door."

I wait patiently as he climbs from the vehicle and rounds the front.

He pops open my door with an over-the-top bow, holding his hand out to me. "Milady."

"Thank you," I say, climbing from the car and glancing around the lot. "This is the secret place you were dying to whisk me off to?"

"Is there a problem, Princess Montana?"

I look up at the billiards pub. It's a rundown-looking building in the middle of a nearly deserted strip mall. There are a few groups of people sitting around outside at tables, smoking cigarettes, sipping beers, and laughing.

While this isn't a place I'd normally step foot in, I'm eager to see what's inside.

"I've never played pool before," I tell him.

"Good. I'll teach you."

He places his hand on the small of my back and steers us toward the entrance.

The first thing I notice is this certain smell to the building, like there have been way too many cigarettes smoked inside in the past, but it's not entirely unpleasant. The carpets are worn and the lighting is dim, but it's not as unkempt as I thought it would be.

We slide into two chairs at the wide-open bar, most of the patrons occupying the many pool tables scattered about the building.

"Do you mind if I get a beer?"

"Just because I'm not a big drinker doesn't mean you can't enjoy yourself. I don't mind. But, fair warning, I'll be taking your keys when we leave, even if you only have one beer."

He reaches into his pocket and hands me the keys. "Two things. One, it's stupid sexy how responsible you are. Two, it's a good goddamn thing we didn't take my bike then."

"I'm sorry, you have a *motorcycle*?"

"Yes, ma'am."

"I've always wanted to go on one. We should have taken that."

"I wasn't sure how you'd react," he says honestly. "But

noted for our next date, because there *will* be another one."

I smile as the bartender appears in front of us.

"Hey, good to see you, Robbie. You want your usual on draft and an hourly table?"

"Please, Not Pam. That'd be great."

"Anything for you, love?" she asks me.

"No, thank you."

She nods and scurries off to grab Robbie's beer.

I turn to him. "Not Pam?"

"You ever see *The Office?*"

"Bits and pieces here and there."

"Remember the secretary? The one Jim's in love with? Pam?"

"Vaguely."

"Well she looks nearly identical to her."

"No way," I protest.

He slides his phone from his pocket and taps the screen a few times before turning it my way.

"See, that's her."

I peer at the image, looking back and forth between the actress on the screen and the bartender standing right in front of me, Robbie's beer in her outstretched hand.

"He's showing you why he calls me Not Pam, isn't he?"

I nod. "The resemblance is...wow."

"I know. I get it all the time. Good thing she's a cutie."

She winks and bends below the counter for a second,

popping back up holding a tray full of cue balls and chalk. "Here you guys go. You know the drill. I'll be around to check on ya in a bit."

Then she's heading back down the bar again, tending to another couple who just walked in.

Robbie hops off his stool with his beer in hand. "Grab the balls?"

"How did you say that with a straight face?"

"I didn't," he admits. "My lips twitched, you just missed it."

I roll my eyes and grab the balls as he leads us over to a table along the wall of windows.

For a place where I'm certain balls go flying off tables all the time, they're quite brave having all the windows and mirrors they do.

He sets his beer on the table and begins racking the balls.

"We're just gonna shoot, get ya used to the table before we start making bets."

"Bets? What kinds of bets?"

"For kisses, fun new positions, butt stuff—the usual."

My lips lift at his nonchalance. "First game starts the bet."

"First game, huh?" He scratches at the stubble on his chin, thinking and studying me. "Okay. What do you want if you win?"

"Ten kisses, anytime, anywhere."

He grins, like he knew that's exactly what I'd say, how safe I'd bet.

He just doesn't know what his kisses do to me.

"Okay, okay. *When* I win, I'll decide what I want." He rubs his hands together, excited. "I'm thinking a new position. I have some crazy things I'd like to do with you. You sure you wanna bet first game?"

I nod. "Positive."

"No exceptions for what I come up with?"

"None."

"Deal."

We shake on it.

He shuffles through the pool sticks, searching for just the right one, testing it on the table before deciding.

"I'll break," he tells me, getting into position.

He scatters the balls with his power shot, sinking a solid and a stripe.

"I'll take solids."

Four shots later, it's my turn.

I sashay around the table, looking for just the right shot, but nothing is working in my favor.

I miss, and he laughs.

"You gotta line it up," he tells me. "Like this. Come here."

He pulls me close until I'm stuck to him like glue. He bends us both down, my butt fitting perfectly against his crotch, and lines us up for the shot.

This continues until we're tied with just two balls

each and the eight ball.

"Think you got this one on your own?" he asks.

"I...I hope so. Guess we'll see."

Within one minute, I sink both balls, call my corner, and win the game.

With a smirk, I rest my stick against the table and take a seat on the stool.

He stands there, gawking for a good minute before finally looking up at me.

"I cannot believe you." His voice is full of incredulity.

"What?" I ask with innocence.

"You know damn well what."

"I have no idea what you could possibly be talking about."

"You hustled me." He lifts a finger my way. "*You*"—he turns his finger his way again—"hustled *me*."

I bat my lashes innocently. "Did I? Is that what that's called?"

He stalks my way, not stopping until his nose is nearly touching mine.

"I could kiss the shit outta you right now."

I lift a shoulder. "You owe me some anyway."

"Nah. You'd like that too much, and after the stunt you just pulled, I'm not giving you the satisfaction."

I grin up at him. "Want to play again?"

"Dammit, Monty," he mutters before sealing his mouth over mine.

His lips press against mine firmly and it's only a

moment before I'm completely lost, wanting to wrap my legs around his waist and put that pool table to good use.

"Get a room!" Not Pam yells from behind the bar.

He laughs, pulling away reluctantly.

Stick in hand, he heads back around the table, racking the balls again. "How'd you get so good at pool?"

"We had a table in our garage. I spent *many* hours out there playing with my dad."

"Explains that wicked bank shot you have." He lifts the rack. "You won, so it's your break."

I get into position and whack them apart as hard as I can.

"Nice," he murmurs.

When I peer over my shoulder, I realize he's not talking about the balls.

It's my butt.

Again.

"Your perviness knows no bounds."

"You're not wrong. I knew pool would be a great idea."

"You brought me here to stare at my bum?"

He leans over the table, lining up a shot, then grinning up at me. "Yes, Monty, I brought you just to stare at your *bum*."

"Quit mocking me."

"Say ass." He shoots and misses. "Your turn."

"No!" I pocket the first two balls of the game. "Stripes or solids?"

"How about *strips* and"—he glances down at his junk

—"this solid."

I roll my eyes and try my hardest to fight my grin. "Just shoot, Robbie."

"How about this: I win this game, you strip and get my solid, and if you win, I'll quit being pervy and actually play."

"Hmm...tough call, because I do adore your solid." He tries to cover his laugh with a cough but it's no use. I know he's getting a kick out of me calling his erection a solid. The jerk. "But I also haven't played a game of pool in ages and was looking forward to playing."

"You're scared I'll actually win."

"You think falling into bed with you scares me?"

"Oh, Monty, I know it does."

You'd think after the many nights we've spent together it wouldn't scare me anymore, but every time we strip each other down to nothing, I get nervous.

It's not because Robbie himself scares me, but because I'm terrified of what he's making me feel so quickly.

We're supposed to be light and fluffy. I shouldn't get butterflies every time I'm around him, shouldn't feel like I have this heavy weight on my shoulders when I'm not.

Yet, I do, and it's frightening.

Thrilling.

And I can't say no.

"You have a deal."

He takes his next shot.

I throw the game.

CHAPTER 19

MONTY

Python: I know it's early, but I just wanted to wish you luck on your first day. You're going to rock this. I just know it. Text or call when you get the chance.

Python: Oh, and thanks for last night. That new position is what dreams are made of.

Me: Thank you, and you're welcome.

Me: I'll try to sneak a text sometime today.

Me: I miss you.

Python: I know you do.

Me: *eye roll*

Me: Please tell me you didn't.

Python: Fine, I didn't.

Me: I needed this. BAD.

Me: Thank you for the flowers, Robbie. They're gorgeous.

Python: Gorgeous flowers for a gorgeous gal.

Python: That was so corny.

Me: But I loved it.

Python: How'd the first day go?

Me: Holy cats. Today was EXHAUSTING! I broke up a fight and spilled my coffee all over myself during lunch. I'm pretty sure three kids already think I'm the worst teacher ever too.

Me: Other than that, let's just say if I were a big drinker, I'd be half a bottle of wine deep right now.

Python: Only half a bottle? Weak.

Python: But you're still cute, so I'll allow it.

Python: Sorry it was a crappy first day.

Me: I wouldn't say that, not entirely. It could have been a lot worse.

Python: But a lot better too. I know you're a bit of a perfectionist, so I'm certain today was slowly killing you inside.

Me: Totally.

Me: As much as I hate to cut this short...

Python: No, no. You're a working woman now. I get it. Go rest. Sweet dreams, Monts.

Python: *sexy not sweet

Python: Sorry, my bad.

Me: I don't know who's more exhausting, the kids or you.

Python: We'll just call it a tie.

Me: Good night, Robert.

Me: SERIOUSLY?

Python: Yep.

Me: You DID NOT have to do that!

Python: Right, but I WANTED to do that.

Me: How'd you know I even like pizza?

Python: Excuse me? EVERYONE likes pizza. It's blasphemous not to.

Python: I'm appalled you'd even suggest it.

Python: Wait, you DO like pizza, right? Now I'm a little worried about my taste in women…

Me: Yes. I love it.

Me: Thank you, but stop sending me stuff. You're going to make me think you like me.

Python: Oh, but I do.

Python: How was day two?

Me: I didn't spill coffee on myself until AFTER lunch today, so there's that.

Python: Oh good gravy, woman.

Python: I wish I could hug you right now.

Me: A naked hug, right?

Python: I'm sorry, did YOU just suggest a naked hug? My, oh my.

Me: I told you, it's been a day.

Python: It'll get better—first week jitters and all that. You'll be a pro in no time.

Me: I hope so. I've always wanted to be a teacher, help kids, and make a difference, ya know. I just didn't think it would be this hard.

Python: It'll get easier, babe. I know it.

Python: Now go rest. I'll talk to you tomorrow.

Me: My feet are killing me.

Python: You texted me at 6AM to talk about your feet? Are you crazy, woman?!

Me: Oh crud! Sorry! I didn't even think about that. You're just always the first person I text nowadays.

Python: I really love that, but I also really love sleep.

Me: Did I wake you?

Python: Nah. I've been up for hours.

Python: Also, if this was a cry for a foot rub, it's not happening. Feet are disgusting, even your adorably pedicured ones.

Me: Well that's just rude.

Python: So, I had a thought.

Me: This is scary already.

Python: Wow. WOW. Really, Monty? REALLY?

Python: I see how you get when you don't get the D for a few days. You get hangry.

Me: Hangry? I don't think you're using that word right.

Python: Sure I am. Horny + Angry = Hangry

Me: Ughh.

Python: 😉

Python: Anyway, back to my thought. I kind of figured I wouldn't be able to see you any nights this week because you'd be dead tired from all the teachering you're doing.

Me: Yes, true. Go on...

Python: Well, how about we go to dinner Friday night then?

Me: You asking me out on a date, Robbie?

Python: Indeed I am, Montana.

Me: I'm in.

Me: Wait, don't you have your son this week?

Python: Therein lies the catch.

Python: I DO have my son this week. He'd be going with us. What do you think?

Me: I think...wow. I...I don't know, Robbie.

Me: That's huge.

Python: That's what she said.

Me: Huh? Who?

Me: Oh. Never mind.

Me: But still. That's a big step.

Python: I know, I know, but... Okay, you know what? I'm calling you so you can't screenshot this and ruin my badass reputation I have going on. You better answer.

MY PHONE LIGHTS UP in my hand and I nearly drop it, which is *so* silly since he just told me he was about to call.

I swipe the green icon over and put the phone up to my ear.

"I'm about to get sappy as shit right now," he says in greeting.

"Well, hello to you too."

"Listen up."

I laugh at his bossiness but do as he says, holding the phone tightly to my ear, ready to soak up every sappy word he's about to fire my way.

He exhales a deep breath, gathering his courage, I suppose.

"I like you, Monty. I like you *a lot*." His words are what some would consider juvenile. The force behind them, though—that's what makes them so powerful.

My knuckles begin to turn white as I grasp the phone even tighter.

"I like you a lot too, Robbie," I tell him.

"No, you don't get it. I can't stop thinking about you, or your ass, your tits...your kissable-as-fuck mouth." I chuckle at how far off this conversation just went, in typical Robbie fashion. "Or your off-the-wall personality and stupid sexy grandma outfits, which is kind of embarrassing if you think about it."

"They aren't *that* bad."

"I beg to differ. Anyway, I like seeing you, spending time with you. I want to keep doing both of those things...often."

The line goes silent, and I worry for a moment that I've lost him.

Then it hits me, what he's saying right now—what he's *trying* to say without really saying it.

My heart picks up its pace and I'm so giddy, so full of energy all of a sudden.

"Robbie, are you...are you asking me to go steady with you?"

"I think so." He mutters something I can't entirely make out, but it sounded very similar to his favorite prayer. "Yes. I meant yes. I am."

"I...don't know what to say."

"I know this was supposed to be light and fluffy and fun or whatever, but it's evolved. I want more than that. I want stability. I want real. I want you."

His words nearly knock the breath out of me, but I manage to squeak out, "You want me?"

"Fuck yes I do. You're the first thing I think about in the morning—after having to pee and my son, of course."

"Well I'm glad to know I come *after* your full bladder."

"Stop making fun of me. I don't do well with this kind of shit."

"I'm sorry. I just...I'm scared."

"I am too, Monty, so goddamn terrified, like my throat is closing right this minute, but I think you're worth it—worth the risk."

"You think?"

He laughs, and I can hear him shuffling around on the other end of the call like he's pacing or something. "I'm usually a wicked good judge of character, but something about you scares me. So, as much as I want to be cocky and be all, 'No, baby, I'm sure,' I can't do that—not with you. You're different than anyone I've ever met before. You make me *want* different things, like something steady, but I'm also really fucking scared by that little fact."

"I think it's brave for you to admit you're just as scared as I am. I want to say yes."

"Then say it."

"I...ugh."

A ping sounds in my ear and I pull the phone away to see I have a text from Robbie.

"Did you just text me?"

"Nope. Wasn't me."

"Hang on."

I swipe my notification bar down to see it's an image.

"What did you send me?"

"I have no idea what you're talking about."

I pull the phone away from my face again and open the text.

Then promptly burst into laughter.

"Oh my gosh, did you just use your bunny to ask me to go steady with you?"

"I have no goddamn shame, Monty, not when it comes to you." He pauses briefly before whispering, "Say yes."

"Yes," I reply without hesitation.

"A-Are you..." He trips over his words. "Are you sure?"

"I'm sure."

"Like *super* sure? The surest you could ever be?"

"Yes."

"Absolutely positive?"

I laugh. "Don't make me take it back already."

"No take-backs. It's our rule...girlfriend."

Me: I just wanted you to know I'm alive.

Python: I was starting to get a little worried.

Python: How was day three?

Me: Much better than the previous two days.

Python: Good. I'm glad to hear that.

Python: Can I call you tonight? Will you still be up after about 9? I have some things to do first, but I should be available after that.

Me: Yes. I'm still at work anyway. Looooong day.

Python: I've got something long for you.

Python: DOWNLOAD ATTACHMENT

Me: I was really scared to open that picture at work but I'm so glad I did. I needed that laugh.

Python: HOW DARE YOU LAUGH AT MY WIENER!

Me: Wait a second, YOUR WIENER?

Me: You're my boyfriend now—doesn't that make it MY wiener?

Python: So you're telling me I just acquired a pussy?

Me: Oh my gosh. Don't say it like that!

Python: Fair's fair, babe.

Me: I gotta ask, why does it look so weird?

Python: Good gravy, Monty. You CANNOT just ask a man why his wiener looks weird. Do you have no class?

Me: Just answer me.

Python: It's a turkey dog. I try to eat healthy.

Me: That sounds…disgusting.

Python: No. Class.

Python: Listen, I gotta run—have to feed my kid. We have someplace we need to be soon. We'll continue this sexument later.

Me: This what?

Python: S-E-X-U-M-E-N-T: a fun, flirty argument that's bound to lead to sex.

Me: You just made that up, didn't you?

Python: I can neither confirm nor deny that.

CHAPTER 20

ROBBIE

"BUT I DON'T WANT to go. First you made me go to day camp here and then regular school and now I have to go at night. *Again.*" He crosses his arms over his chest in a huff. "No thanks."

"And I don't want to work and pay bills and do all the other stuff I have to do but it's part of growing up, so pull those pants up and let's get moving. We're going to be late."

"That's your fault. You were on your phone at the dinner table."

"And you were eating slower than a snail."

"You cooked dinner late."

"It was a hotdog! Those should take like two minutes tops to eat. I didn't know I had to give you a thirty-minute window of time."

He shakes his head, his curls bouncing all over. "You don't even know your own son."

"I know I'm gonna stuff him in the nearest trash can if he doesn't walk faster."

"You wouldn't."

I side-eye him. "Test me."

His eyes spark with worry and he takes off running down the hall.

"Walk!"

He skids to a half stop, his shoes squeaking across the floor.

"Thank you," I call out as he disappears around the corner.

Little shit.

I hustle to catch up with him, because I wasn't kidding—we *are* running late because he took forever to eat, and being late is so not my thing.

Sure, some of it had to do with me texting Monty like a goof, but let's just shift the blame to Xavie. It's totally his fault in the end anyway.

I barrel around the corner and come to a dead stop when I nearly collide with the last person I expected to see standing at the end of the hall with my son.

"Monty?"

Her head shoots up at my voice and our eyes collide.

Shock. Confusion. Worry.

So many reactions in such a short amount of time.

"No," she mutters.

"Beat ya, Dad! Guess who's getting stuffed in the trash can now," Xavie taunts, doing a little dance.

"Still you," I tell him.

"No way! I won fair and square. Didn't I, Mrs. Andrews?"

There it is. The confirmation I needed.

Monty Andrews, the girl I'm steadily falling for—the one I just asked to be my girlfriend last night—is my son's teacher.

Fuck. Me.

When Xavie mentioned his teacher's name was Andrews, I immediately thought of Monty. But he said Mrs., and there was no way that could have been Monty because she's not married. Plus, I was certain she was teaching middle school, not first grade, so I pushed it out of my mind any time he said her name.

There was no way this beautiful girl standing before me could be my son's teacher.

But, I was wrong.

So fucking wrong.

"*Miss,*" she corrects. "It's true, he did."

"Who's side you on?"

"It appears I'm straddling quite the line," she comments, the double meaning in her words clear as day.

"Why don't you head into the room, son? I'll be there in a moment."

He races inside, leaving just me and Monty standing in the hall.

I want to run.

I want to scream.

I want to kiss the hell out of her.

I want to do so many things right now, and none of them are the appropriate reaction.

She takes timid steps my way, her uncertainty showing in the way her shoulders square as her eyes harden.

"What are you doing here?" she asks.

"What are *you* doing here?" I echo.

"This is where I work."

"This is where my son goes to school."

"I..." Her hand flies to her head as my words sink in. "But how?"

"Um, because he's seven?"

"I mean, how is your child seven? Aren't you my age?"

"I'm twenty-six," I tell her.

"I...I thought your son was younger, like two, three max...not seven." Her brows scrunch together. "How old were you when you had him? Eighteen?"

"Nineteen," I correct.

"Oh. Wow."

There's judgment in her eyes. It's something I'm used to, but not from Monty.

She realizes the way her words sound, and her mouth drops open. "Crud. No. I'm sorry. I didn't mean that to sound so...well, rude. I am *not* judging you for being a teen father."

"Good, because I refuse to be ashamed of it."

"You shouldn't be."

"I know."

The hall grows quiet and I'm worried as shit she can hear my heart trying to pound its way out of my chest.

How in the fuck is this happening right now?

"How come we never talked about this?" The words tumble from her mouth so fast I almost miss what she says. "I mean, in all the conversations we've had together, how did none of this ever come up?"

I shrug. "We made assumptions and stuck to them."

"I've never been one to make assumptions."

"You also weren't the kind of person to make out with a stranger in the bathroom, but you did."

"I did." She smacks a hand to her forehead, the other clutching her stomach. "I take one step out of my comfort zone and *this* happens. Karma, that's what this is—for leaving my family, for not following rules, for—"

I grab her pacing form, stilling her movements.

"Stop. You're making me dizzy."

Her eyes are brimming with unshed tears and worry as she glances up at me. "I'm sorry," she whispers. "This is all my fault."

"No, Monty. It's just a weird-as-shit coincidence."

"Why weren't you here last week?"

"Why wasn't I where?"

"Here. Parent-teacher meetings. You weren't here." Her eyes widen. "Oh gosh, I met your ex—Holly. She was so nice, so pretty...*so* not me."

"I like you better."

Though the comment is true, it's also a tactic to get her to calm down. She doesn't laugh.

"I'm sorry. Last Wednesday was my Wednesday to cover the late shift at the center. You knew that."

"I knew that when you were just Robbie, the guy from Lola's, not my boyfriend and *father* to one of my students."

She sucks her bottom lip between her teeth and I want to reach down and pull it out with my own, but I can't.

"It'll be okay, Monty."

She shakes her head, trying to pull out of my grasp, but I don't let her go. I can't—not yet.

"How? How did we not talk about all this?"

"Well, to be fair, this all started out as just sex, nothing else."

"But it evolved."

"It did, but we were supposed to still be light and fluffy." I pull her closer, wrapping my arm around her waist and bringing my lips to her ear. "You weren't supposed to be so addicting."

"Robbie...what does this mean?"

Our entire relationship so far flashes through my mind.

I met her in a bar. I fooled around with her on top of a bathroom counter. I had my fingers buried inside her sweet pussy. I charmed her via text for weeks, kissed her against a brick wall, had countless dirty dreams and cold showers with her in mind.

And then, I fucked her, again and again and again.

All over my apartment. All over hers.

I bent her over the couch, the bed, and though we swore we hated shower sex, I even had her in there.

She's my son's teacher, and I can't keep my goddamn hands off her.

I blow out a heavy breath and step away from her, missing the contact as soon as she slips from my fingers.

"It means you're my son's teacher and we had sex—a lot of sex. We just committed to a relationship *last night*, and it means..." I rub at the back of my neck, the tension building and building. "It means things just got a whole lot more complicated."

"FINALLY, I want to thank you all again for coming. I appreciate you taking the time to meet with me. I look forward to working alongside you all this year."

My heart swells with pride.

My girl did good.

Ha. *My girl*—I don't know how much longer that will be true after the discovery we made tonight.

How did we miss that? How did we not even think to check? I've been so wrapped up in getting her naked that it didn't even cross my mind to ask her what grade she taught. Besides, what were the chances anyway? How is it even possible that the random girl I met in a bar would turn out to be my son's teacher?

One by one, the parents shake Monty's hand, exchanging pleasantries and asking about a few things she didn't address.

Then, it's just me, Monty, and my son.

She eyes me from across the room and I can see the trepidation in her green gaze.

I'm scared too, I want to scream.

She crosses the room to stand in front of me, clasping her hands together, looking every bit like the teacher she is.

"Did you have any questions, Mr. Cross?"

There's a stirring in my pants at the way she says my name, and I want to punch myself in the face for having that reaction.

"Several."

"I have a few myself."

"Perhaps we can discuss things later?"

"9 PM work for you?"

She's referencing when I said I'd call her earlier, and I nod.

"Good. We'll talk then." She turns to the kid. "Xavier, it was great seeing you again. I'll see you tomorrow."

"Good night, Miss Andrews," he says through a yawn.

I guide my son to the door without another word.

I can't say anything. I'm too worried about what might come out of my mouth.

The drive home is short, way too short for my liking tonight, and our bedtime routine seems to take half the time it normally does.

Xavie's conked out by eight thirty and I'm left pacing the small apartment, question after question floating through my mind.

My heart races as I stare the clock down, the minutes ticking by too fast and too slow all at once.

What am I going to say to her? What will she say to me? How in the hell are we going to fix this mess we've gotten ourselves into?

At nine on the dot, my phone rings.

"Hey," she says quietly when I pick up.

I fall back onto the couch, all my muscles suddenly so tired I can't seem to hold myself up any longer. I sigh heavily and take a sip of the beer that's helping calm my nerves right now.

"We're a goddamn mess, Monts."

She laughs lightly. "I know."

"What are we going to do?"

"I'm not sure."

"What do you *want* to do?"

"I'm not sure about that either," she admits.

I don't know what I want to do.

I don't want to give her up, but I'll do whatever makes her feel comfortable.

We sit in silence for a long time, so long I worry she's fallen asleep on me.

"Are you still there?" I ask in a hushed tone.

"Yes, just thinking."

"About us?"

"Of course. How can I think about anything else right now?"

"I don't know. I was hoping you found a distraction that was working and could share it with me. Nothing, not even alcohol is working. I've been sipping on a beer for the last half hour."

More silence.

Long sighs.

Exhaled breaths.

"We should quit while we're still ahead, right?" she asks.

"We should, but I don't want to."

"I...I don't either."

"Are we *allowed* to date? Does the school have any policies against it?"

"I'm not sure. I didn't exactly look for information in the handbook when I received it. I never thought it was something I'd have to worry about."

There's a bite to her words but I know she's not directing it at me, rather at the situation we're currently in.

"Can I say something kind of weird?"

"Go for it."

"When your son walked into my classroom, there was something familiar about him, but I couldn't put my finger on it," she tells me.

"His eyes—they're the exact same as mine."

"That's it, because other than that, he doesn't look like you at all. Why don't you share the same last name?"

"His mother's request." I sigh. "I regret agreeing to that every day. At the time, I didn't care, didn't think I'd mind my kid not having my last name. Now I want it so fucking bad."

"Can you change it?"

"Yeah, but I want to make sure it's something Xavie wants too."

"Xavie? Is that what he normally goes by?"

"Outside of school, yes."

"Xavier Levy." She says his name with such wonder.

"Xavier *Zachary* Levy. I got to pick the middle name at least."

"He's named after your goat-loving bestie?"

I chuckle at her description. "The one and only."

"That must really go to his head."

"You have no idea."

I listen as she shuffles around on the other end of the call.

"What are you doing?" I ask.

"Getting into bed."

"Are you naked?"

"No!" She laughs. "You can't talk to me like that anymore."

"Why not? We're still dating, right?"

She goes quiet. I can't hear her moving, but I can still hear the faintness of her breathing.

Two full minutes pass before she speaks again.

"Yes."

My heart swells at the three-letter word.

So small, simple, yet packed with so much power.

"How are we going to navigate this?"

"Carefully, and together. It's not illegal to date you, and it's not entirely unethical either. We have to be careful, though, tread lightly, and probably not let Xavier know about this. We also shouldn't have sex again until we can figure this out."

I spring forward on the couch in shock.

Oh hell no. There is *no* way I'm giving up sex. Not going to happen, not when I know how fucking good it feels to be inside her.

"I'm sorry, did you just say what I think you just said?"

"Yes, Robbie." She sighs loudly. "No more sex. It's too much."

"But we've already had sex. That's the dumbest argument I have ever heard."

"I..." She clicks her tongue. "Ugh. Fine. You're right. I just wanted to feel like I had *some* control over this situation. Let's just...be careful, *very* careful—like, no one can know we're together."

"We're sneaking around then?"

"In a sense."

"Huh. I kind of like the idea of that. Sounds...sexy. Fun. *Dangerous.*"

She giggles, and the genuine happiness I hear in it puts me at ease for the first time this evening.

"Hey Monty?"

"Yeah?"

"I'm glad you're still my girlfriend."

"I'm glad too."

CHAPTER 21

MONTY

Me: Rule #1, no more dirty texting me when I'm at work and YOUR SON is in my classroom.

Python: It'll be hard, like me, but I can live with that rule. Next.

Me: Rule #2, I can't come to your apartment anymore. It'll feel weird now. You and Thumbelina will have to come over here, or we can meet somewhere public.

Python: Stop trying to get me to have sex with you in public, Monty.

Me: I'm not!!!

Python: You just keep telling yourself that, babe.

Me: Rule #3, no calling me babe. I like it too much.

Python: Fine, babe. I won't anymore, babe.

Me: You're horrible at this.

Python: How does that saying go? Rules were meant to be broken?

Me: No, rules are there to be FOLLOWED. It is very important to follow rules, especially our rules.

Python: I had no idea I was dating someone so lame.

Me: Yes you did.

Python: You're right. We should break up.

Python: KIDDING. Don't leave me. I like you too much.

Me: I like you too, which is the problem.

Python: And by problem, you mean the best thing to ever happen to you, right?

Me: That is yet to be determined.

Python: Noted, Monty. NOTED.

Me: I could lose my job!

Python: No you couldn't. You said there was nothing in the handbook when you looked it over. We're good. We just need to keep it professional and on the DL until he's not in your class anymore.

Me: So basically for THE ENTIRE SCHOOL YEAR?

Python: YES. STOP YELLING AT ME, DAMMIT. IT IS NOT MY FAULT I HAVE A MAGIC DADDY DICK YOU CAN'T RESIST.

Me: It is absolutely your fault.

Me: Also, don't call it that anymore. It's creepy now that I know your son.

Python: Ew. Yeah. You totally ruined that for me. Thanks, bore.

Me: *kisses*

Python: Since we had to cancel our date tonight, can I take you out Sunday evening? After I drop the spawn off at his mom's?

Me: Hmm...I think I can pencil you into my schedule.

Python: I'm gonna pencil into you.

Python: Wait. No.

Python: I think I just compared my dick to a pencil, and we both know it's more like a Pringles can.

Python: And that was a horrible attempt at being all sexy and funny and whatever else.

Python: I'm just gonna be quiet now.

Me: That's probably best.

Me: P.S. You're my favorite flavor of Pringles. 😊

Python: Wow. You suck too.

Me: I do, but you know that.

Python: OH FUCK. Montana Andrews, did you just make a BLOWJOB joke? You little minx!

Me: Stop. It.

Python: Nope! I just took three fucking screenshots of that shit just in case I accidentally delete one. I am printing that out. Just wait.

Me: That's it, we're breaking up.

Python: Sorry, you're stuck with me.

Python: You're excited, I know.

Me: *not (You missed a word there.)

Python: Ooooh and sassy too. Me likey.

Python: Do you like tacos?

Me: Do you like air?

Python: I'm not entirely certain, but I think that was a death threat.

Me: I mean, it wasn't, but it could be.

Me: Yes, I like tacos. Why?

Python: Just making sure for our date tomorrow.

Me: We're getting tacos tomorrow?

Python: Guess we'll see.

Me: If we're not getting tacos, then why ask me about tacos? You can't just tease a gal with tacos and then not deliver.

Python: Geez. Someone likes their tacos. I'll make a special note of that.

Me: Sorry. I'm hangry right now.

Python: Why are you horny? Been looking at those pics I sent you again?

Me: Robbie...

Python: I'm gonna go ahead and exit this convo while I still have my balls intact. I do cherish them and was hoping to maybe keep them, have another kid down the road. So, yeah. Bye now.

Python: For clarity's sake...I DID NOT mean have a kid with you.

Python: Not that you're, like, disgusting and I'd never consider it, but yeah, not right now.

Python: You know what? This just went really fucking south. We're going to pretend this never happened and I left a long time ago.

Python: Bye.

Me: Robbie?

Python: Yeah?

Me: I really like you.

Me: But please stop talking.

Python: Done.

Me: What time is our date tonight?

Me: And how should I dress for this occasion?

Python: I'll pick you up at 7. Feel free to be naked.

Me: You want to take me out in public naked?

Python: No, but I can always have an appeteazer before we head to dinner.

Python: I'm talking about you, Monty.

Python: More specifically, your pussy, in case you were wondering.

Me: I...ahem...yes, I got that, but thank you for the, uh, visual there.

Python: Visual, huh? What are you thinking about?

Me: You know.

Python: Explain, and in great detail, please.

Me: I will not!

Python: Fine then. Be naked.

Me: Or what?

Python: Oh, Monty. If you think your defiance has done anything to diminish this boner I have, you're wrong.

Python: Be. Naked.

CHAPTER 22

MONTY

"I AM *SO* GOING TO HELL."

He climbs back up my body, hovering over me with a wicked grin. "You gonna save me a seat when you get there?"

"No. I can't believe I just let you do that to me."

"I can. It's impossible for you to resist me."

"Sometimes I wish I could. You're a little much at times. Plus, you know, there's the whole me being your son's teacher and all thing. That would really lessen the worry hanging over my head."

"Then how about for tonight, we're just Monty and Robbie? I'm not a dad and you're not my kid's teacher. We're just two people trying really fucking hard to not fall for each other too fast. We're just out to have a good goddamn time. Maybe we'll kiss. Maybe we'll hug. Maybe I'll bury my face between your thighs again. We'll just have to see where the night leads. Sound good?"

My legs squeeze together at his words and I nod.

"Yeah?" His grin grows. "Which part?"

"You know."

"You're damn right I do, baby." He leans down to kiss me, and I push his face away. He sticks his tongue out, licking my hand instead.

"Oh my gosh, put that thing away!"

"That is *so* not what you were saying just a couple minutes ago."

I groan and grab the nearest pillow, whacking him with it before covering my reddening face.

Just as Robbie requested, I was naked at seven sharp... or as naked as I was going to get when still having to answer the door.

When I pulled it open for him, all I had on was my robe, pulled tightly against me, my nipples straining against the fabric at the sight of him.

He knew it too.

Without a word, he backed me inside, not stopping until we reached my bedroom. He stripped the thin material from my body, laid me down on the bed, and used his tongue to bring me to the point of no return...twice.

He drags the pillow from my face, smiling. "You're welcome, by the way."

I lift a brow. "I'm not going to fall to my knees thanking you."

He slams his eyes closed and draws a heavy breath. "The images floating through my mind right now..." He shakes his head. "But no time. We need to get going soon before we miss it."

"Miss what? Tacos?"

"Yes. There's a food truck I want to take you to and it's only at certain locations during certain hours. We need to get moving if we want to make it."

"People eat food out of trucks?"

He looks at me incredulously. "Yes. Now put clothes on, my little sex vixen."

I roll from the bed and begin pulling on the outfit I laid out. Robbie heads out of the room and down the hall, to the bathroom I assume.

"I'm using your mouthwash!" I crinkle my nose at the thought then he continues, "I won't put my mouth on it. Stop panicking."

Warmth passes over me as his words sink in. He knows me so well already that it's a little scary. It hasn't been that long since we met, and we've been officially dating for an even shorter amount of time, but he knows me.

It's moments like these that make this so difficult.

When I saw Robbie walking down the hall toward my classroom the other day, my heart began beating a mile a minute because I genuinely thought he was there for me.

Then I connected the dots, and just as quickly as my heart had started pounding, it stopped.

What we're doing, us seeing one another, it's not *bad*... but it's not necessarily good, either.

According to the handbook, we're not breaking a single rule set forth by the school. But, in the eyes of many, we're breaking an ethical one or two, and that's just as bad.

I would never, *ever* use my relationship with Robbie to give Xavier an academic advantage, and I know Robbie would never expect that of me either.

It's explaining all that to a seven-year-old that might be difficult, which is why we have to keep this strictly on the down low while I'm still his teacher. Next year, when he's out of my class, we can tell him.

Next year.

My lips tug into a smile at the thought of spending that much time with Robbie.

That would also mean hiding us, our relationship, for the entire school year, and that part makes me want to cry.

A wall of warmth crashes over me as he approaches from behind.

His heavy hands settle on my waist and his lips drop to my ear. I shiver at the contact.

"As sexy and fuckable as I think you look in those ridiculous skirts of yours, they've gotta go."

With one quick move, he unbuttons the fastener and the garment drops to the floor, leaving me standing here in nothing but my shirt and panties.

"Robbie!"

He smacks my bottom hard enough that I know it'll hurt to sit for the next several hours and then he falls back on my mattress with a bounce.

"What? I brought the bike. You can't wear a skirt on the bike."

"The bike?" The words come out as a squeak and I clap my hands together. "I'm so excited!"

"Me too. I can't wait to feel your legs wrapped around me. Now pull on those skintight jeans again and grab a jacket." He taps on the watch adorning his wrist. "Clock is a tickin'."

I race around the small room, pulling my jeans from the drawer and sliding them on. "You know, we'd have had plenty of time to get where we're going had you not requested I be naked when you got here."

"I'm sorry, are you actually complaining about orgasms right now? Because I can always just stop giving you them if they're that much of an inconvenience for you."

"No!" I shout too quickly. I shove my feet into my sneakers and stand, bumping my head on the rack lining the small space. "Ow! *Cats*."

"Just say fuck, Monty," he teases.

"No." I emerge from the closet wearing the jacket he requested, then pull my hair to the side and twist it into a quick braid. "And no taking my happy endings away either. I like those."

He pushes off the bed and comes to a stop in front of me. He tucks a stray hair behind my ear and says, "I know you do. I think your neighbors might too."

I gasp at the suggestion because I *was* quite loud during that last one.

"They do not! Let's go before I change my mind about dating you."

He laughs and rolls his eyes as I stalk away.

I can feel him at my heels, trailing closely behind me as I lead us down the short hall and to the front door. I grab my purse and pull out my keys, yanking him from the apartment because he's suddenly the one dragging his feet.

He stands dangerously close behind me as I stick the key into the door to lock it, so close I can feel his breath on my neck.

I hate that it gives me shivers.

"You're always threatening me, and it's so fucking hot," he whispers.

Then he promptly drags his tongue across my neck.

"Robbie!" I yell, slapping at him.

He just laughs, and I fall for him a little more.

"THESE MIGHT BE the *best* tacos I have ever had in my entire life."

"Right? I knew you'd like them. I found this place on accident one night when I was out for a ride and I've been stalking their social media pages since. That's how you know where they'll be."

"It's so good. So...*fresh*, and I love that you can get it

any way you want. It's like...like..." I snap my fingers together. "Oh my cats, I get it!"

His brows pinch together. "Get what?"

"The name! TacoWay! Like Subway, only for tacos. You can make your own concoction."

"You're just now getting that?"

"Stop judging me and just eat your taco."

"I could always eat your taco." He winks and takes another bite of his food.

I stare up at him in disbelief.

"I meant your puss—"

I slap my hand over his mouth, looking around to make sure no one heard what he just said. The other patrons pass by without a care in the world, minding their own business and doing their own thing.

He laughs against my hand and I glare.

"I know what you meant, you perv."

"You love my perviness."

"Sometimes. Sometimes it makes me blush so much I think I might turn into a tomato or something. I'm certain one of these days you're going to make me blush so hard it'll stain my cheeks and that'll just be how I look from now on."

"I like your blushing. It's cute."

"It's blotchy and embarrassing and ugly."

He sets his empty bowl down and stares over at me as I shove another bite in my gourd.

"What?" I ask through a mouthful of food, something

that is so unlike me.

He shakes his head. "Nothing."

I chew and swallow before speaking this time. "No, tell me, please. I detest when people do that. All these thoughts of what they could be thinking run through my mind and it's never pretty. So, please, just tell me, even if you think I won't like it."

He sighs. "Haven't you realized by now that I think you're beautiful no matter what? Those freckles you hate so much are sexy as shit. Your—"

"I thought we established that there is nothing sexy about human excrement."

"Stop interrupting, it's rude."

"Sorry. Continue."

"Anyway, as I was saying," he jabs. "The red hair you think is 'bright and unattractive' is alluring. It *calls* to me. Your body, which you often complain about, is what most would call perfection. Your long legs that make you 'look like a giraffe'? Fucking hot, especially wrapped around me. Hell, even your Casper complexion is hot."

His words make me want to throw my arms around his neck and kiss him over and over again.

My eyes sting with unshed tears, and I do my best to blink them away.

I've never in my life felt like I fit in. I've always been that pale, ginger girl who could turn as red as a bottle of ketchup at the simplest words or comments. I've never felt beautiful. I've never felt sexy.

Until Robbie.

"Casper complexion, huh? Gee, thanks."

"I'm saying you're sexy as fuck, Monts, and I don't ever want you to feel like you aren't. I don't ever want you to feel like I don't want you because of your self-designated flaws. I love you just the way you are."

His back goes ramrod straight as he realizes the words he just spoke. His lips part as if he's going to say something else, but nothing comes out.

I wait.

And wait and wait and wait.

He doesn't say anything.

Neither do I.

It does nothing to counteract the way my heart begins to beat faster and faster.

Love.

He said it. He knows he said it. *I* know he said it.

Yet, we ignore it.

"How'd you like riding on the bike?"

"It was..."

"Scary?" he provides, laughing at me. "Because I sure as shit heard you yelling in my ear when we got on the highway."

"I would prefer to never to do that again."

"I'll take the backroads home."

"There are backroads?" I nearly shout. "Why didn't you just take those to begin with?"

"And miss all the screaming? Nah."

We fall back into a comfortable silence as I finish eating my food, setting the empty container on top of his. I wonder if it will always feel like this with him, if things will always be so easy between us.

Well, as easy as they can get with me being his son's teacher and us having to hide our growing relationship.

Maybe this isn't so easy after all...

"Talk to me. What's going through that head of yours?"

"Huh?"

He brushes his fingers over the crinkle that's formed between my brows. "You're thinking about something you don't want to think about it. What is it?"

"Everything."

"Us, isn't it?" he guesses.

I nod.

He sighs and pushes himself off the concrete wall we're seated on. His long legs carry him back and forth and back again as he paces, hands on his hips, a frown slashed across his mouth. "We're at a real fucked-up cross-roads, aren't we?"

"We're screwed, and not just literally."

He coughs out a laugh but continues pacing. "Good one, but yes, we are—though I think if we're creative enough, we can make this work."

"Should it really have to be that hard though? Should we have the need to be 'creative' to enjoy our relationship?"

Robbie grins at me as he does another pass. "I like it when you call it a relationship, makes me all mushy and shit on the inside."

"Stop making me laugh. I'm being serious. *This* is serious."

"I know, Monty. I know it is. We can make this good though. It's gonna be hard, in more than one area"—he throws me a wink—"but it *will* be worth it. Put the work in now, enjoy the results later."

"Later as in end of the school year later? As in about ten months from now later?"

"Yeah, that later."

"You planning a future with me, Robbie?"

In a flash he's right in front of me, his hands cradling my face and pulling me toward him. His face is hard, eyes serious. He's holding on tight, like he desperately needs me to listen to him.

"Damn fucking straight."

He smashes his mouth to mine and a tremor rattles through me. I was not expecting the weight that slams down on me.

It's heavy, but not in a bad way.

It's good—*really* good.

"You're not giving up before we even really get started, are you, Monty?" he asks, his forehead resting against mine, his breath coming in short gasps.

I swallow and shake my head. "No."

"Good."

He takes my mouth again, and somehow, it's so much more than it was before.

That weight? It was nothing, not compared to this.

I'm falling for him.

Hard and fast, it's happening, and I don't want to stop it.

A whimper escapes when he begins to pull away, and he laughs breathlessly against me. "I can't keep kissing you like this in public."

"Yes you can," I tell him.

"Do you want me to strip you naked in front of that family over there? That wouldn't be very appropriate for a teacher to do."

"That wouldn't be very appropriate for *anyone* to do."

"Eh, we'll agree to disagree on that one." He gives me another chaste kiss before pulling away and grabbing my hand, lifting me from the wall too. "Dance with me."

"I am not dancing with you in the middle of the street."

"Sure ya are."

He tugs me along, dragging me out into the center of the boardwalk. You'd think on a Sunday night this place would be dead, but the weather is perfect and there's no way anyone could pass up being out tonight.

There's a man busking on the street corner across the way. His croon carries over the crowd, and everyone within earshot is mesmerized.

We're in the middle of the crowd when Robbie drops my hand.

"Stay. I'll be right back."

He crosses the street to the performer, whispers something in his ear, and drops a bill in his guitar case. The performer laughs as he shakes his head, then they bump fists.

My eyes follow Robbie's strides as he makes his way back through the crowd, a secretive smile on his face the whole time. He curls his arm around my waist and drags me toward him when he reaches me.

"Let's dance."

"There's no music."

"There will be in just a moment."

"What'd you do?"

His lips twitch as he fights a smile. "I don't know what you're talking about."

Just then, the crooner begins to pluck away at his guitar, producing the familiar riff of *I Got You Babe* by Sonny and Cher.

"Cher? Really?"

He lifts a shoulder. "I know you have a huge crush on her."

I laugh and snuggle in closer to him as we sway to the music. We're not far into the already short song when his hands begin to wander, slipping his palms into my back pockets, cupping my rear end.

I shake my head at his advances. "I think this would be

deemed inappropriate too."

"Would it though?" he tries to reason.

"Yes."

"What a shame."

He pulls me closer, using only his hands on my rear, just as the song ends. The singer moves seamlessly into his next number, *Can't Help Falling in Love*.

If Robbie feels me stiffen in his arms, he doesn't show any sign of it.

"Did you..." I lick at my dry lips, trying again. "Did you ask him to play this?"

"No," he says quietly in my ear.

But I don't believe him.

There's something in his voice...it's different, not as sure and sturdy as it usually is.

I want to tell him it's okay, that I'm feeling it too, but I'm too scared.

Besides, I don't want to read too far into things. I *can't* read too far into things, not with the current state of our relationship, how it hangs so closely to the edge of destruction.

He squeezes me closer and I try my best to focus on right now.

Us.

The musician plays another song, this one a little more upbeat than the last, but we don't let each other go. It's like we're glued together and there's nothing coming between us.

The dark, spicy scent of his cologne fills my senses, and I can't help but nuzzle into him more.

He chuckles. "Are you smelling me?"

"No."

"Fibber."

"Am not." I take another whiff. "Okay, maybe I am. You smell so good though—like, *so* good. Clean, fresh."

"You're welcome for showering," he teases.

That dull, achy need I always feel between my legs when Robbie is near begins to grow. Our closeness, my lips still stinging from his earlier kisses, his hands on my butt...I can't take this anymore.

I dart my eyes around the crowd, looking for a place for us to be alone.

"I have an idea." My words come out rushed, excited.

He pulls back and grins down at me. "Why are you smiling like that?"

"Like what?"

"Like you're about to do something *very* naughty to me."

"I have no idea what you're talking about."

I grab his hand and pull him through the crowd, moving purely on adrenaline and need because there's no way I'd typically be doing this.

There's a lone photo booth sitting at the edge of the crowd, and I'm certain no one will notice if we slip inside.

"We are *not* doing a photo booth. It's so juvenile and

cutesy. I'm not doing that shit," he says when we approach it.

"We *are* doing this. Get in."

He lets out a frustrated groan as I push him inside.

"What are you doing?" I ask as he reaches into his back pocket and retrieves his wallet.

He pulls two bills from inside and inserts them into the machine. "Um, it's a photo booth—they require money to work."

"That is not what I had in mind."

I swing my leg over him and climb onto his lap.

"Oh," he says with surprise, his hands landing on my hips. "I like this. This I can get on board with."

"Good. Now kiss me."

The rush of power my words give me has me slamming my mouth down on his. He laughs at my ferocity and takes over, working his mouth against mine with the finesse I've only ever experienced with him.

His hands dive into my hair, pulling at it with just the right amount of pressure. He holds me close as he works my lips apart, tasting and teasing me with his tongue.

The heat of the kiss becomes too much, and I don't know about him, but I am *dying* for a release.

"You have to touch me," I whisper to him.

"Why'd we have to bring the bike? Bikes are lame. Jeans are lame. I miss your skirts so I can just slide my hand up them."

"It's all your fault."

"I am the worst." He pushes my jacket off my shoulders. "But I can work with this."

The light material falls from my body, landing on the floor of the booth, and I don't even care that it's probably disgusting and dirty down there.

Robbie is about to set my body on fire, and I can't wait to feel the flame.

I'm suddenly so thankful I wore my off-the-shoulder top as he tugs the material down.

"Another white one—go figure."

"Stop it. You know I'm boring."

"I like that you're boring," he says, his attention solely focused on my breast as he pulls the cups of my bra down, my bare chest now on display. "I also like the way you taste."

He closes his mouth over my nipple and I try my very best not to moan too loudly at the contact. I hold his head close as he works his lips over me, giving the occasional nip that sends a zing straight to my core.

"Why did I have to wear jeans?" I murmur.

"Touch yourself," he says against me.

"What? I-I can't do that!"

He lets my nipple slide from his mouth, dragging his teeth over the sensitive bud as he goes. His eyes are glazed over with lust as he stares up at me.

Without breaking contact, he unsnaps my jeans. "Put your hand in your pants."

"No!"

"Monty, put your hand in your goddamn pants or I will rip these sexy-as-sin jeans from your body, turn you around, and fuck you loud and hard in this goddamn photo booth. We're bound to make a scene. Your choice."

Oh my.

His words spur my movements and I do as he instructs, sliding my hand into my jeans. The first contact is bittersweet, my swollen clit so sensitive it almost hurts because it feels so good.

He works his hand between us, his thumb pressing against mine. I let out a low moan when he begins moving us in slow circles.

"Th-That's nice."

He gives me a deep, throaty laugh. "I know."

When he removes his hand from mine, I halt all movements.

"Don't stop, Monty. Keep going. Take yourself there."

"I...o-okay."

I slam my eyes closed as embarrassment washes over me. I'm so terrified to be doing something so intimate in front of him. This is the most naked I've ever been while still wearing all my clothes.

Eyes still closed and fingers still on my clit, Robbie begins to shuffle around, and I hear the familiar hiss of a zipper.

The sound of flesh working against flesh fills the small space, the noise of the crowd growing louder outside as the street musician continues rocking out a rhythm.

My fingers play a beat against my own body, matching whatever song it is he's playing.

Robbie's warm mouth clamps over my nipple again and I explode.

Bright lights flash behind my eyelids and I swear I'm seeing those fireworks everyone talks about in this very moment.

I slow my movements but don't completely slide my hand from my pants, still enjoying the last of the zings racing through me too much to quit now. That euphoric floating feeling takes hold and I want to sink into its warmth, stay there forever.

The sound of Robbie still working himself over calls to me and I open my eyes. My gaze automatically drops down, watching as he strains against his own touch.

I can't take my eyes off his movements. They're steady and sure and hurried all at once. Watching him touch himself causes that familiar stir to strike again, and I can't help it when my fingers begin to move over my aching clit.

"Jacket."

"You are jacking it," I say back, still watching as he strokes his hard length.

He laughs huskily and gives me his classic prayer before grunting and emptying himself all over the front of me.

I can't even be mad. It's the most beautiful thing I have ever seen.

His head is thrown back, eyes squeezed tightly shut,

chest rising and falling in rapid succession.

Robbie is a beautiful creature on his own.

Robbie coming? It's *breathtaking*.

He sags against the booth and I fall against him, exhausted.

"Get off me, you're a mess."

"You're the one who made me dirty."

"I like it when you get dirty," he murmurs quietly in my ear. "Getting you dirty is my favorite thing to do."

"You're a horrible influence on me, Robbie. I would have never done this before you."

"Is that a bad thing?"

"Yes, but it's also the *best* thing. You're..." I blow out a shaky breath. "You're that thing I never knew I wanted until I had it. You're fun and adventure and temptation all wrapped into one, and I want to give in to you so badly."

We both know I'm talking about so much more than what's at the surface of my words.

I'm not just talking about giving in to the impulses he awakens in me.

I'm talking about giving in to what he makes me feel.

Love.

"Then give in."

The words.

Hushed.

Whispered.

Pleaded.

"I already have."

CHAPTER 23

ROBBIE

SHE DIDN'T HAVE to say it.

I know.

I know because I feel the exact same way, which is real fucking crazy when you think about.

There are so many logical reasons why we shouldn't be falling in love, but love isn't logical, is it?

Her breasts are heavy in my hands as I pull the cups of her bra over her exposed chest. It kills me to cover such a beautiful sight, and I want nothing more than to strip her completely naked and fuck her into tomorrow, but we've already pushed our luck enough.

We're damn fortunate no one pulled back that curtain and caught us.

She works her shirt up over her arms and snaps her jeans closed as I tuck my half-hard dick away. I reach down and grab her jacket, passing it to her.

"You might wanna use this to hold in front of that

mess you caused. I have a spare shirt in my saddlebag that you can put on once we get back to the parking garage."

She glowers at the mention of the mess, but there's no malice behind her stare, having loved every minute spent in this booth just as much as I did.

Monty pushes off my lap, standing as best she can in the crowded space. "I can't believe you talked me into this."

"Me?" I slap at her ass when she steps from the booth, laughing as I follow behind her. "You're the one who was all, 'Oh, baby, take me into the photo booth, baby. I wanna do something naughty.'"

Walking backward, she points at me with a grin. "I have never and will never talk like that."

"A man can dream." I wink.

She shakes her head and spins around, running smack into a passerby.

"Oof!"

I rush to her side, glaring at the careless moron who just nearly knocked her over.

He grabs hold of her shoulders, steadying her, and I want to rip his stupid fucking hands off.

"Miss Andrews? Is that you?"

That voice...I know it.

Monty smiles up at the guy. "Brandon, hi. Funny running into you here."

"I was out for a bite at TacoWay. They're darn hard to track down, but they have the best tacos in the city."

I try really fucking hard to not roll my eyes when he says darn and not damn. *Give me a break.*

"What are you doing out here?" he asks.

My girl would make a horrible spy; she can't stop herself from glancing back at me.

Douchebag notices.

I see the spark of familiarity in his gaze as our eyes connect.

"I was out doing the same thing. I heard from a, uh, friend how good they were and decided to check it out."

He points in the opposite direction. "The truck is that way if you're lost."

"Oh, no. I already had some. I was...um...I was in the photo booth."

His eyes dart that way, then briefly to me again before he returns his attention to her. Fucker is observant. I see it as he rakes his eyes over Monty, noting her messy hair and off-kilter clothing.

We both know nothing is ever out of place with her appearance.

He knows what she meant to say was *we* were in the photo booth.

"Oh yeah? Wanna get a picture together?"

"No!" she shouts too loudly and too quickly. She brushes a lock of hair behind her ear. "I mean, no. It's not working. It's broken. I tried."

"Ah, well, what a shame. I bet we could have some fun in there."

My fists curl at my sides, and I want to deck the smarmy fucker. I'm not one for violence, but if he makes one more flirtatious comment to my girl, it's on.

"Well, I better get going, Brandon. It was great running into you, but I have to get home and get some rest. We have a busy day tomorrow."

"I understand. Can you let me walk you to your car? I'd be a jerk not to offer."

"That won't be necessary."

"Monty." He says her name like he fucking knows her, and it makes me want to scream. "You can't walk out here on your own."

She shakes her head. "I won't be. My friend is just using the restroom and will be back any moment."

Smart.

"Good thing for your *friend.*" He nearly spits the last word from his lips, darting his eyes my way again. "I guess I'll see you tomorrow then?"

So much hope in his voice, so much inflection, like his words mean more than they actually do. I want to march over there, grab the prick by his collar, and give him a good shake to remind him that woman he's trying so desperately to pick up is *mine.*

"Yep. See you tomorrow," Monty agrees.

He reaches out and gives her shoulder a squeeze, and I nearly let my feet carry me his way at the contact.

"Good night, Monty."

"Night," she says, moving away from his touch.

He finally turns away, getting lost in the crowd, and I should be happy the shithead is finally leaving.

But I can't be, because everything just changed for us in a big way.

He's Monty's coworker.

And last year he was my son's teacher.

He knows exactly who I am, and he knows what we were doing in that photo booth.

THE MOMENT she's certain Brandon is gone, my girl flounces back over to me, grinning.

"Whew. That was close."

I nod but don't say anything. I don't trust myself.

I take her hand and lead the way back to the parking garage, not wanting to risk running into anyone else we know.

"That's the guy I've been telling you about, my coworker who kept asking me to go for drinks and such over the summer. He's your competition."

I know she's teasing, but it doesn't mean I hate the words any less.

"Monty, he's—"

"Kind of a creeper?" she interrupts.

No, he's going to rat us out. He was Xavie's teacher.

"I know," she continues. "He gives me such weird

vibes. Sometimes he's not so bad, but some days it's hard to handle. I think he might just be going through a tough time. He was a kindergarten teacher last year before moving up to second this year and was dating one of the secretaries. They were engaged. Turned out she was *engaging* in some not-so-clothed activities with the gym teacher too."

I hear it in her voice—sympathy. No matter how hard of a time the dude has taking a hint and not leaving her alone, she still feels bad for him.

Which is *so* like my Monty.

She leans into me, pressing her body against mine, and I throw my arm around her shoulder, bringing her in closer.

"Thank you for tonight," she says shyly. "It was...nice."

My heart is hammering in my chest, and I pray she doesn't hear it.

Tonight *was* nice...until Brandon ruined it.

He won't keep his mouth shut about this. If there's anything I learned when he was Xavier's teacher last year, it's that this dude is a douche with a capital D. We butted heads...*a lot*. I'm fairly certain he hates me too, because I wasn't afraid to call him on his crap.

He will rat us out. There's no way he won't.

He'll wait though. He'll drop the bomb when we're least expecting it, let us get comfortable and close and fall completely and utterly in love before pulling the rug out from under our feet.

I can't let that happen.

"You okay?" she asks as we approach the bike.

"Yeah, everything's great," I tell her, giving her the best smile I can muster and throwing my leg over the seat. "I'm great. *You're* great."

"I know." She winks and gives me a saucy grin before sliding her helmet over her head and climbing on behind me.

There's something different about her on the ride home, and not just because she has her arms outstretched against the wind as we barrel down the highway.

It's more than that.

She seems so...free. Adventurous.

Ready for whatever life throws her way.

And she needs that right now.

Because tonight? Tonight is going to be the last time I see Monty for a long damn time.

I just don't know how to tell her that.

"I DID SOMETHING REALLY FUCKING STUPID."

"Color me surprised," my best friend says with a lopsided grin.

When I don't laugh or even smile at his remark, he sobers up, sitting straighter in the chair and turning all his focus on me.

It's Monday morning and I'm sitting on the other side of Zach's desk at Embody Positivity.

Considering we spent the better part of the last several years running his business from his basement, it's weird to see him behind a desk again.

But here we are.

And here I am asking for his help...again.

"What happened?"

"Monty is Xavie's teacher."

Zach's right bushy brow rises, but just the right one. "How long have you known?"

"Long enough—almost a week."

"And you're just now telling me why?"

"Because it's fucking complicated, you ass. The fewer people who know about it, the better."

"But I'm your best friend."

"Play that butthurt bestie card later. Right now I need help."

He sits back, pretending to slide something off his desk and tuck it away in a drawer. "Butthurt bestie card has been stowed for later. Tell me what's up."

I roll my eyes at his joke and sigh. "We went out Sunday night. I took her to TacoWay and—"

"She totally orgasmed from those amazing tacos, didn't she?"

"Yes, but stop interrupting. *Anyway*," I continue, "I'm pretty sure I told her I loved her, we danced, and then I'm pretty sure I told her again."

When Zach doesn't say anything like I expect him to, I keep going.

"Then we kinda sorta...um, fooled around in a photo booth."

Both brows lift this time and a smile curves across his lips, but he still doesn't say anything.

"Then I'm pretty sure she told me she loved *me*, which is still kind of blowing my mind, but I digress." I scrub a hand through my already messy hair. "We ran into her coworker when we came out of the booth, both of us looking guilty as fuck."

Zach steeples his hands together, resting his chin on the tips of his fingers. "So? It's not like he knows who you are."

"Remember when I said Monty is Xavie's teacher?" Zach nods. "Well, that means Monty works at the same school he went to last year."

"And?"

"*And* I know her coworker. Actually, in a way, you do too."

A crinkle forms between his brows. "You're gonna have to start elaborating."

"Remember how I was having issues with Xavie's teacher last year? The one who kept sending him to the principal's office for *really* stupid things?"

"Mr... Oh, shit—what was his name? Mr. Dipshit? Douchebag? Dickweed?"

"Donahue, Brandon Donahue, and that's who we ran into Sunday night."

Zach's eyes light up at this revelation. "Oh fuck. He knows you. He *really* knows you, and he absolutely hates you."

"I know."

"You're fucked."

"I know," I say again. "And it's not even in the fun way."

"I mean, from what I hear happened in that photo booth, it was."

He barely dodges the stapler I throw at him.

"Hey! That was heavy, you ass!"

"Deserved too, you dick."

"Fair enough." He scoots around in his chair, too lazy to even get up, and grabs the stapler, putting it back in place. "What are you going to do?"

"Well..." I draw out.

"Okay, what stupid-as-fuck thing did you *already* do?"

"I haven't...yet, but I'm going to. I *have* to. I can't see her again, not after last night, after almost getting caught—not when that douchebag knows about us."

"You can always keep it on the DL."

"That was our plan, but now that means not even going out for fucking tacos." I let out a frustrated groan. "It means being holed up in our apartments for fear someone will see us together and take this to the extreme."

"You're not doing anything wrong, you know," he tries

to reason. "It's not illegal, and it's not even entirely unethical, just...frowned upon."

"Frowned upon is enough for Monty to freak out. Frowned upon is also enough to cause problems, especially for a first-year teacher."

He winces. "I didn't realize this was her first year."

"Yeah, and *I* don't want to be the reason things get fucked up for her, or the reason she gets a bad rap, or for this to cause *any* drama. I'm not worth it."

"I think Monty would say differently, but that's your call, Robbie." He taps his fingers to his chin a few times before huffing out a loud breath. "For what it's worth, I don't think you'll be wrong whatever you decide to do. This is a really tough situation, and I won't judge you if you break up with the best broad that's ever happened to you *or* if you continue to bang your kid's teacher. Up to you, man."

"You're so eloquent."

He spins himself around in a circle, grinning like an idiot. "I've been told that a time or two."

Zach continues to spin as I mull his words over.

Monty *is* worth the fight—there's no denying that—but when that fight isn't just something that's tough to handle but something that could affect her career? It becomes a battle I don't know if we *should* fight.

"What are you gonna do?" he asks, still spinning.

"I don't know."

"Well, I don't either. You gotta figure that shit out on your own."

I push up to stand and stare down at him. He is *still* spinning. "I hope you puke."

"Think I could get my boss to give me the day off if I do?"

I shake my head at him and head for the door as I call out, "You're exhausting."

"You love it!"

CHAPTER 24

ROBBIE

Monty: Hey. I haven't heard from you today, which is kind of unusual because you're always super annoying.

Monty: I was kidding. I like it when you're super annoying.

Monty: Robbie?

Monty: Huh. Guess you're busy or sleeping. I'll leave you be. Just text me when you get the chance. *kisses*

Monty: Good morning. 😊

Monty: Okay, it's now after lunch on Tuesday, and I'm starting to get worried. I haven't heard from you since Sunday night. Are you okay? Please, just answer me.

Monty: Maybe your phone isn't getting texts? I'll try calling.

Monty: I tried calling. Nothing. So that means you're ignoring me. Noted.

Monty: Your son came in today wearing an "X Gon' Give It to Ya" t-shirt. That is SO not appropriate. Funny, but not appropriate. He was sent to the principal's office.

Monty: Obviously, it wasn't by me. It was by one of the administrative assistants.

Monty: Just thought you should know though.

Monty: Okay, fine, it was an obvious attempt to get you to talk to me, but I guess that's not going to work seeing as you're still silent. It's been almost a week, Robbie. Please, just tell me what I did wrong.

Monty: More silence. I'm just going to assume your phone is broken. That's going to help me sleep at night.

Monty: I went by your place tonight. At first I was really mad because you wouldn't answer the door. Then your neighbor kindly informed me you were out with a "very sexy brunette."

Monty: So...yeah. Enjoy your night out. I'll leave you be now.

Monty: DOWNLOAD ATTACHMENT

Monty: CALL ME ASAP

Me: Oh fuck.

Me: Listen, I'm in the middle of an important meeting. Can I call you afterward?

Monty: You had better.

Monty: There is A LOT of explaining you need to do.

Me: I know. I'm sorry.

Monty: Don't you dare apologize to me right now, and definitely not via text.

Me: You're right.

Me: Give me thirty minutes.

Monty: You have ten.

Me: I'll make it work.

# CHAPTER 25

MONTY

NINE MINUTES LATER, my phone lights up in my hand.

I debate not answering it.

Anger is flowing through my veins. It used to all be directed at Robbie. Now it's directed at Brandon too.

That traitorous, inconsiderate, moronic...*jerk!*

"Explain."

"Well, that's one hell of a greeting, Monts."

"Nope. No. You don't get to 'Monts' me, especially when it makes my insides do these stupid flips. You need to explain yourself—*now*, Robbie."

"I really don't want to do this over the phone." He gives a dry laugh. "Actually, I don't want to do this at all. I *never* wanted to do this, which is why I've sort of—"

"Ignored me? Abandoned me?"

"It sounds really bad when you say it like that."

I scoff at his words. "It *is* really bad, Robbie. You took

me back to your house, made love to me, and then sent me on my merry way only to ignore me for nearly a week."

"Monty...there was so much more to it than that. I didn't want to have to do this, so I hid from it like a little bitch. I should have pulled my goddamn big boy pants up and hit this head on, but I couldn't. We were so happy, and I wanted to hold on to that for a while longer."

"You think dodging my texts and just disappearing from my life is holding on to happiness?"

"That sounds really bad too." He laughs dryly. "I'm an idiot and clearly really fucking bad at relationships."

"I think that is putting things mildly."

He laughs again, and I hear how disappointed he is in himself.

I'm disappointed in him too, yet I can understand why he did what he did. I didn't face my problems in Montana; I ran. So, get it.

Which makes me feel like an idiot too.

"Was it Brandon?" I ask him.

"That...yeah." He clears his throat. "Yes. He was Xavie's teacher last year. I know him. He recognized me Sunday night, and I knew he wouldn't keep his mouth shut. I thought if we separated and took time apart, he wouldn't have any ammo against us."

"But the pictures."

"The pictures."

When Brandon walked into my office this morning

and slid a white, bookmark-sized slip of paper my way, I was confused.

"Thought you might want these, and just a note: what you're doing with him? It needs to end. This kind of...indiscretion is not tolerated at our school. End it, or you'll be answering to Principal Gladden Monday afternoon."

That was all he said, staring down at me victoriously as my hands shook, flipping the paper over and gasping.

There were four pictures of me and Robbie in the photo booth.

My top was clearly off, his face was buried in my chest, and my head was thrown back mid-orgasm.

I glanced back up at the traitor, and his grin grew. Then he slipped from my classroom like he hadn't just wrecked my entire world.

"How did this happen, Robbie? How do those even exist?"

"I...*fuck*. Remember when I put money in? I didn't even think about it. The booth must have been on a timer and it went off."

"The fireworks," I whisper into the phone.

Those weren't fireworks I saw when I came. It was the camera flash.

I am an idiot.

"What?"

"I...I..." Even though he can't see me, humiliation washes over me. "Nothing, it's nothing."

"I didn't even think about it once you climbed onto my lap."

"I didn't either."

"The photos must have printed out and that fucking douchenozzle grabbed them." He lets out a string of curse words. "God, Monty, I want to rip his goddamn head off. Just knowing he's seen you like that...it has my fucking blood boiling."

"Trust me, it doesn't make me happy either. I just...I can't believe he'd do that. I can't believe he'd be so...*mean.*"

"I think mean is going easy on him."

"Probably."

I hear him moving around and want to ask him what he's doing, but I almost feel as if I don't have that right anymore, not when I haven't spoken to him in nearly a week.

Him ignoring me hurt. It hurt *bad*, especially since I practically confessed that I was in love with him on Sunday.

"I'm sorry this happened, Monty."

"Me too. It stinks."

"No," he says, and I hear it in his voice before he even speaks the words.

This is it.

This is goodbye.

"I'm sorry we let this keep going on. We shouldn't have. We should have kept it light and fluffy and parted ways when we found out you're Xavie's teacher. What we're doing...it's not right. You can't put your career on the line for good sex, Monty. I won't let you."

I've been fighting back tears this entire phone call, and I'm not surprised when they finally begin to fall at his words.

He's saying goodbye, and it hurts just as bad as I thought it would.

The worst part? He's wrong. He is *so* wrong.

What we have isn't just good sex. It's more—*so* much more—and I thought he knew that.

Maybe I was wrong though.

Maybe Robbie isn't the guy I thought he was, isn't my new adventure.

Maybe he's just a stepping stone.

If that's the case, why does this hurt so much?

I do everything I can to muffle my cries, but I think he hears them anyway.

"Are you okay?" he asks.

Gathering myself as best I can, I wipe away the tears making their way down my face. "Y-Yes. I'm good. I'm fine."

"Good. That's good. This is for the best," he says, trying to convince us both.

Another unsteady sigh from him.

Another strangled cry from me.

"Goodbye, Monty."

There's a click on the other end of the call, and I break.

CHAPTER 26

ROBBIE

MISSING someone you aren't sure you ever really had is strange.

At first, you can't eat. Nothing is appealing, not even the slice of gooey, greasy pizza you know you shouldn't be eating anyway.

Then, sleep slides through your fingers like a slippery bar of soap.

And finally, the cold sets in.

There's a void—a hole—and you're not so sure it will ever be filled.

It's only been a little over thirty-six hours since I said goodbye to Monty, but it feels like a fucking lifetime. It's as if seconds and minutes never existed and all that's there are decades and centuries.

I miss her laugh, her smile, her silky red locks...her ridiculous sense of humor and her inability to say even the tamest of dirty words, the way she looks when she comes, and that blush that steals up her cheeks.

I miss her.

It's as simple as that.

I steer my car into Holly's driveway and throw it into park.

I'm here to pick up Xavie and I need to get my shit together. I can't wallow in front of him, especially when I can't explain the why to him.

Time to pull up my fucking big boy pants and move on.

Move on.

Like it's so simple.

I drag my hand over my face, scratching at the beard I've managed to grow in the last few days, another sign of my wallowing.

Shit. I should have shaved.

The front door opens and out runs my son, a big grin on his little face, his arms stretched wide.

"Dad! You're here!"

Showtime.

I climb from the car and he crashes into me. "What's up, dude? You miss me?"

"A little bit. Can we go see Thumbelina?"

"Ah, I see what this is: you only want to hang with your old man because he has a bunny."

"And crabs. Don't forget you have crabs too."

I try to hold back my laugh. "Yes. How could I forget

about those? Did you bring yours?"

"Mom has 'em." He sidesteps me and pops open the door to the back seat. "I'll be in here. Hurry up. Thumbelina's missing her brother."

I shake my head at the impatient little shit and head toward the open front door, where his mom stands.

It doesn't escape me how different she and Monty are from one another. From their looks to their personalities, they're complete opposites.

Monty is reserved, and that word doesn't exist in Holly's world.

Where Monty is all legs, Holly barely stands five-four.

I'm fairly certain thanks to Holly's naturally bronzed skin, courtesy of her Latina heritage, Monty would disappear standing next to her. That's how different their complexions are.

Xavie must have gotten most of her genes, because save for his eyes, that kid looks nothing like me.

"Hey, Hol," I say as I walk up onto the porch. "Heard you have crabs too. What a shame."

She laughs and holds the portable tank out to me. "Here. You can have them back. Creepy little things. I can't believe you let him get those."

"Hey, he's your kid. He got his weird taste in animals from you."

"For the billionth time, liking hairless cats does not make me weird."

"Save the speech for someone else," I tease. "How you been?"

She crosses her arms over her chest and eyes me up and down. "Better than you it seems. Who screwed you over?"

"Me."

"Huh?"

I shake my head. "It's nothing."

"Robbie Cross, don't 'it's nothing' me. We have history, but we're still friends. Talk to me. Maybe I can help, offer a woman's insight and all that."

She's not wrong...

I glance back at the car, making sure Xavie's still okay, and lean in close, dropping my voice to just above a whisper.

"You've met Miss Andrews, right?"

Her dark brows slash together. "Our son's teacher? Of course I have. What about her?"

"She's...um..." I scratch at my beard again. "We were kind of dating."

She balks at my confession. "Shut the fuck up, Robbie. No you weren't."

"We were, Hol, and it was getting serious too."

"Was? What happened?"

"Well, we found out she was Xavie's teacher, thought we could make it work and keep things quiet during the school year. We went out on Sunday and, yeah, things did *not* go as planned. We ran into Mr. Donahue."

Holly groans. "Oh god. Of all the people, it had to be that fuckhead? I *hated* him. He was such a twerp to Xavie."

"I know, and of course he remembered me."

"Probably because you threatened his life a time or two."

"I think you're exaggerating that a smidge."

She squints, tilting her head. "Am I?"

I chuckle and continue. "Anyway, we tried to play it off like we weren't together."

"But that dick is perceptive."

"Yeah." I nod. "Let's just say he's not too happy about my relationship with Monty and is threatening her with the...information he has on us."

"You're choosing your words very wisely, which is unlike you. That means there's something you're not telling me."

I open my mouth to speak again and she holds her hand up, silencing me.

"It's fine, I get it," she says. "Now when you say things were getting serious between you two, you mean..."

"Dating. We were dating. It was official boyfriend-girlfriend type shit."

"Ah, I see."

"Is this weird for you? To talk about this?"

"We are *way* past that. I just want you to be happy, Robbie. If it's with Miss Andrews, then that's who it's with."

"Monty. Her name is Monty."

"That's...different, but I suppose it fits her. She's not your usual type, huh?"

"Not in the slightest, and I think that might be what I like about her most. She's unique, fresh, fun."

"Stupid pretty," Holly interjects.

I wince at the jealousy I hear in her tone and she notices, waving her hand.

"Nope. No. Sorry. Ignore me."

"She said the same thing about you, if that makes you feel any better. We didn't know she was Xavie's teacher until the second parent-teacher meeting."

Holly's brown eyes widen. "How is that possible? Did you two not discuss...well, anything?"

"We were doing the light and fluffy thing."

"Ah, yes. Makes sense. No strings attached—that's your MO."

"It's hard to attach strings when you have a kid in the mix."

She lifts her hands. "Trust me, I get it. That's why I kept crawling back to you. It was easy, and easy is always nice." She huffs. "Look, I'm gonna say something, and I don't want you to get mad, okay?"

My sagging shoulders lift at her tone, ready for whatever she wants to throw at me. Holly has always been a straight shooter, and it's one of my favorite things about her.

"Hit me with it."

"First, I think you're a fucking moron for breaking up with her."

I laugh at her bluntness, because it's so Holly.

"Second, you're running because you're scared, because you're used to easy. You fell into that pattern and it's hard for you to break it. This girl, though, she challenges you. You like it, but you're afraid to like it too much." She gives me a sad smile. "Though based on the way you look right now, I think it's a little too late for that. So, just give in. Fight for her."

"Fight for her?" I repeat.

"Oh yeah. Women love it when men do that shit. You'll learn eventually."

"You broads are complicated."

"We just like keeping you on your toes is all."

"That you do. That you freakin' do."

"Seriously, though, Robbie, I've never known you to be a quitter. Don't quit on her when the going gets tough. You didn't quit on me when I got pregnant and put you through hell the first five years of Xavie's life, and look where we are now."

Again, she isn't wrong. I didn't quit on her. I couldn't.

Just like I can't quit on Monty—not really.

I have to fight for her, for us.

I nod in agreement. "We're in a good place."

"Damn straight we are. We're civil. Hell, I'd even call us *friends*."

"That sounds scandalous."

"I think a lot of people would agree. Now, take your spawn and get the hell off my porch. There's a glass of wine calling my name and *The Bachelor* starts in like five minutes."

I roll my eyes. "Some things never change."

"When they're good, why should they?" She winks. "Make sure my kid calls me tonight before bed. I'll see you on Sunday."

"See ya Sunday. Oh, and Hols? Thank you. Your talk really helped."

She waves me off. "I know. Now go. Shoo!"

The door slams shut in my face and I can't help but laugh.

She's still the same girl she was when I first met her: obsessed with her wine—even though she wasn't even legally allowed to drink it yet—and in love with those cheesy reality TV shows.

I climb back into the car and hand Xavie his crabs.

"Here. Hold these creepy critters and buckle up."

"On it, Pops."

"Pops? That's a new one."

"Just something I'm testing out."

I chuckle and pull out into the street, turning right to head back to our apartment.

"So how was your day, dude? Do anything fun?"

"Mom let me have not one but *two* donuts for breakfast, *and* a Yoo-hoo."

I cringe but remind myself he's just a kid and deserves

a treat every now and then. Besides, a donut sounds damn good right now.

"You guys go to Magic Holes?" *Worst donut shop name ever.*

"Yep. They were yummy like always. Oh, Dad!" he says excitedly. "Can I take a donut to school tomorrow?"

"Tomorrow? A donut on a school day? I don't know about that. Donuts are weekend treats, you know that." *And only when you're with your mom,* I want to add but don't.

"It's not for me."

"Then who's it for?"

"Miss Andrews."

That pit that's been forming in my stomach grows at the mention of Monty.

"You want to take your teacher a donut? Why?"

"Because she's sad. She's been super sad all week. She keeps smiling like she isn't, but I can tell, Dad. I can tell."

"Yeah? How can you tell?"

"You just know it when you know it," he says, like he's a little Yoda or some shit.

And people say kids don't know anything—bull. They can be intuitive little turds sometimes.

"Do you know why she's sad?"

"Nope. I just know she is. I can ask her if you want."

"No, buddy, don't do that. It's rude."

"Is bringing her a donut rude too?" he asks hopefully.

"No, that's not rude at all."

"Then can we?"

"Well, I guess if it's for Mon—Miss Andrews, then we can get up early and get a donut."

"Maybe one for me too."

"We'll see."

My throat tightens as I pull into my apartment complex, thinking of the last time I saw Monty.

It hurts to know she's miserable, hurts even more to know she's hurting so much the kids are picking up on it, and it's all my fault.

The urge to cry begins to swell, which is really fucking stupid because I do not cry, dammit.

I want to though. I also want to scream, and I want to drive to Monty's place right now, bust down her door, and tell her I'm a dumbass and we should be together.

I should fight for her and for us.

I want a future with her, and I don't want to give up.

I fucking love her.

I want to tell her all that, because I do.

I love Montana Andrews, and I'm going to make damn sure she knows it.

CHAPTER 27

MONTY

"MONTY!" Denny rattles me from my sleep with her loud screech. "Get your scrawny, pale ass out of bed. You're going to be late!"

"No, I have another ten minutes."

"Yeah, ten minutes until you have to leave."

I spring from the bed, glancing at my phone sitting on my bedside table. *Oh cats.* "I'm going to be late!"

"That's what I've been trying tell you. Get up!"

"I am, I am!"

I race around my room, pulling clothes on and trying to get my messy mane under control.

I've never been late before.

I've also never been heartbroken before.

But here I am, doing both.

To say these last few days have been hard would be putting it mildly. I knew ending things with Robbie would hurt, but I didn't anticipate the sleepless nights or desire for...well, nothing.

I thought I'd wallow for a day or two and that'd be it.

I didn't think I'd be scrambling to get out the door and get to work on time because I spent most of the night staring at my phone trying to convince myself not to text or call or make every single type of social media account just so I can stalk him.

It's official, I've gone insane.

Mad.

For him, at him.

Me, us.

Everything in between.

I am a complete and total mess right now.

After I finally talked myself down from my near leap into the dark abyss of social media, I made a plan.

Today, I am going to march into Principal Gladden's office and tell him everything about Robbie and me, all of it—well, maybe not all the crazy sex parts, but still, most of it, and from the beginning.

I'll tell him this won't interfere with my job, I will *not* play favorites with Xavier, and we won't let him know until he's out of my classroom. And, if that's not good enough, I'll offer to move classes, or districts—anything. I will *beg* if I need to.

It's kind of crazy, but I think it'll work.

Robbie is worth the fight, whether he thinks so or not.

Denny's standing at the door, holding my lunchbox

out to me with a frown as I hastily make my way into the living room.

"I'll kill him," she says. "I'll do it. I have no problem going to jail for my girl. I bet I can make a mean shank."

"You've never seen a shank in your entire life." I grab my lunch from her hands. "But thank you for the support. I appreciate it. I'll see you tonight. Love you."

She grabs my elbow as I go to pass.

"Denny, come on, I'm going to be late."

Her eyes are filled with worry. "It's going to be okay, Monty. I promise."

"I know it will."

She's taken aback by my words, but I don't give her the chance to question me, racing off to my car as fast as my feet will carry me.

The drive is quick, or rather, *my* driving is quick, because I can't be late.

I skid into the parking lot with just five minutes to spare, throwing my car into park, grabbing my bag, and racing toward the front door.

I barrel into my room and toss my things onto my desk just as the first student arrives.

Whew. I made it.

Coincidentally, it's Xavier.

"Mornin', Miss Andrews."

"Good morning, Xavie." His little brows scrunch together because I only call him Xavier. "Oh, sorry. Xavier," I correct myself. "How was your weekend?"

"Good. I got to have donuts yesterday with my mom. Then when Dad picked me up, I asked if we could get *more* donuts and he said yes, so I got you one."

"You brought me a donut?" I ask.

"Yep!" He holds his little finger out to me. "One sec."

Dropping his backpack to the floor, he spins around and drops to his knees to unzip it.

I can't help but smile at the fact that he stashed a donut in his backpack.

"Here you go." He holds a crushed box out to me and frowns when he notices the state it's in. "Oops. It got smooshed. Dad said that might happen."

I take the box from his hands. "Thank you, Xavier. That's very kind of you." It's also very convenient since I didn't have time for breakfast and I am *starving*.

"What's the special occasion? Why'd I get a donut?"

He shrugs. "Just because."

"This is the best *just because* donut I've ever been given. I'll go ahead and eat it now if you don't mind."

He leans in conspiratorially. "Can I have half?"

I burst into laughter and open the box, ripping the donut in half without an ounce of hesitation.

"Here you go, little man. Enjoy."

He shoves the sugary treat in his mouth, then holds out his thumb and mutters a muffled, "Thanks," on the way to his seat.

I lift the other half of my donut to take a bite, but then

something catches my attention out of the corner of my eye.

There is a bright blue sticky note attached to the lid of the donut box.

What the...

I lean in closer to read it.

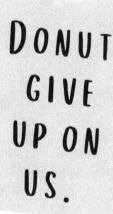

Robbie.

My heart jumps into my throat for all the right reasons.

I scramble to dig my phone from my bag, forgetting all about my hunger and the delicious donut sitting in front of me.

Me: I didn't plan on it.

Python: Good. Me either.

Me: That's not what it seemed like the other day.

Python: Let's just say I had a lapse in judgment and I'm a fucking idiot.

Python: I am much more smarterer than I was then. 😉

Me: And still just as exhausting I see.

Python: You know you missed me.

Me: I did, but we're not in the clear yet.

Python: But we will be.

Python: Look, I have a meeting in like two minutes. We'll talk tonight. Lola's at 7?

Me: I'll be there.

Me: Donut go getting dumb in the meantime.

Python: I am 96% positive that wasn't proper in English. Shame, teach. 😉

Python: And I won't.

For the first time in days, I feel good, *hopeful.*

We're not done.

Not even close.

THE SECOND THE last student trickles out of my classroom, I'm on my feet and racing off to Gladden's office.

This isn't over for me and Robbie. This can't be where our story ends. I won't let it.

As I round the corner, I see Brandon for the first time today. He's turning into the next hall...toward the offices.

Oh no...

I race forward and, without much grace, slide my way into the front offices.

"Miss Andrews, how can we help you?" the head assistant asks.

I try my best to calm my voice, but I know it's no use. "I'd like to speak with Principal Gladden in regard to a personal matter."

Her brows lift—at the shakiness in my voice, I'm sure —but she remains professional. "Of course, dear. I do believe he has a guest in there now, so you'll need to wait a moment."

I'm too late.

"No!" I shout.

"What was that?"

"N-No. This can't wait. It has to do with his guest."

"Are you certain, dear? I don't see how that could be possible if it's a personal matter."

"It is. Trust me. Please, let me in there."

She frowns. "I'm afraid I can't do that."

"I-I..."

I am so getting fired for this...

I don't wait another second. I push past her and barge into the room.

"Miss Andrews!" she calls after me, obviously upset.

"Principal Gladden! I need to speak with you *immediately.*"

I hear her footsteps race after me. "Sir, I am so sorry. She ran right past me."

The balding man sitting behind the desk raises a hand. "It's fine, Mary Ann. I'll take it from here."

I can feel her glare as I stand ramrod straight, not breaking eye contact with the principal.

The door clicks closed behind me and Gladden smiles my way.

I give him a tentative smile in return, my nerves beginning to eat at me.

Raymond Gladden is one of the biggest reasons I took this job. He's welcoming, inviting, and kind while also a no-nonsense type of guy.

I liked him at once.

"Miss Andrews, to what do I owe the pleasure?"

"Sir, I...I, um...I-I..."

His lips twist into a grin. "Yes?"

"I-I'm sorry, sir. I'm nervous."

"Yes, I can tell, Miss Andrews." He leans across his desk, folding his hands together. "What's going on, Montana?"

"Sir, I...I've been seeing a student's father since summer. W-We were not aware of our...predicament until the second parent-teacher meeting. We had *no* idea—I swear, sir."

He nods, rubbing a hand over his jaw. "I see. And after you found out? Then what?"

"We...uh..." I wince. "We continued to date, sir, but I swear, I did not treat Xavier any different. I—"

"Xavier?" he questions. "Xavier Levy, correct?"

"Yes."

"He's a good student."

"He is, sir, very bright and kind."

"Yes, I agree." He nods again. "Please continue."

"I... Well, I read the handbook and couldn't find anything about this...unique situation. However, I wanted to be very transparent about my...uh, relationship with Mr. Cross."

Gladden begins to laugh.

I stand here, dumbfounded, because I have no idea what's going on. I can feel Brandon staring holes in the back of my head and I'm surprised he hasn't spoken up yet, but I can't turn around and look at him. I won't give him the satisfaction; I'm already embarrassed enough as it is.

"Uh, sir?" I say when he still hasn't calmed down.

The principal shakes his head. "I am sorry for the outburst, I just find this whole situation to be funny."

"Why is that?"

"Montana, there are no formal rules against dating the parent of a student. It's not even in our ethics handbook because this issue is complicated and unique to each situation. Would I prefer it not happen? Well, yes, as the pitfalls should the relationship turn sour are something we'd like to avoid. But, we understand there are sometimes things that are beyond our control, such as you two beginning to date *before* Xavier was your student. You're allowed to have a life outside of school."

The weight that's been sitting on my shoulders for weeks begins to lift.

"However, there are a few precautions we would like to take."

And it's back.

He waves his hand toward the couch behind me. "You had a wonderful idea—care to share it again, Mr. Cross?"

Mr. Cross...Robbie!

I whirl around, and there he sits. It's Robbie, not Brandon like I thought.

He gives me that lopsided grin I love so much. "Hey, Monts."

"*Hey, Monts*—that's the best you can come up with?" I smile back at him.

Robbie shrugs. "We have company."

Our company clears his throat, and we both try not to laugh.

"As you were saying, Mr. Cross," he prompts with obvious humor in his voice.

"Right. I suggested that, since it's still the beginning of the year, we move Xavie to another class."

"Another class? I-I don't want him to miss his friends, Robbie. That's tough on a kid."

"I know it is, but hear me out...what if we moved him to second grade? Last year, Holly and I were approached by Principal Gladden himself about pushing him up a grade. We didn't talk about it again, but he called this morning to see if we'd thought about it more before the school year progressed much further. Figured we'd use the opportunity to chat." Robbie sits forward on the couch. "Xavie's smart. He's gifted, and he's already in two enrichment classes. Why not move him up?"

I mull over what he's saying.

Xavier *is* smart, probably the brightest kid in my class. There's no reason he shouldn't be in second grade, and if he's going to move up, he should do so at the beginning of the year.

"What does Xavier think?" I ask him.

"He's open to it. He said he'd miss his friends and his teacher"—Robbie grins—"but I think he'll adjust rather quickly. Besides, he's smitten with the idea of being 'just like Uncle Zach' and skipping a grade."

"You never told me Zach was a bookworm."

"Oh, did I leave that out?" he teases.

"I think this is a great start," Gladden interjects. "Miss Andrews, if you don't mind, we can continue discussing this tomorrow if you feel we need to. I'd like to speak with Mr. Cross more before I head home for the day."

"I, um, no...*sir*. I don't have anything else I'd like to discuss."

"Great." He stands, moving around his desk to the other side. He takes my hand in his, shaking it. "Breathe, Montana. It's good for your soul. We'll get this figured out. You did nothing wrong."

I want to throw my arms around his neck and squeeze the life out of him, but that would be *so* inappropriate.

Instead, I return his handshake. "Thank you so much, Principal Gladden."

"Of course. Oh, and that other issue of yours? We'll get it taken care of."

I look at him, puzzled.

"Your coworker's antics will not be tolerated, and they're real rich coming from him considering all the drama he caused last year after cheating on his fiancée with another teacher."

My mouth drops open, then I snap it closed at once, surprised by this information but trying to remain professional.

"That is an...interesting development in the story I heard."

"I'll speak with him," he promises again. "You have a good night. I'll see you tomorrow."

"Yeah, get out of here. I have an appointment at seven and we have things to chat about," Robbie says as I turn to exit.

I grin over at him, relief washing over me.

I have a date to make.

# CHAPTER 28

ROBBIE

THE LAST TIME my heart was trying to jump out of my chest from nerves was when I was in the delivery room waiting for Xavier to be born.

But this, waiting on Monty? It's a close goddamn second.

My meeting with the principal ended about thirty minutes after Monty left and then I raced over to Holly's with Xavier in tow.

We spent some time going over everything, signing all the papers we needed to, and getting our son set up to begin second grade tomorrow.

Who knew the little swimmer that won would turn out to be a fucking genius?

I look around the nearly empty bar; it's Monday and there's not much of a crowd. I sip on the water sitting in front of me, waiting.

Someone slides onto the stool next to mine, and I don't have to look over to know who it is.

"I'm going to say something very forward, and you'll have to excuse me for this—it's the alcohol talking."

I grin as she repeats the words she spoke that first night, the ones that led us straight to the bathroom.

I turn her way. She's wearing the same outfit she was when we met here the first time, and I can already feel my cock beginning to grow.

"You have the most kissable lips I've ever seen in my entire life." She leans toward me. "And I want to kiss them."

I haul her off the stool and straight back to the women's bathroom, not stopping until she's sitting on the countertop and I'm planted firmly between her legs.

She grins up at me. "Hey, Python."

"Oh, fuck." I laugh, and then I capture her mouth with mine.

Home.

We've only been apart for a week, but it feels like a fucking lifetime, especially when my heart is bursting with love for this buttoned-up bombshell.

When I finally pull my mouth from hers, I say, "I missed the hell out of you, Montana."

"I missed you more. How about you don't do that to me again?"

"I won't, I promise. I told you, it was a momentary lapse in judgment. I'm not always so stupid."

"Better not be. I don't think I could survive it again."

"I know, but I think we're in the clear...if you're good with that. What do you say?"

"*Yes*."

I rest my head against hers. "I'm sorry for not having faith in us. I was just worried. I didn't want you to lose your job or get in trouble. I didn't want to put that pressure on you. I'm not worth that."

She grabs my face, bringing it up until our eyes meet.

"You're worth *more* than that, Robbie—*so* much more."

Her words hit the center of my chest and it knocks the breath out of me.

"How can you even say that?"

"Because I love you, you dumbass."

I rear back at her words. My perfect, girl-next-door, goody-two-shoes Monty...she just cussed.

And it sounded as absolutely ridiculous as I thought it would.

Laughing, I push my forehead against hers again. "Yeah?"

"*Yes*—so much."

"Good, because I love you too."

I seal my lips to hers again, and this time I don't stop.

EPILOGUE

MONTY

One year later

"MISS ANDREWS, can I have another donut?"

"Call her Monty, dude. How many times have we told you?"

Xavier smiles sheepishly from his perch at the counter. "Sorry. Monty, can I have another donut?"

"May you," I correct him.

"Yes, I may." He grabs the last donut sitting inside the box and takes a huge bite of it. He pats his stomach. "Hits the spot."

We did it.

We made it through the school year without letting Xavier know we're dating.

There was a lengthy discussion about whether or not we should tell him, especially since there was no longer any chance of a conflict with him moving to second grade, but we decided it'd be best to keep things under wraps. He did start the year as my student, after all, and it only felt right.

The afternoon school let out, we went for ice cream, all three of us together for the first time.

It was the best afternoon I'd had in a long while.

"Once you're done with your donut, can you go grab Thumbelina?"

Xavier sits up, mouth twisted in confusion. "What for? It's not time for her to be out yet."

Robbie lifts a brow at his kid. "First, because I said so. Second, because I said so. And third, in case you were wondering if there was one, be—"

"Because you said so," his son interrupts. "Yeah, yeah. I get it."

I try hard not to laugh, and I find myself doing that a lot lately.

Xavier might favor Holly in looks, but he is *all* Robbie in personality, right down to the sarcasm.

He finishes off his donut, hops down from the stool, and then snaps his fingers. "I remember!"

I stare after him as he sprints down the hall, having no clue what he's going on about.

"Your kid is weird," I tell Robbie once he's out of earshot.

"He gets it from you."

"Me? I'm hardly ever around him!"

"I wouldn't be so sure. Besides, kids are *very* easily

influenced—all it takes is like five minutes a day and boom! They're walking and talking just like you."

I glare at him over the counter. "Uh huh, and what if you spend, oh, about eight years with them?"

He grins and mutters, "Dammit."

"Monty 2,243, Robbie 4."

He points at me. "But at least I have four."

"It's way better than the zero you *did* have."

"My thoughts exactly."

"Dad! Dad! Come quick! You won't believe what Thumbelina did!"

I charge down the hall, worried about Xavier *and* the bunny. I skid into the room and stop dead in my tracks.

"Seriously? You scared the you-know-what out of me!"

Xavier falls into a fit of giggles. Robbie comes up behind me, wrapping an arm around my waist and resting his chin on my shoulder.

"Oh my gosh, she's at it again, huh?"

"You think you're really clever, don't you?"

He nods. "The cleverest."

I stare down at the bunny, warmth and love spreading through me. She's tucked inside her cage with a cardboard sign resting against her.

Sprawled across the sign in what can only be Xavier's handwriting is a question meant just for me.

Will you move in with us?

Robbie's lips brush against my ear and a chill runs down my spine. "What do you say, Monts?"

"You're telling me I'd have to live here with *two* boys? Two boys who fart and can't pick their socks up to save their lives? One's a good cook, but the other leaves something to be desired." I look left. "No offense, Xavier."

He holds his hands up. "None taken."

"Is that what you're saying though?"

"That's what I'm saying."

"No, that's what *we're* saying," Xavier corrects, eyes glistening with hope and excitement.

I turn my head and see that Robbie has the exact same look on his face.

"Say yes, Monty," he whispers. "Say yes."

"Yes."

He grins triumphantly and smacks a big wet kiss to my cheek.

"Yay!" Xavier shouts, doing a little dance of his own. "No take-backs!"

"Yeah, girlfriend, no take-backs."

I wouldn't dream of it.

THE END

Psst...

Want more Monty & Robbie?

Take a look at the sweet note Robbie wrote for Monty on their wedding day...

MONTY,

Remember when I asked if you wanted to see
my python and you thought I was a total perv,
but you went into that bar bathroom with
me anyway?
That was the single greatest night of my life.
Sure, I've had countless other great moments,
like when Xavie was born, but that night?
It changed everything for me.
Because that's the night *you* happened.
And you? You've been the best part of me by far.
Which is why I'm so fucking glad that today
is the day we finally say "I do." I can't wait to
marry you. I can't wait to officially make you mine.
I can't wait for forever with you, because I know
it's going to be damn good.

I love you, Monty.
Always, always, always.

Yours,

ROBBIE

P.S. I plan to show my python allllll night long.
(And yes, I do mean my pants python this time.)

OTHER TITLES BY TEAGAN HUNTER

CAROLINA COMETS SERIES

Puck Shy

Blind Pass

One-Timer

Sin Bin

Scoring Chance

Glove Save

Neutral Zone

ROOMMATE ROMPS SERIES

Loathe Thy Neighbor

Love Thy Neighbor

Crave Thy Neighbor

Tempt Thy Neighbor

SLICE SERIES

A Pizza My Heart

I Knead You Tonight

Doughn't Let Me Go

A Slice of Love

Cheesy on the Eyes

TEXTING SERIES

Let's Get Textual

I Wanna Text You Up

Can't Text This

Text Me Baby One More Time

INTERCONNECTED STANDALONES

We Are the Stars

If You Say So

HERE'S TO SERIES

Here's to Tomorrow

Here's to Yesterday

Here's to Forever: A Novella

Here's to Now

Want to be part of a fun reader group, gain access to exclusive content and giveaways, and get to know me more?

Join Teagan's Tidbits on Facebook!

Want to stay on top of my new releases?

Sign up for New Release Alerts!

ACKNOWLEDGMENTS

I always have to give a special, and very well deserved, message to my Marine. You make my world go 'round. Thank you for being you. For getting me. For always being there. I love you more than words can explain. Also, thanks for always letting me put your anecdotes in my novels. You're the real MVP.

Mom, thanks for always being there no matter what... and no matter where. I love you.

A big, HUGE thanks to my readers. You don't even know how much your support means to me. You guys are the reason I'm still writing, the reason so many things in my life are possible. I see you and I appreciate you.

Teagan's Tidbits, you finally got a book dedicated to you! HUZZAH! I would be lost without you wonderful peeps. Thanks for giving me a safe place to hang out. I love you all...even Aubrey.

Laurie, I swear, I would be lost as fuck without you. Thanks for wrangling this crazy cat.

Christine, I still don't like you. But then again, I kind of do. That felt so gross to type, but whatever. Thanks for all your help...I guess.

Kristann, my #soulmate, I love you. So, so much. Diann too, just don't tell her I said that.

Caitlin, my fabulous editor (Editing by C. Marie, you guys. Go check her out!). You work your magic and make my crazy readable. Thank you. I don't know what I did in my career before you. You're my hero.

My fabulous proofreaders, Julie Deaton and Jennifer Van Wyk. You two gave this manuscript a good polish. Thank you for catching those last-minute errors I sure as shit would have missed. You're the best!

Sara Ney, you're the best and worst dance mom I have ever had. Thank you.

Jessica Estep, my fabulous publicist...THANK YOU! Thanks for navigating me through this crazy publishing world and doing it even though I ramble and can't seem to make up my mind about anything. I adore you.

To the rest of the InkSlinger family, you're the greatest and I still pinch myself every time I realize you've let me in to your little family. It feels like home already.

I feel like Oprah handing out all these thanks yous, so I'm gonna cut this off. To anyone else I'm forgetting...oops! My bad. But you guys know how scatterbrained I am half the time. I adore you and I feel your love and support. Promise.

With love and unwavering gratitude,
Teagan

TEAGAN HUNTER writes steamy romantic comedies with lots of sarcasm and a side of heart. She loves pizza, hockey, and romance novels, though not in that order. When not writing, you can find her watching entirely too many hours of *Supernatural, One Tree Hill,* or *New Girl.* She's mildly obsessed with Halloween and prefers cooler weather. She married her high school sweetheart, and they currently live in the PNW.

www.teaganhunterwrites.com

9 781959 194187